Johnnie
the Pirate King

DS WHITAKER

ISBN: 978-1-7342595-9-9 (EB)
ISBN: 978-1-954794-00-9 (TP)

Author photo by Diana Lang
Cover Design by DS Whitaker

To Tim with all my love

Prologue

W ithout warning, the hitman, dressed in black, stepped from the shadows, his eyes like red lasers.

It made little sense, but he went with it. His heart pounded. "What do you want?" Johnnie asked.

His tall adversary held a long spear, like Neptune's trident, that glowed silver. A bolt of lightning burst from the storm clouds, striking the forks in a spray of embers. Like Magneto in X-Men, Smith held up his gloved hand, redirecting the electrical energy at him in a blinding light.

Johnnie's muscles shuddered, his brain on fire from the pulsating, crippling shocks. Convulsing, he held up his arms for protection, but nothing helped. His body felt like pudding; Johnnie cowered on the sand, sure of his own demise.

The man in black chuckled. "You will die for what you did. Look at my face."

Where he expected to see the scars from their earlier battle—where he hit Thomas Smith with a garden shovel—the killer now had a donkey's face, with fluffy pointed ears.

Johnnie was floating on the open ocean now, face down on a battered boogie board that smelled like rotting fish.

Smith lifted the spear high, ready to strike him through the chest. "Johnnie, I'm going to fuck you up. Because I love you."

The hot spear pierced his ribs and he woke with a shout, his arms flailing.

Johnnie rolled to the side and hit his jaw on the nightstand. Perspiration pocked his brow and his back was damp. As he took deep calming breaths, he wondered what the hell it all meant.

Just a bad dream, Johnnie told himself. The threat from Smith had to be latent anxiety; the butthole was likely dead or long gone.

Unable to fall back to sleep, he got a glass of water and checked all the window latches again. Across the yard, he noticed a light on in his landlord Gertie's house. Which seemed odd, but she seemed unsettled these days, her anger at her new love interest, Cudlow, palpable.

Johnnie changed his pillowcase to a dry one and got back into bed. The clock read 2:14. Meaning only three more hours until his alarm went off. He turned his thoughts to more pleasant images, like the Goddess sailing across the bay on her stand-up paddle board. The sun glistening off her golden hair. Even in his imagination, he didn't know what to say to her. How to make her notice him.

It was downright pathetic.

Chapter 1

Johnnie, dressed in his Park Service uniform, arrived at Hawksnest Beach and sat at the water's edge, hoping for an uneventful day. The sun rose behind the hill, fracturing the sky in hues of pale pink and bright magenta. Stumpy scurried toward him and hunkered down at his side. Johnnie rubbed the top of the iguana's head with his thumb. Stumpy's mouth froze open in what could appear to be a smile, then rested his head on his front legs and settled down.

Palm trees swayed in the warm breeze. Off in the distance, sailboats and fishing boats appeared tranquil, moored at their assigned spots. A peaceful start to his work day on St. John.

A short text message from his boss listed a couple extra chores, ones which would easily fit into his usual maintenance routine. He yawned audibly, and rubbed his eyes, still salty from lack of sleep.

As his focus returned to the bay, something didn't look right. Because a boat seemed to come closer. He polished the lenses of his glasses with the end of his shirt, and stared, keeping his eyes on the same spot. Yes, a boat sailed into the swim zone, which was wrong on many levels.

Did this moron not know boats prohibited here? He waved his arms.

Oh, shit. Based on the direction and rate of speed, the boat was on a collision course.

Johnnie jumped and shouted, "Hey!"

The thing was going to run aground. This couldn't be good. No one else was on the beach, leaving the decision to him. But without superpowers, his only choice was to swim out and try to get the vessel under control. Getting wet first thing in the morning was never on his list of enjoyable activities.

He unbuttoned his shirt and unzipped his pants, unlaced his high-top hiking boots and kicked them off. As the ship came closer, it was clear no one was present on the elevated flybridge—the captain's helm—of the forty-foot fishing vessel.

Johnnie ran to the water and swam toward the boat. About eighty feet from the shore, the large vessel shuddered to a grinding halt, obviously hitting the ocean bottom, listing to one side.

Too late. He swam around to the stern of the boat. The decal letters with the ship's name were missing, leaving an obvious outline of the words, "Bert's Folly". The port-side panel had an odd graphic, like an octopus with twenty arms. He pulled himself onboard with the short ladder.

From the rear deck, he yelled, "Hello!" He clenched the side of his wet tighty whities to keep them from drooping.

No answer.

He climbed the ladder to the fly bridge. The engine was off, but the key was in the ignition.

Did the boat simply break loose from its mooring ball? Weird things like that happened especially after Irmaria. Once secure mooring points spontaneously broke free. It had taken years after the hurricanes to remove all the boat wreckage around the island.

Johnnie looked through the cubbies on the bridge for clues. Just some navigation charts. No registration, no paperwork. Like a ghost ship. None of it made sense. Inside the cabin, he looked for more clues. A dark stain on the floor looked like blood. But there were empty wine and beer bottles on the lower floor of the kitchenette. Probably red wine from a party.

He retreated from the cabin and climbed back to the bridge to think of his next step. Visitors were arriving on the beach, including a family with two small kids. It wouldn't be right to leave the boat in the swim zone.

Johnnie sat in the captain's chair and turned the ignition key. The engine roared to life and he pushed the throttle into reverse; trying to dislodge the ship gently to limit any additional damage to the sea floor. He backed out, turned the boat around and picked a spot close to the other boats to park it. After tying up to a free mooring site, he realized he needed to report this to Kemper. *But how was he supposed to get back to the beach?*

He waved to one of the other boats. A couple, seeming in their 50s, waved back. Johnnie shouted to them, "Can you give me a ride in?" It occurred to him he must look like a maniac in his soaked underwear. But getting a ride would be preferable to swimming back.

The husband picked up John with his zodiac tender.

As Johnnie got into the dinghy, he grimaced. "Hey, thanks." Not knowing what to say, he blurted, "Sorry, I usually wear clothes."

"We saw you swim out. Is that your boat?"

"No. I work for the National Park Service. Did you see what happened?"

The man kept his hand on the steering handle of the small electric outboard motor. "Not sure. It sailed by us with no one up top."

"Weird." He wondered how someone loses a boat this size.

After he got back to shore, Johnnie waved goodbye to his rescuer, and got dressed where he had dropped his clothes earlier. An older woman, holding hands with a three-year-old girl, walked along the water's edge; she gave him a stink eye and veered away. As they passed, she muttered, "Pervert."

His hand formed into a fist and he thought of some choice things to say, like "hag!", "mind your own business!" or "what's your problem?" plus a string of obscenities he ached to spew forth, but remembered his calming exercises. And he didn't have time for anger or confrontations. He focused on taking some cleansing breaths instead. *One, two, in. One, two, out.*

He dusted off his cell phone and called his supervisor Kemper.

"Kemper, it's Johnnie. An abandoned yacht ran to ground in Hawksnest bay. Can you call the Coast Guard or whoever?"

She exhaled. "Sit tight and I'll see if they can send someone over."

"Roger that." They ended the call.

His anger vanished as he regarded the boat from afar. It was a pretty sweet vessel. Perfect for deep sea fishing trips. Surely someone would claim it.

Stumpy ran up and put his foot on his boot. [Hey Johnnie, what were you doing?]

"I found a boat." He pointed. "Do you want a cheese puff?"

[Yes, yes, YES!] Stumpy swished his unnaturally shortened tail, bouncing up and down on his front legs, bobbing and jiving in excitement.

Johnnie tossed two puffed corn pieces to his friend and went back to his chores. He hoped the authorities would be there soon because he had more work to do at Cinnamon Bay.

A half-hour later, while he was sweeping sand off of the pavilion's concrete floor, Kemper Snow arrived. Under her iconic Ranger hat—with her straight shoulder-length dark blonde hair tucked behind her ears—Kemper's sky-blue eyes showed concern. "Johnnie, which boat is it? Did you get the mooring number?"

The mooring number. An important piece of information he should have noticed, he thought. "See out there? The one on the far right?"

His underwear, still soaked, turned his green cotton trousers dark in an unflattering configuration. But worse, they created a wedgy. He resisted the urge to pick at his butt in front of Kemper. Instead, he shifted his weight from foot to foot, hoping the wad would dislodge on its own accord.

She squinted. "Ah, got it. The Coast Guard said if the boat is stable, they'll get to it by tomorrow afternoon."

"Hey, do you know what happens to lost boats?"

She rubbed her chin with her long, pale fingers. The brim of her flat hat obscured her expression. "Well, they try to track down the registration. If they can't locate the owner, they place a public notice. Then if no one claims it in thirty days, they hold an auction."

He lifted the tinted lenses on his round glasses, gazing in the ship's direction. "It's a nice boat."

She crossed her arms and began walking back to the parking lot. He walked behind her, finally pulling on the seat of his pants out of her view.

Without turning around, she asked, "If it goes to auction, are you interested in bidding?"

"Could be. I'm going a little stir crazy." Somehow, pulling on his trousers made the wedgy worse. It didn't seem possible. While her head was turned, he gave into his desperation and shoved his hand down the back of his pants to smooth out the lump.

She took off her hat and brushed her hair behind her ears as she walked. "Ha. I know what you mean. I grew up in Minnesota." Kemper stopped and gazed off into the distance. "I miss leaves changing color in fall and the snow in winter. Never thought I would. But I guess we all want things we don't have." She fit her hat back on snuggly and turned without warning.

Johnnie jumped back and took his hand out of his backside. "Um. Yeah. I guess."

She chewed on her thumb-nail. "What would you do with the boat…if you got it?"

His mind blanked for a second. *Maybe she didn't notice…* "Not sure. Go to different islands on the weekends. Explore good fishing spots." Now at the parking lot, the sun's rays reflected off cars, sending heat across his face. He took a step back under the shade.

"A ship like that would be perfect for romantic dates." Kemper elbowed him in on the arm and grinned. "Some string lights, a bottle of wine, drifting under the stars." Her eyes danced upward. "Heaven."

Discussing romance with his boss made his face twitch and skin itch. "Maybe for other people."

"Oh." Her face turned serious. "Okay. Well, see you, Johnnie. Be good now." She waved goodbye and walked away toward a white Park Service pickup truck.

* * *

About an hour later, close to eight, Johnnie finished his usual maintenance chores at Hawksnest, leaving him time to tackle some repairs. Kemper wanted the tool shed repainted.

He rolled on brown paint and daydreamed about what he would do if he owned a nice boat. Foremost, get off the damned island for a change of scenery. Also have a few moments where he wouldn't have to worry about Thomas Smith behind every tree or fence. But also have something of his very own. Where he was in charge. And no one would criticize him.

His reverie was dashed when a limousine entered the parking lot. His carefree thoughts were replaced with contempt and confusion, knowing what this meant.

Weddings were the worst. Maybe he just hated love. Seeing a couple so happy. Not knowing what they were in for. The woman was far too old to wear that style of dress, low cut on top with a poofy cotton candy princess skirt. And the groom in his late 40's had a bad haircut and adult acne. Johnnie tried not to watch. But after the ceremony, they didn't leave. Taking pictures for a half-hour in an assortment of poses. Their feet in the surf, twirling each other, and lots of kissing. It was the fake sort of play-acting happiness which really irked him.

His own wedding day was like that—full of smiles and laughter. Only, at the time, he thought it was real and would last forever. Marrying your high school sweetheart could be that way. Young and thinking nothing could ever hurt them. Oh, how wrong they were.

This particular couple was bothersome for two other reasons. Namely, the infractions. First, they brought champagne and glasses onto the beach, and park rules strictly prohibited glass containers. A totally dumb move. Really, the officiant and photographer should have known better. He'd have to report it. And second, they brought a small pot-bellied pig with them on a leash. It was cute, but made a lot of noise, running around and squealing. Johnnie was sure the pictures would be adorable.

But the rules were clear. No pets allowed. Yes, he could simply give them a warning. But, no, the lump of spite in his throat told him to report this shit.

He dialed Ranger Merv.

"Hey, Merv, it's Johnnie. I need your help."

"My man, what do you need?"

"There's a wedding at Hawksnest, with lots of wrong stuff going on."

Merv asked, "It's not one of those nude weddings again, is it?" He chuckled, "I'll be right over."

"Eww. No! Don't be gross, man. They have champagne and a pig."

"Like, what? Like a pig roast?"

"No, a live animal."

Merv's voice rang with glee. "Dang, sounds freaky. Yeah, I'll be right there. Hey, I sent you a text. Happy hour, next week. Let me know."

"Bye."

Johnnie didn't want to wait around. He put away the painting supplies, got in the service truck, and headed to Cinnamon Bay. It was more crowded there. As he was pulling into the parking lot, he saw her. His jaw dropped and he slammed on the brakes.

It was the Goddess. She was carrying her stand up paddle board through the parking lot. Easily six-foot tall, the muscles in her long arms were defined but not bulky; her skin lightly golden. She stopped at a dark green jeep with a hard-top roof rack.

She was more stunning up close. Her hair had a straw-colored beach wave on one side, the opposite side shaved close. And she had the cutest nose with freckles. And high cheekbones. Sure, there were sun-kissed wrinkles around her eyes. He guessed her age was between thirty-five and his own age, forty-five. But the Goddess ruled over women half her age.

When she reached upward, standing on her toes to shove the board onto the Jeep's roof, her butt cheeks peeked out from the bottom of her cut off jean shorts. Like smooth works of art.

Panic set in. Should he talk to her? Say hello? *But then what?*

A car honked behind him. A man's voice called out, "Get out of the way, loser." Without realizing it, he had been sitting in the truck in the middle of the parking lot staring. He shook his head and turned into the spot labeled Park Service Only. After exiting the vehicle, he continued to surveil the Goddess, while pretending to look for something in the rear bed. He removed a shovel, knowing he didn't need it. His eyes darted between the shovel handle and the Goddess. Time slowed down. But his reverie ended when she got in the driver's seat, put her Jeep in reverse, and drove away.

At least she was alone, he thought. No sign of her presumed boyfriend, a guy labeled Fabio for his long thick hair. *Did his absence mean she was now single?* Did he have a chance?

Not that he would know what to say to her. She would probably think he was a creep. And he felt creepy, gawking like a teenager. From the back of his truck, he traded the shovel for some trash bags and headed towards the pavilion. *What would the goddess want with a garbage man like him anyway?* A woman like her would never give him a second look. No, even if he had all his brain matter, she would still outclass him.

And it was best not to dream.

Chapter 2

At the end of the workday, Johnnie rushed home for his video session with Dr. Louisa Phillips. He couldn't put it off any longer. Robin was hounding him and he needed his prescription renewed. The events of the last month seemed so distant now. Like they happened to someone else. Or like a movie where he couldn't remember the exact sequence of events. Regardless, it was time to fess up and tell his psychiatrist the truth. He opened his laptop for their five o'clock video call.

After the usual pleasantries and routine questions, he went for it.

"Wait. You did what?" Lou stripped off her tortoiseshell glasses.

"It was self-defense." He shrugged at the video screen.

"But you didn't call the police?"

Lou sat with a window behind her, and the glare on the monitor put most of her face in shadow. But he could make out her frown.

"I guess I wasn't thinking clearly."

She stared at him, eyes narrowed. "The truth."

"Yeah, okay. I didn't want to explain myself to Chief Tobias again." The police chief hated him and the feeling was mutual. Tobias was itching for any good reason to hassle him.

She put her glasses back on and scribbled on her notepad. "So, let me recap. Three weeks ago, you face down a known murderer, stab him with your fishing spear, incapacitate him, and instead of calling the authorities, you swim him over to a remote island and strand him there? Johnnie, I have to say, I…wait. I don't know what to say."

"Sorry."

"I'm glad you're all right, but the lying and deceit needs to stop."

He hung his head. "I know. I know. Sometimes I don't think things through."

"Look, I'm not your moral compass. That's on you. And maybe I would have done the same thing in your position. I've never had someone try to kill me."

"See, the thing is, I don't know if he's alive. I keep looking over my shoulder. And I've had a couple nightmares…like the ones about the accident…and I wake up in a cold sweat. Not that I'm afraid. But the not knowing is messing with me."

"You could still tell the police and FBI. Or your sister. She works for the government. You said it was self-defense." Lou gave him the look. The look, staring over the top of her glasses, which reminded him of his sister Robin. The look that meant, 'cut the crap.'

He rubbed the back of his neck. "I was hallucinating on the swim back. Maybe the whole thing was a bad dream."

She paused for a long time. In a measured tone, she asked, "John, are you saying you don't know reality from a dream?"

Now he stepped in it. "No! I mean, yes, I know the difference. Really. Can we let it go? Maybe I shouldn't have told you." He sighed, feeling remorse in so many ways he couldn't count. But mostly for bringing up Thomas Smith.

She took off her glasses and shook her head. "I need time to process this. I'm glad you finally confided in me. But I can't help you when you lie to me. Even by omission."

"I know. I know."

Lou squeezed the bridge of her nose with her head tilted down. When she righted herself, she said, "All right. Let's move on. How are things? Your moods, energy, vision?"

"I feel good. Sometimes lonely. I miss Cud. Robin is spending time with her new boyfriend. A ranger invited me to join a group for happy hour. Though I'm not sure I want to go."

"You don't want to—why?"

"Merv is kind of phony."

"Why else?"

"Do there have to be more reasons?"

"Since you left Miami, you never mention going out with groups or going to parties. Have you talked with any of your former Marine buddies lately?

"No. I don't see the point."

"Why?"

"They have families and live in North Carolina, and I don't remember enough to talk about old times. And I don't want their pity. It gets awkward."

"But what about on St. John? You've been there four years. What do you think is keeping you from socializing? Why aren't you dating? Surely you must have considered it."

"Maybe I don't like people."

"Because…?"

"Look, my head hurts. Can we call it a day?"

"Sure, Johnnie. But I want you to think about this and journal your feelings. And think about telling the truth to the authorities. Deal?"

"Fine. Deal."

Dr. Phillips asked her usual parting question.

He answered, "I'm grateful for being alive, and Robin is happy, and the awesome fudge Gertie made for me."

They said their goodbyes and Johnnie ended the video call.

It was pretty lousy of him to lie to her those weeks ago. He expected her to be furious. The disappointment on her face was worse than anger.

* * *

Dear Diary,

Cud's been away for three weeks now. Gertie's been calling him, but now his voice mail is full. She says, if he wants to talk, he can face her in person. You would think she would appreciate a bank account with ten million dollars. She said Cudlow is a horse's ass, which made me laugh. I said, I'll take the money, and she rolled her eyes.

Anyway, I'm going to stay out of it. Because what do I know about relationships? Nothing.

Dr. Lou is mad and wants me to tell the FBI about my encounter with Smith, but I hate him and hope he is dead. Plus, Robin would lose it if she knew the truth. Maybe Smith will come back and kill me. I had a dream where he stabbed me with my fishing spear and told me he loves me.

And no, I'm not telling my therapist about that one.

With Robin busy with her new boyfriend and Cud gone, I'm feeling stir crazy. The boat was really sweet and got me thinking. Not that I can afford a real yacht. I want to get off this island so badly.

Robin says I should try writing stories. I have an idea about a

Pirate King who gives to the poor, but then I realized I don't know much about pirates. I need information on real pirates and not the Pirates of Penzance or Disney movies. Because, face it, Captain Sparrow spent more time putting on eye makeup than directing his crew.

Also, I need to read mermaid lore. There's a theory early sailors were just horny for manatees. Although, I saw manatees all the time in Florida and they are far from attractive.

Sweet dreams, Diary. Love, Johnnie.

* * *

It was a beautiful morning for the first Wednesday of May and Johnnie had finished cleaning the surfaces in the pit toilets at Hawksnest Beach. He stripped off his rubber gloves. Ranger Merv Hartley walked past the orange cone blocking the men's restroom and leaned against the cinderblock wall.

"Hey, Johnnie, I saw you feeding that deformed iguana earlier." Merv crossed his arms and grimaced.

Johnnie regarded Merv with his tall forehead and deep cheek creases. "Yeah. He likes cheese puffs. I only give him two a day. What do you care?" He rose off the floor and picked up the bucket of dirty water with hints of suds. Johnnie dumped the contents into the pit.

"It isn't good to feed wildlife."

Johnnie walked past Merv, moving the cone with his free hand and bringing it to a small alcove. "What? Are you going to report me? Don't be a douche."

"Nah. But you should lay off, okay?"

Johnnie walked to the maintenance shed and Merv followed. "It makes Stumpy happy. But, sure, whatever." In his mind, he wanted to say, "Fuck you," but didn't.

"Hey, speaking of wildlife, what happened to your homeless friend? What's his name?"

"Cud."

"Where did he go?" Merv chuckled, "Did he finally go splat on the road?" He slapped his hands together in a loud clap. He snapped his fingers rhythmically, as he sometimes did when he was in a good mood.

Merv was very chatty and upbeat today, and this made him suspicious.

Johnnie flipped up his sunglasses to get a better look at Merv's face.

"No, man. He went home to the Bahamas. Might be temporary, but I don't know."

Merv slapped his hands on the side of the shed with rhythm, like he was playing bongos. "Do you like soccer? Me and some other guys get together to watch games and have a few brewskies at the Yellow Parrot. You should join us on Friday, after work. Make some human friends."

Was Merv implying Cud wasn't human? Or was he thinking only of Stumpy? Either way, a dick comment. "I don't know. I'm not great with groups or parties." This was true. People at parties talked loudly, which made his head hurt. People screaming at televisions in sports bars were the worst.

"Well, I'm texting you the details in case you change your mind."

Johnnie wondered why Merv was so friendly all of a sudden. He blurted, "Why are you being so friendly?" He opened the shed door and placed the bucket inside, and then grabbed a broom.

Merv finished typing, put away his phone and sighed. "Look, man, I'll be honest. I know Kemper really likes you. I mean, not *like* likes. But she cares about you like a friend. And well, I'm looking to ask her out. Which yes, I know, I know, 'don't date your boss', but there's something about her I really dig. So, I figure, if she sees us pal-ing around, she might like me more…give me a chance. What do you say?"

"Kemper? Doesn't she have a boyfriend or husband or something?"

Merv clasped Johnnie on the shoulder and grinned. "Her boyfriend dumped her two months ago. She's fresh meat, if you get my drift."

No, he didn't get his drift. "Don't be a dick."

"Right! You're right. I didn't mean it like that. I mean…" Merv shook his head. "Sorry. Look, man, I'm trying to be a better guy. Honestly. I think Kemper is the sweetest woman I've ever met. And I'm done with the bimbos. I want to be worthy. That's why I think you're the best person to help."

There were many things to unpack in those statements. First, Kemper was sweet, and yes, far too nice for Merv. Second, Merv seemed genuinely sincere, which was odd. And third, Johnnie knew he wasn't the best person to help in any type of situation, barely dealing with his own mood swings and depression. "Yeah, sure. Maybe I'll come by for one beer."

Merv clapped him on the shoulder again. "Thanks, dude." He walked off.

Stumpy came by while Johnnie locked the shed. [What did he want?] He chuckled at his elderly iguana friend. "I think Merv is in love."
[Love is nice. Why don't you have a girl friend?]
"Why don't you?"
Stumpy cocked his head. [I'm too old. What's your excuse?]
"Hmm. Brain damage?"
[Cheesy puff? Yum time?] Stumpy rested his front leg on Johnnie's boot.
"Nope, no more. Sorry."
The iguana cocked his head and then scooted away under a bush.
Johnnie swept the concrete floor of the picnic pavilion. *Maybe Stumpy had a point.* Maybe he needed to open up to the idea of more friends and possibly a girlfriend. Because if a tool like Merv had friends—including girlfriends—why couldn't he?
His scant memories of his ex-wife Darla flooded in. He didn't remember the early happy times all that much, but the fall-out and terrors after his accident in Afghanistan were always present. How he pushed her away with his self-loathing and frustration. Flying into rages over how much butter she put on his toast or when he couldn't find the remote control. And the very terrible time in Miami when the small dog next door whispered to him incessantly for him to kill himself; leading him to barricade himself onto the balcony of their eleventh-story apartment, threatening to cut his own throat. It couldn't have been easy on her. Still, when she left him...
He pounded his skull with the palm of his head. *Think of something else...*
A seagull flew onto the picnic table and chirped at him, breaking Johnnie's train of thought.
"Hey, bird."
The gull stared at him, like he was peering into his soul. [Johnnie, lighten up. Why can't you be happy?]
He thought a bit. "Great question."
The bird shook its head and ruffled its neck feathers in disapproval. It flew onto his broom handle, and inched its head close to his ear, like he wanted to whisper a secret.
Johnnie grew still and leaned his head toward this strange bird, wondering what divine truths of the universe it might divulge.
The gull lunged for the metal temple of his glasses, pressing his

clawed feet against his cheek. Downy feathers erupted in the battle as Johnnie swatted and yelled, "Stop!" He took off his cap and swung it at the insistent thief.

The bird flew off, its wings thumping the air.

"Fucking bird." Johnnie shook his head, dusted feathers from his face, fitted his glasses back on, and drew in calming breaths to cool the heat of embarrassment.

Sure enough, there was a witness to the mayhem. A teenage girl, close to thirteen, standing on the path a few feet away, smiled at him. He recognized her as a regular at this beach. He turned his gaze away. This wasn't the first time the girl witnessed him battling an aggressive animal.

She came toward him and leaned against the pavilion's support post. "Animals are crazy."

It was obvious she was trying to be nice. And he wasn't going to argue, although in this situation, he was probably the crazier one. He kept sweeping.

"You know, I did a report on seagulls last year."

Why couldn't people leave him alone. "So?"

"Did you know they can drink salt water? They have these special glands…"

As she spoke excitedly about seagulls, his attention wandered and his thoughts returned to Darla. In hindsight, he didn't blame Darla for leaving him. *Not really.* Although he wondered if he would ever find love again.

And admittedly, despite talking to random wildlife and near constant anxiety in social situations, he'd made tremendous progress over the last five years since the bullet shattered his skull. He thought about what Lou said.

But the idea of dating scared him more than a demonic, mind-melding Chihuahua.

Chapter 3

After finishing his rounds at work, Johnnie arrived home at four o'clock and needed to get thoughts of Darla out of his mind. He had finished reading a book last night and had nothing new to read. After some internal debate, he decided to try his sister's suggestion to try writing. With a stack of loose-leaf paper and a chewed-up pen, he sat outside on a bright yellow Adirondack chair next to Gertie's vegetable garden.

Where should he start the story of the Pirate King and his mermaid girlfriend?

Many scenes came into his head yesterday, but now he struggled to recall them. Gone like morning mist. Something about fighting a sea monster? But where did the pirate live? Where did he venture to? He had no idea.

He wrote a list of characters. Even if he didn't know the story, he could give characters names. Next to Pirate King, he wrote Captain Cecil. The king would have a pet iguana named Grumpy. The mermaid would be Coraline. She would have a pet starfish named Zena.

And then his mind blanked again.

A starfish? Dumb.

This wasn't working. He needed to learn about real pirates, both legend and lore, or his story would be a trash fire.

The public library was closing in one hour. If he left now, he might have twenty minutes to find some useful reference material.

Johnnie grabbed his keys and jumped on his red Piaggio scooter, the Flying Pig.

Forty minutes later, he arrived in Cruz Bay and parked outside the library. It was relatively small, and the hours were limited to weekdays, but it was better than nothing. The librarian, Ms. Teller, always gave him scornful looks. Losing a book completely and bringing ten others back four months overdue didn't help. But after that first disaster, his return scorecard improved with the help of reminders on his phone.

He walked in at 4:43 and flipped up his round sunglasses. Only seventeen minutes left until closing. He didn't have time to dick around and made a bee-line to the check-out desk.

"Hi, I'm looking for information on pirates."

A woman in her mid-thirties—someone he'd never met before—looked up from the terminal at the counter. She was short and curvaceous, with long shiny strawberry-red hair, thick eye-lashes, and a round face. Her nametag—fitted to her loose blue linen dress—read *G. Hobbs*.

The librarian smiled and saluted. "Ahoy, matey! I like your glasses." This new librarian was happier than he expected, beaming with too much energy.

Saluting back seemed silly. He replied, "Um, ahoy?"

"Hmm. We have books in the children's section, and also in the history and folklore sections. Do you have a particular pirate, time period, or geographic area in mind?"

Again, he had no clue and wondered if he was wasting both their time. "I don't know. I need to know where they went and what they did." His brain chided him, *yeah, that was specific...so lame.*

"There were quite a few pirates living north of Haiti, and some close to here. Blackbeard is one of the most famous. My favorite is Anne Bonny. She was a badass. But Francois L'Ollonais was especially cruel."

Her blue eyeshadow looked nice but it temporarily distracted him; causing a distant memory to flicker about an elderly second-grade lunch lady who always wore blue eye makeup. Plus, he liked the way the red-haired librarian grinned when she used the word 'badass'.

"Lo-lo who?"

"LO-LO-NAY," she enunciated, "a Frenchman, also called Flail of the Spaniards. You should read up on him. He makes Negan from The Walking Dead seem like Mr. Rogers."

He shrugged. "I'll take whatever you got."

"Sure. Follow me." She walked around the wooden L-shaped desk and talked as she led him to the room next door. "Did you see the recent news about the drug cartel out of Puerto Rico? They're calling them modern day pirates; with a fleet of ships running drugs and money across the Caribbean."

The librarian seemed to be a fountain of knowledge. In contrast, his own memory was so bad he often forgot which day of the week it was. Plus, he rarely watched the news, opting to watch sitcoms or more upbeat shows. "No, haven't heard about them...do they attack other boats?"

The next room was filled floor-to-ceiling with dark wooden bookcases. Without turning, she said, "Yes, brutally. They steal private boats from unsuspecting owners, tossing them overboard to die slowly or kill them if they try to fight back. A way to evade the Coast Guard. At least temporarily." She stopped in the far corner of the dimly lit space. "Hmm, we have a really awesome book, but I'm not sure if it's checked out. My name's Greta. What's yours?"

"John."

"Nice to meet you." She pulled several books and stacked them in his arms. "These are probably the best. This one," she showed him the cover, "is a review of all the known pirate shipwrecks and how they went down. Like storms or battles. Good maps, too."

The weight in his arms increased. He shifted his grasp to get a better handle on the tall pile. He said, "I think...this should be enough."

She turned and blushed. "Oh, geez. I'm sorry, John. I got carried away."

"No. No, it's fine. Thanks, Greta."

She looked at her watch. "I should check you out."

"What?"

She shook her head. "Check your books out. I...you...you have a library card, I presume?"

He detected a flush in her face. "Yes."

She pumped her fists in unison. "Great."

They walked back to the circulation desk.

Johnnie plunked down the books and her hands flew, opening back covers and scanning the bar codes. After she scanned the last one, he handed her his library card. It was white plastic, like a credit card, with his name, QR code and the words St. John Public Library in blue script.

She scanned his card. The screen beeped. But not a good beep. More of an alarm noise which meant, '*denied.*'

Greta pursed her lips, squinting at the screen. "It says...your borrowing privileges are suspended."

"What? No, I don't—"

"Hold on. There's a pop-up note from Ms. Teller, saying you have an outstanding book."

Ms. Teller was the head librarian. A large-boned woman in her 50s with short silver hair, bright red lipstick reminding him of fresh blood, and a scowl that could kill puppies. He often wondered what would happen if she and Chief Tobias had a baby. They would probably name it Adolf.

He threw up his hands. "Oh, no, not that crap again."

"Excuse me?"

"Sorry. I worked it out with her two months ago. I paid all the fines and the cost of the book. Jeez, I think it was over fifty dollars."

"I…it doesn't say…maybe I could call her."

He crossed his arms, glancing at the clock on the wall behind her. *4:58.* "Yes, could you?"

Greta's face showed defeat. "Oh, I just remembered. Ms. Teller flew to Georgia." She checked her watch. "I think she's still on the plane."

He huffed. "I'm telling you the truth. I even have the receipt at home. Or call my sister. She works in the legislature. She knows I paid the fine." He landed a palm on the counter with a loud thunk.

She twirled a finger through a lock of her red hair and chewed her lip. "It's not that I don't believe you. I'm not authorized to override the computer."

He closed his eyes. His fingers gripped the edge of the counter. *Don't be a dick*, he told himself. Slowing his breath, he calmly said, "I don't want you to get in trouble. I'm trying to write a novel about a pirate, and I got stuck. At this rate, my story will be total crap."

Her eyes went wide and she spread her fingers on the counter, leaning forward. "You're writing a book? That's amazing!"

Instinctively, he backed away. Why did he have to mention writing? *Dumb.* "Probably *not* amazing. I've never written a story before."

"No, really, that's wonderful. I used to write short stories in high school. But that was decades ago. What's your book about?"

He told her the premise.

"A love story? With sea monsters? Yes, you have to write that. I would love to read it."

"You would?" His eyes widened and he took an unsteady step backward.

"Only if you want me to. I can't get enough of stories." She twirled her hair again.

"I read lots of books. Although, I usually forget them as soon as I finish."

She walked to the front door, turning over the 'open/closed' sign. Then she strode back to the counter and lifted the stack of pirate books. "Just take them."

"Really?"

"Yes, but you must promise two things." She held up two fingers. "One, return them on time. And two, let me read your pirate story when it's finished."

"Greta, thank you." He regarded her face. Not an epic beauty like the Goddess, but pretty. Her eyes were kind, sparkled with intelligence, and made him feel at ease. "I promise."

"Ha, for good measure, you can name one of the characters Greta. It's only fair." She smiled, then lifted the counter to pass back to her terminal and seemed to cancel out the transaction on the computer, hitting the delete key repeatedly.

"What kind of character would you want to be?" Johnnie took the stack of books in his arms. He wasn't sure if he could get them all home on his Piaggio. The seat compartment only had about a cubic foot of space. Some books were oversized.

"Let me think…maybe a barmaid spy or a rival mermaid." Her hazel eyes beamed, "Someone sinister or cunning."

"You don't seem sinister."

She winked, "A girl can dream."

He sorted through the books and placed three of the seven back on the counter. "I don't think I have space to cart these back home."

"No problem. I'll keep them behind the desk for you."

"Oh, wow. Thanks!" Suddenly, he was nerves again. Because if she was within arms' reach, he would have hugged her. And he never hugged anyone, except Robin. "Well, since it's past closing time, I'll get out of your way. Have a good evening, Greta."

"You too, John. Nice meeting you!" She waved.

He pulled on the window-paned door. It rattled but didn't budge. *Was it stuck?* He pulled again, harder. He looked over his shoulder. Greta pointed. Then he saw the small sign, 'push'. He tried again, successfully. As the door closed behind him, he saw Greta give him a thumbs up through the window.

Back at his scooter, he was relieved to find the four books fit in the compartment. There was a smile in his heart as he donned his helmet.

Greta was one of the nicest people he'd ever met.

Pretty and sweet and smart.

Maybe the kind of woman he could date. Even if it was only an experiment. Dr. Lou wanted him to socialize. It could work.

He wanted to walk back in and ask her if she liked food; to go out and have lunch or dinner with him sometime and maybe talk about books.

But then the lights in the building shut off.

Johnnie decided he could ask her when he returned the books.

Giving him a few days to work up the courage.

Chapter 4

Dave Jones walked down Calle de la Forteleza in old San Juan, holding hands with his boyfriend Renaldo. Ren wore tight pastel pink shorts, a teal Izod shirt, and blue tinted aviators. As they wandered past a store selling sunglasses, Dave stopped to check his reflection in the shop window. His black jeans and black T-shirt made a sharp contrast compared to Ren's more colorful style. The bandages across his nose and chin made him look like a burn victim. But they would come off in a month.

"Ren, let's stop in here."

"Sure, babe."

Dave tried on different sunglasses, trying to envision them sitting correctly on the bridge of his new nose without the gauze.

"How do these look?" He put on the gold wire frames with dark brown and tan ombre lenses. Almost seventies style. But the wall racks were filled with mostly retro-inspired styles.

Ren adored himself in the next mirror down, fussing with his dark shaggy bangs. With a quick glance, Ren said, "Gorgeous."

"I should grow a mustache. Maybe buy a wig."

Making pouty faces in the mirror, Ren chirped. "I know a place."

"Are you sure you want to come with me to New York?"

Ren ignored his question. "Babe, you worry too much."

They went to the counter and paid for the sunglasses.

When they exited the store, Dave patted Renaldo's tush. "You know, I saw my picture at the security screening area at the airport last week."

Renaldo pecked Dave on his ear, one of the few spots on his head not covered in gauze. "After the swelling goes down, no one will be looking for this handsome devil. They won't recognize you. I'm an artist."

They walked down the busy lane. "Wait, wasn't I handsome before?"

"Babe, that's not what I said. Don't fish. It's trés gauche."

"You know, I thought I would like retirement." They sauntered down the sidewalk.

"Are you unhappy? When you called me a month ago, saying you were done, I was surprised. Men like you never retire."

"Well, I know when I'm beat. I got stupid near the end. Could have died."

"New York isn't the most relaxing."

Dave scratched his chin next to the sticky tape. He didn't mind getting stitches but the adhesive on the tape irked him. "We could stay here. Real estate is cheap. We could build a dream house. With an infinity pool. And a home gym."

"I wouldn't mind staying." Ren winked.

They came to a small park and sat on a bench. Renaldo took Dave's hand. "We could have a life here. A good one."

Dave traced Renaldo's cheek with his fingertip. "You make me happy."

"Ha. I saw the way you looked at that girl at the restaurant last night. The petite one with the huge titties. It would take a harem to keep you happy."

"Maybe I've changed."

"Maybe…" Ren took off his sunglasses and swung them in the air to amplify his point. "Or maybe next month, when the bandages come off, you'll bang everything in sight, like the old days."

"Hey, I called *you*. Not anyone else. You. Because you're special."

Ren folded his glasses and hung them from his shirt placket. "No, you called me because I'm a plastic surgeon. And you were in a bad way."

"Maybe at first." He leaned over and kissed Renaldo's neck.

Ren squirmed as if tickled. "See, this is why I can't stay mad at your thicc ass."

"Come on, let's go get some rum punches." He whispered something in Renaldo's ear, resting his palm over his boyfriend's thigh.

"You know how to sweep a girl off her feet."

They left the bench and walked back toward the water. Their favorite bar was only three blocks away.

Dave glanced over at Renaldo as they strolled. They could have a perfect life, he thought. Thirty million in Puerto Rico was more than enough to retire on. And maybe Renaldo was right. Settling down with one person might be a stretch. He would have banged that girl at the restaurant if she gave him a second glance. Adjusting to monogamy would be difficult.

But then again, life would be different now. All his old rules were gone and he could give it a shot.

* * *

After work on Friday, Johnnie went home to change and still arrived at the Yellow Parrot before five o'clock. The place was hopping and reggae music played. On the far end of the bar, a group of decidedly drunk men tossed back beers and danced in a circle, like ska moves, which made no sense. A group of young women in short dresses huddled at another corner of the bar, giggling and hooting about something. He scanned the room for any men wearing black. *The coast was clear.*

Merv had invited a mix of his buddies and some other rangers. Johnnie knew a few of the rangers in passing. Like Tanya who worked mostly at Annaberg and Charlie who patrolled all over where needed.

His fears about being too early vanished when he found Merv, Tanya and Kemper standing in a cluster, each with a beer. It felt odd seeing everyone in regular clothes instead of their uniforms.

Kemper looked especially thin without the uniform and bulky belt. And she looked feminine in her orange Bermuda shorts and tight polka-dot puff sleeve t-shirt. Or maybe it was the floral headband that screamed 'I'm a female'. Merv also looked different, but not as much. He had the same weird grin no matter what he wore.

Johnnie waved and walked up to the three. "Hey."

Kemper said, "Johnnie! Glad you made it out. Good to see you." She tapped her fist lightly on the shoulder.

"Um, yeah."

Tanya gave him an odd look. "Hey, Johnnie. I didn't think you'd come."

"Hi, Tanya."

She looked at him, "Taylor."

"Oh, right, Taylor. Sorry." *Why did he always get her name wrong?*

Merv laughed, "You remember my name right, Jock-o?"

"Yeah, it's Perv, right?"

"Ha! Ha! Good one." He wrapped his arm around Johnnie's shoulder and shuffled him to the side. He whispered, "Dude, *not* cool. Be my wing-man, all right?"

"Geez, I was just kidding."

"Yeah, but not in front of Kemper, got it?"

Johnnie shook his head, "Sure."

They rejoined the women.

Johnnie asked, "So when does the game start?"

Taylor pointed to the wall-mounted screen. "The game just started. Manchester versus Liverpool. An epic battle."

Over the music, it was impossible to hear the game. But the games were closed-captioned with the score information displayed in the upper corner. Johnnie asked, "Sooo…who are we rooting for?"

This was a big mistake. Because Taylor and Merv got into a lengthy debate on the merits of each team. A debate Johnnie had no clue about and didn't care for. He extricated himself from their loud voices and sat at the bar, pretending to watch.

Mandy, the bartender, handed him a frothy beer without him asking.

Kemper sat down beside him. "I don't care who wins either. Just trying to have a social life."

"Same here. But I suck at it."

She swirled her beer, staring into the foam. "I'm sure you've heard."

"Heard what?"

"My fiancé broke off our engagement."

"I heard something. Sorry. It's his loss."

"Thanks. You don't have to say that. He wanted us to move to Argentina. But I didn't want to leave. I guess I brought this on myself."

He took a sip and wiped foam from his upper lip. "You'll be okay. I bet lots of guys would be interested…"

One of the soccer teams scored. The bar erupted. Over the din, Merv's voice rose above, shouting, "Yes! Boom dinga lingy!" More finger snapping.

Kemper leaned on a bent arm to face Johnnie. "Lots of guys?"

Johnnie kept his eyes on the screen. "Sure. You're pretty, easy to talk to. Caring. God knows you've put up with my shit…I mean, problems."

She ran her index finger over her bottom lip. "Johnnie, I like you too."

Merv popped up behind them, throwing a sweaty arm about each of their shoulders. "What are you two conspiring about? Do you need a re-fill? On me." He waved to the bartender. "Round on me."

He slithered onto the stool to Kemper's right and leaned in close to her. "So, which team are you rooting for?"

Johnnie couldn't stand to listen to Merv and his explanation of soccer rivalries. He nodded along for a few minutes, but ached to go home. He checked the time on his phone. A message from his sister, Robin. She was getting off work and asked if he wanted to have dinner. *Perfect.*

He texted back. "Please save me. At the Parrot. ASAP."

It became easier to listen to Merv's droning voice now he knew Robin was coming to his rescue.

Sure enough, five minutes later, Robin and Arturo arrived. Robin was in her suit with her dark hair in a barrette; Arturo was in plain clothes instead of his police uniform. Robin waved to the group. "Hey, hi everyone!"

Kemper smiled. "Hey, Robin! Nice to see you again."

Robin put her hand on Johnnie's shoulder and turned to Merv, "Is it okay if I steal my little brother?"

A wave of relief washed over Johnnie. He couldn't get away fast enough.

Kemper looked at him with big eyes. "But he just got here! You and Arturo should join us!"

Johnnie darted his eyes at Robin, trying not to be obvious, but internally screaming, 'Get me out of here, now!' He settled up his tab by putting a ten-dollar bill next to his glass.

Robin took the hint. "Oh, I wish we could. We have reservations. In fact, we need to get moving. Maybe next time?" Without waiting for a response, she hooked Johnnie's arm and they strode out of the bar with Arturo in tow, waving goodbye.

A half a block away, clearly out of sight and sound of the bar, Johnnie said, "Thanks. You saved me. Merv talks so loud he makes my head hurt."

Arturo said, "Where are we going? Did you really make reservations?"

Robin said, "Let's go to my place and order a pizza. Okay?"

As they walked, Johnnie blurted, "I met the new librarian."

Robin laughed. "I'm surprised you had the courage to in there after your last battle with Ms. Teller. I've never even used the library and I'm fucking afraid of her."

"Her name is Greta. I like her."

"Cool."

"I'm thinking of writing a story."

Arturo was walking ahead of them, seemed to be scrolling on his phone. He asked, "Is pepperoni okay for everyone?"

Johnnie and Robin said in unison, "Yes."

Arturo tapped buttons on his phone while he walked.

Robin said to Johnnie, "What kind of story?"

"You'll think it's weird."

Robin kept her stride as her condo building came into view. "Weird stories are always my favorite."

"I'm thinking of asking Greta out."

She stopped cold. "Really?"

He nodded. "But I'm scared she'll say no."

Arturo who was steps ahead of them, not aware they had stopped, backtracked. "What's wrong?"

Robin laughed. "Johnnie has the hots for the new librarian."

Arturo smiled. "Congratulations."

Johnnie wondered how much Robin had told Arturo about his accident, mental issues, and complete absence of a love life. Usually, Robin was pretty cool about letting him keep things private. "Well, I don't know. I haven't asked someone on a date in..." He didn't know for sure. Probably the last time was Darla and that was high school.

Arturo said, "Look, be friendly. It will all be okay. You'll see."

Robin beamed, "Yes, if it's meant to be, it will all work out."

Johnnie sensed she was talking about her new found romance with Arturo.

The three continued forward and Robin entered the key code for the exterior gate to the building.

He hoped they were right. Maybe it wasn't *such* a big deal to ask Greta out.

Act like a friend.

Like a pal.

He imagined Stumpy in a dress and chuckled to himself. Could he feed Greta cheese puffs as they gazed across the early morning waves? No, that would be truly crazy.

And kissing Greta would be way better than hanging out with Stumpy.

Chapter 5

Johnnie headed home after a couple slices with Robin and Arturo. The pair made eyes at each other and laughed at inside jokes he had no clue about. It was awkward. But still better than being around Merv and obnoxious sports fans.

It was dark as pitch outside when Johnnie parked the Pig on the broken concrete outside Calabash Market. Just a box of cereal, some milk and a loaf of bread; a quick stop. It was dark and he wanted to get home. He planned to put on some music, play computer chess for a half-hour, press his uniform, write in his journal and hit the sack.

And there she was. The Goddess. In the canned foods. Wearing a hot pink backless sundress and one large silver hoop earring.

He retreated, walking backwards, slowly, casually, like it was normal, which it wasn't. He had to regroup. *Think.* Could he pretend to bump into her and say hello? Should he grab a box of cereal and run to the checkout and leave before she finished shopping? He went to the produce section, picked up a melon and inspected it. He didn't know exactly how to inspect melons, but it gave him cover. Next, he picked up a squash. He knew things about squash from Gertie's garden. The produce here paled compared to Gertie's and was crazy expensive.

A voice, smooth and melodic, behind him, "Hi, can I get in there?"

His shoulders seized. Slowly craning his neck around, he got a glimpse of her hair. He stepped to the side with his head down.

"Thanks." Her arm—long and slender, with stacks of delicately beaded wrap bracelets—reached across to select two bags of baby spinach from the rear of the display.

She tossed them in her red handbasket. She said, "The squash? Are they good here? I usually get mine at Starfish Market."

He needed to say something. "I like asparagus." *No, wrong thing.*

Why did he say that? He detested asparagus. "I, ah, don't know."

She clicked her tongue and said, "Um, okay, thanks," and walked away.

Shit, shit, shit. Not smooth.

He raised his eyes and craned his neck to see her walk away. Her golden hair caressing her defined tan shoulders. Her calves were chiseled and breathtaking.

She placed her items on the counter at the register and completed her transaction.

Still holding the squash, he dropped it back onto the pile, and went the long way around to the bread aisle. When he got to the register, the Goddess was leaving, hand in hand with Fabio; the bell chimed above the door.

 He placed his loaf of bread on the counter.

Mr. Bravos was working the register. He snapped his fingers in the air, "Johnnie? Earth to Johnnie."

"Sorry, what?"

"Um, are you sure you want this?"

Johnnie looked at the bread. It was mashed and mangled. In his despair, he had crushed it between his fingers. "Oh, um. Yeah, my bad. I'll pay for it. No problem."

"Are you okay?"

"Mario, do you know her name?"

"Who, the one who just left?" He fiddled with the bread's plastic bag to smooth out the bar code.

"Yeah. I see her around a lot."

"Oh, sure. She lives a few houses down from me. Her name's Mildred."

"Nah. Really? That's an old lady name."

"I think she goes by Lilly."

Lilly. A much prettier name. A name fitting a true Goddess. "Hmm. Well, thanks." He paid for the bread and headed to his scooter. As he mounted the Pig, he sighed. He'd forgotten the cereal and milk. But he couldn't go back.

The entire day had been full of social failures.

Describing his pathetic behavior in his journal tonight would not be easy.

Maybe he'd leave this last part out.

* * *

Dear Diary,

I like the new librarian. I was thinking of asking her out. But would it be wrong if I'm actually in love with the Goddess? Also, did you know The G smells like Irish Spring? Weird right? Do they even sell that brand of soap anymore?

It was nice seeing Robin so happy. Her and Arturo make a sweet couple. I hope it works out with them. Because one of us should be happy.

I skimmed through some of the pirate books. Grog sounds disgusting. And keel hauling is pretty nasty. I don't think I could have been a real pirate. But I saw nasty stuff in Afghanistan, which makes me wonder about the presence of evil in the world. The Taliban cut off people's ears and noses and left them to die in the mountains. Or worse. Much worse.

Is it because of greed? Or fear? Or disliking other people outside your clan?

I dislike lots of people but I would never drag them under a boat to get ripped apart by barnacles. Well, maybe Chief Tobias.

Yes, I'm kidding. I think.

Anyway, I had a bad evening. See you tomorrow, Diary. Love, J.

* * *

Cudlow stared at his computer monitor, reading more emails. It was nearly midnight and his eyes were dry. His dress shoes and socks lay in a messy pile under his desk. He reached for another bite of his candy bar and knocked over his can of Red Bull.

"Bollocks!" The fizzy drink streamed across his papers and onto the expensive silk area rug.

He looked for napkins; not finding any, he took off his white dress shirt and got down on all fours to mop the puddle. It wasn't effective at all; instead of the fabric soaking it up, the soda beaded on the smooth fabric. He called out to his butler, "Hugh!"

Jackson, wearing sweatpants and a T-shirt, appeared at the door. "Paw, what happened?"

Cud stood, now in his white undershirt. "Sorry. I'm a clumsy arsehole. Did I wake you?"

"No. I was in bed reviewing that contract you asked me to look at."

"Good. Good." Cud stared at his desk and the jumble of paper, binders and sticky notes. He rubbed his eyes and face. "Maybe I need to go to bed."

Jackson yawned. "You can't keep going like this." He examined the trash can and picked up a wad of empty wrappers. "Did you even eat a proper dinner tonight? Or is it still on the counter? Grandpaw, you can't live on these blasted things."

"I had a banana earlier." He bit his lower lip, thinking. "I gave Hugh the weekend off, didn't I?"

Jackson chuckled. "Yes."

"The flight to Orlando leaves in six hours." He slunk down in his tufted leather chair.

"Tell me what I can do." Jackson straightened a stack of papers on the corner of the desk.

"No! Stop! I know where everything is."

His grandson dropped the stack. "Sorry. Please, give me more to do."

Cudlow waved his hand. "I didn't mean to raise my voice."

Jackson came around the desk and kissed him on the top of his head. "I'll pack your overnight bag and leave it by the door. By the way, Gertrude called again."

"Did you answer?"

Jackson pulled a phone from his pocket. "No. You told me not to. She also texted. Why won't you talk to her? I thought you loved her."

Tears came to his eyes. Maybe it was the exhaustion. Maybe he was feeling sorry for himself. There was no way for him to know objectively. "I love Gertie like the morning mist loves the new day." He closed his eyes and leaned back in his chair. He recalled how the sun glistened on her face as she worked in her garden. Her deep brown eyes that struck him to his core and left him breathless.

"I don't know what that means." Jackson took a seat in the club chair to the right of the desk.

Cudlow chuckled. "Good point. In any case, she can never know what I did."

"I still don't understand. Her life was in danger. Why can't she know?"

"Look, this will all be over in thirty days, regardless. Either I'll have bankrupted the company or save it. Either way, I can go home to her."

Jackson frowned and shook his head. "She's so angry. Are you sure she'll take you back?"

"No. But I can't process that thought right now. I'll call her tomorrow."

"Go to bed. That's an order." Jackson stood and placed his hand on Cud's shoulder. "You are no good to anyone without proper sleep."

Cudlow grimaced. "Five more minutes. I promise." He placed his hand on Jackson's. "Thank you."

His grandson huffed, held up his five fingers for emphasis, and left the room.

Cud sighed. He picked up the pile that Jackson had started to straighten up and worked the pages into shape.

A cool breeze billowed the toile curtains.

He rubbed his eyes again. A thin beam of moonlight illuminated the silver-framed family photos on the fireplace mantle.

"Freddy? Is that you?"

No answer.

"I miss you, sweetheart."

Again, no answer.

He pulled a green leather-backed diary from his desk drawer and ran his hand over the worn cover. The gold initials read, "WAL" for Winnifred Anne Loughton.

After his wife passed, he should have tossed the damn thing. Reading it those ten years ago was a mistake. One he couldn't erase. All her inner thoughts, hopes, and secrets. *Secrets she had kept from him.*

He opened an earmarked page. She had written the word "Galapagos" and inked a sketch of a penguin and a crab. Cud mumbled, "We should have gone. I should have listened."

Pain clutched his heart, remembering how he had brushed her off, choosing to work instead of celebrating their twenty-fifth wedding anniversary. How, in response, she didn't talk to him for a week. Not that he noticed at the time.

He racked his brain trying to remember what deal had been so important. But his memory was foggy.

The curtains billowed again. "Freddy?"

Whispering, he said, "I'm different now. I swear."

He turned off his computer monitor. It was time for bed; for clearly, he was mad and seeing ghosts that weren't there.

Cud scooped up shoes, socks, and damp shirt and went to the window to close the latch. Outside his window, beyond the flower garden, lights twinkled across the dark water. The world was asleep. He shuddered, shut his eyes and whispered, "I love her. Please let me go."

Pausing for an answer, none came.

He locked the window and closed the drapes with his free hand.

Perhaps he had gone daft. The pressures of trying to build back three hundred million in corporate wealth—and save hundreds of jobs—were simply taking a toll on his health. And all those Red Bulls couldn't be helping. Yes, he needed to eat better and learn to delegate.

Before closing the office door, he said, "Goodnight, love."

And he turned off the lights.

Chapter 6

he never understood men, no less billionaires.
Gertie sat at her dining table, looking at the bank statement, while on the phone with her boyfriend, on speaker.

"Gertie, are you still there?" Cudlow asked.

"Yes."

"I wish I could explain. I'll be back in four weeks. Don't be cross."

Her frustration grew. "What could be so important? I thought you gave all that up."

"I did. But there are problems. Too great for Jackson to handle alone."

"So, you lied."

"No, this was unforeseen. Can't we talk about something else?"

"Sure. How about the ten mill you dropped on me? I never asked for it. You need to take it back."

"Yes, I know I should have asked first. But I want you to have it."

"First you call me a gold digger and then you give me millions? Like I'm a prostitute?"

"Wait, a what? No. It's for our life together."

"I'm not your kept woman. I'm nobody's property."

"Oh, for goodness…you are exasperating."

"Me? Ha. I'm also hanging up." She smashed the red icon on her phone, blocked his number and put her phone face down on the table. "Asshole!"

Since the bank manager told her three weeks ago, she called Cudlow nearly every hour, only to be directed to his voicemail over and over until his mailbox was full. Then she sent him emails; also unanswered.

Each night, lying awake wondering how to give the money away to charity and distribute it among good causes. The IRS would want at least half. She would need an accountant to deal with this mess.

Gertie didn't want to get married and it was clear Cudlow took her for granted. And even if they patched things up, she had everything in life she could ever want. All she wanted was a *normal* boyfriend. Like Helen Hunt in As Good As It Gets. Or maybe a friend with benefits. With the money hanging over her, she couldn't think straight and figure out *what* she wanted.

Her first husband had been a real prick. Controlling the bank account, giving her a meager allowance, rifling through her dresser drawers and kitchen cabinets to make sure she didn't save enough to leave him. Refusing to let her get a job.

The bad situation got worse when he hit her, after he discovered she was on birth control against his wishes. She had been in her early twenties then and was naïve to have stayed those five years.

The divorce was messy. When she moved back in with her mom, Sebastian broke into the house and tore up the place. Threatened suicide. Threatened their lives. And he left her saddled with debts. She had to borrow from relatives to settle legal fees and avoid bankruptcy. It took years to get her life and credit history repaired.

Now Cudlow was playing an equally dangerous game, tilting the balance of power, and she wasn't about to sacrifice her independence to anyone.

He could keep his damned money and his mind games.

She never asked for this. The sweet, affable destitute man she connected with was gone. Replaced by someone she didn't recognize.

But who was Cudlow? The version who had lived on the beach was equally a stranger. How did he live in the wild all those years? With no real shelter?

What did Johnnie say that night on the beach? Pointing to the west end?

She put on her sandals and grabbed her car keys.

It was after ten at night. Hardly any cars on the road, which was helpful because the adrenaline coursing in her veins made her driving erratic. She took a turn off the dirt road too wide and had a close call, almost sending her back wheels off the side of the steep hill. A voice in her head said to turn around and be sensible. That same voice was drowned out by her need to know the truth of Cud's former situation.

She pulled into the deserted parking lot at Hawksnest Beach. Could she find it in the dark? Not knowing exactly what to look for?

Turning on her phone's flashlight, she scanned the dark forest. She wove between the mangroves heading west. The wind was warm but strong, plastering her clothes against her torso. Branches bobbed and swayed, and she shielded her face from blowing sand.

She found it. Cudlow's 'nest'. Where he had lived off the land for the last decade. It was quaint, like a child's playhouse, but with no rigid structure. The branches created a semi-arch over the entrance. There was a broken boogie board on the ground, like a bed, a cooler with a broken handle. and a folded green tarp.

She turned off the flashlight app and sat on the board. Hunkered down, the surrounding vegetation and rocks provided an adequate windbreak. Through the branches, the stars looked beautiful.

Lying back, the board was hard and hurt her spine and shoulderblades. *How could he sleep on this for ten years?* But she would give it a try. Maybe if she could walk in his shoes—or in this case, sleep in his nest—she could understand the man.

She rolled to her side and draped one of his filthy beach towels over her legs. Then propped another under her head. The sand irritated her face and neck. *Were those sand fleas biting her?* There was no rational way …

What would drive a person to live like this?

It had to be some kind of trauma…

Or insanity.

Was Cudlow insane?

She really knew how to pick 'em.

Gertie sighed and rolled on her back. Her chest heaved, and she hugged herself, wondering who was crazier. Her homeless billionaire boyfriend? Or herself, a woman who invites a man she barely knows into her bed on the first date?

But admittedly, the spark was real. The way he looked at her, with those magnificent green eyes, emotionally bare and spiritually alive. He stirred a passion buried deep for decades, like a volcano, reducing all her caution to ashes and scattering them into the wind. Plus, she had always been a sucker for a British accent.

Was it wrong not to ask him more about his past? Probably. Yet neither of them wanted to break the spell.

She recalled something Cudlow said, how he described enjoying his evening baths in the ocean.

Should she?

No half measures...

With a damp and sandy beach towel in hand, she walked to the water's edge, disrobing quickly, leaving her clothes in a heap, keeping the towel handy. *This is nuts...*

In her birthday suit, she walked into the water, the wind almost pushing her back. The ocean felt freezing, like a million tiny needles on her skin, even though she knew the water temperature was likely in the upper 70s. She plunged forward, yelping into the night air, "Oof, ah, ow, agh, aaaa."

It seemed like a bad idea, but too late to stop now.

After she submerged completely, the temperature shock subsided.

When the discomfort went away, the effect was liberating. Decadent. Amazing. Like she was alive for the first time. Her skin was slippery like a sea lion. Short waves rolled through her, lifted her body, the starry sky enveloped her. Gertie dipped her head back, floating on the soft roller coaster, admiring the island.

Yes, maybe Cudlow was on to something.

And in that moment, she missed him. His kisses, his adorable dimples when he smiled, his dancing for no reason except joy for life itself. And how they made love like teenagers. Giggling one minute and love-struck the other. All the things she appreciated about him that had nothing to do with damned money...

A floodlight on the beach stabbed her eyes. A booming man's voice called, "Ma'am, please exit the water."

Oh, shit.

She paddled closer to shore. "I'm...I'm not dressed."

"We know. Someone called it in."

She didn't recall seeing anyone else. But there was another car in the parking lot. *People needed to mind their own damned business.* "What? You're arresting me?"

"Sorry, ma'am. We can't make an exception."

"Fucking assholes..."

"Please exit."

At least she had money for bail. She strode out of the water, arms wide. "Take a good look! Happy now?"

The officer averted his gaze. "Ma'am, please get dressed."

She toweled herself off and pulled on her clothes. Her phone and her car keys were in her pocket. "Now what?"

The officer used his pen light to write out a ticket. "Name?"

"Gertrude Brown."

"Address?"

This is ridiculous. "I promise not to do this again, all right? Can we forget about this?"

"Procedure."

"Son, I'll show you procedure." She grabbed his note pad and threw it on the sand.

Two minutes later, she was handcuffed in the back of the patrol car, heading to Cruz Bay.

Humiliation burned her face. She made a mental list of all the people she could contact for her one phone call. *Johnnie?* No, he didn't have a car and slept like the dead, plus she refused to sit on the back of his damned scooter.

Dottie? But Dot was such a gossip. The whole church would know by day break.

Maybe Johnnie's sister? Robin seemed like she could keep a secret.

This was all Cudlow's fault. *Why couldn't he be normal?*

Maybe she shared some blame, letting him get under her skin like this.

Her life had been simple and serene before. None of this situation was healthy.

But she knew one thing. The bastard wasn't going to get away with this shit.

* * *

Officer Arturo Bell walked through the corridor of the police station in his civilian clothes. A sight for Gertie's sore eyes. Sitting in the cell was embarrassing. Luckily, she was alone.

He opened the cell and shook his head. "Gertie, what were you thinking?"

"I was just having a moment."

"I'd say. When Robin told me…"

"Look, Officer Roberts was being unreasonable."

"He was only doing his job."

"Well, I told him I wouldn't do it again."

"I spoke with him. He knows you've been through a lot. Being kidnapped at gunpoint is traumatic, even weeks later. But you assaulted him. He couldn't let it go."

"Assaulted him? Ha! What a pussy…"

"Gertie! Shut your mouth right now."

He escorted her into the interrogation room. The room was cinderblock without windows and a checkerboard linoleum floor. "Look, I know you are good folk, but you need to get a hold of yourself. Hear? What is going on with you?"

She leaned on the wall, closed her eyes for a long time, and tried to swallow back emotion. "You're right. I'm not right in the head."

"Do you want to see a doctor?"

"No." She whispered, "Artie, did a romance ever turn you crazy?"

"Ha!" He chuckled and crossed his arms, his stance wide. "Yes, I understand. Between you and me, Robin is a bit of a workaholic. But we try to compromise."

"Well, Cudlow is off in the Bahamas, hardly returning my calls, and he did something so stupid…"

"Yes, men are troublesome. And hard to change. My advice? Tell him how you feel. Or move on. New love is not something you need to wreck yourself over."

"That's easy for you to say. I haven't been in a relationship in forty-five years. At my age, there may not be more chances."

"Oh, don't sell yourself short. You are still a fine-looking lady. But no one is gonna come around if you act like this, cursing and fighting and running around bare-assed."

Part of her wanted to explain the skinny dipping. But it was late. "So, can I go now?"

"Yes, I smoothed it over. But I will say, you could send Officer Roberts a couple dozen of your homemade ginger snaps as an apology…" Arturo winked. He handed her phone back.

Gertie pocketed her phone and scratched her chin. "Yes, the least I can do. Thank you, Artie."

He walked her out of the interrogation room down the narrow hall to the exit. "I'll drive you back to your car. No more nonsense, promise?"

"Yes. And Artie, can you keep this between us?"

Outside the building, at the curb, he held the car's passenger door for her. "I hate to say…"

"What?" She got into his white Toyota Corolla and slammed the door.

"I already got a call from Aunt Dottie."

"No! How? How did she find out?"

He sat in the driver's seat and rolled down the window. "Police scanner."

"Lord give me strength. Why am I not surprised?"

Arturo laughed. "My mom says all the time, God Knows All and Dottie Knows More."

"Did they say my name on the radio?"

"No, but Officer Roberts mentioned a seventy-year-old female and the indecent exposure charge. Dot called Janice for the scoop. Those two are incorrigible." Arturo started the engine. "You can make a formal complaint. Janice knows better."

Janice worked in the 9-1-1 dispatch center. She was part of her church circle of friends and Gertie had known her for decades. Regrettably, Janice believed the only way to deal with the chaos of her job and avoid PTSD was to tell everyone every minor detail of her day—without filtering caller's private details. As a group, her friends confronted her, warning her to stop blabbing. Unfortunately, this admonishment only changed her tactics. Instead of broadcasting secrets to large groups, she merely cornered people individually after church to share the latest 'news'.

"Shoot." Gertie turned on her phone. Sure enough, there was a text from Dot, *"You okay, girlfriend?*

A complaint would have absolutely no effect and only create tension. "Take me back. I've had enough drama." Gertie turned her phone off and stared out the window as the car accelerated down the hill.

Chapter 7

Gertie arrived at the Freeport airport at ten the next morning and hailed a taxi. On the short ride, the driver asked her questions. "What brings you to our lovely island? Where are you from? What activities do you have planned?"

She tried to be polite, but stayed evasive. Because she was going to speak her mind, and get back on the next available flight. In fact, she didn't even bring luggage. Only a large straw handbag with a shawl, her e-reader, a personal check in her wallet from the Carib Bank for $9,999,442, and her latest cross-stitch project.

As the driver pulled up to the wrought iron gates, he whistled, "Fa-ewww." He swiveled his neck to face her. "Lady, you want to go in *there?*"

"Yes. Buzz them. Tell them Gertrude Brown."

"Okay, you say so." He rolled down the window and pressed the white button on the intercom stanchion. Gertie noticed a security camera mounted to the iron fence swung in their direction.

An unfamiliar male voice over the intercom said, "Proceed straight," and the double gates opened.

"Shiiiit," the driver said under his breath, gawking at the house as it came into view.

Gertie felt underdressed in her yoga shorts and V-neck cotton T-shirt. The taxi pulled up to the front of the grand estate. It reminded her of pictures of Martha Stewart's house in the Hamptons, but with stucco exterior, and a wrap-around second story porch. Lush vegetation and mature palm trees surrounded the house. A young man, early twenties, with short brown hair, a royal blue polo shirt, and black Bermuda shorts, waited on the steps to welcome her.

The driver said, "Your total's twenty-one."

She handed him twenty-six dollars US and opened the back door. "Thanks, have a nice day."

The driver said, "That's it? I'm a bit down on my luck these days. Kids school tuition..."

She slammed the door shut.

The driver yelled something crass and gunned the engine around the circular drive.

The thin young man with dark eyelashes, a square jaw, and handsome roman nose approached and extended a handshake. In a British accent, with a voice reminding her of Cudlow's, the man spoke, "Hello, Miss Brown, I'm Jackson."

The Jackson?

The fury in her veins vanished. Jackson was an innocent in this whole debacle. She remembered her manners and shook his hand. "Jackson, I've heard such nice things...I hope you'll forgive my abrupt arrival, but I have some things I need to work out with that excuse of a man."

"You mean grandfather?"

"Yes, I'll apologize in advance. Some of the language out of my mouth may be...let's say, unladylike."

He shook his head, "I'm terribly sorry. You just missed him. Pawpaw is off to the US mainland today for some business."

"Why am I not surprised?" She pulled out her phone and texted, "You can't avoid me forever," to Cudlow.

"Please, come inside. Can I get you a lemonade?" He gestured toward the door.

"Sure. Maybe something stronger. I need a drink." She followed him inside.

The house, despite its size, seemed cozy, with overstuffed arm chairs, nature inspired wallpaper, and wood floors. The ornate fireplaces revealed the home's age with their sandstone mantles and wide dimensions. They walked through a grand hall before heading through a doorway to the kitchen.

Jackson said, "Would you like a brandy? Or we have wine."

It was before noon. Orange juice seemed like a suitable compromise. "Would it be too much trouble to ask for a screwdriver?" She scanned the kitchen. "Are you alone here? I expected a team of servants to greet me."

Gertie's gaze wandered around the gleaming kitchen. Baking would be a dream with its four wall ovens. A tinge of jealously struck her chest. She ran her hand over the veins in the white marble countertop. *Marble was ideal for rolling out pastry dough…*

Jackson opened the refrigerator and took out a carton orange juice. "Our butler Hugh is off this weekend. The cleaning crew comes on Sundays. So, I take it he didn't know you were coming today?"

"No. I wanted to catch him off-guard. When is he getting back?"

Jackson unscrewed the cap from a bottle of expensive vodka. "Can't say exactly. He often brings an overnight bag. Some of his meetings drag on."

She took the glass he offered, and downed half in one gulp. "Ah. Yes. I needed that."

"Would you like a tour of the house?"

She downed the rest of her screwdriver and set her handbag down on the counter. "Sure, why not?" The next return flight wasn't for three hours.

He led her back through the vaulted-ceiling living room. Framed portraits of family members lined one wall. The sofas were white and plush. But the space didn't look lived in; like there could be velvet ropes around the furnishings.

"Who else lives here?" she asked.

"Only me and Pawpaw. Father and mother live in London. When I turned eighteen, he asked me to be the caretaker. Sometimes my girlfriend stays over, but she says it's too quiet."

"A young man like you rattling around in this place by yourself?" It broke her heart.

"No, it isn't bad. Come on, I'll show you something." He led her up a Victorian-era staircase with ornate oak spindles. At the end of the upstairs hall, he opened a door.

She entered the small empty white room. "What can you show me? There's nothing in here."

"Wait." He plucked a set of large goggles and some oversized gloves off the wall behind her. "Put these on."

"What for?"

"Humor me. Please?"

She put them on. *Blackness at first.* "What is this…?"

Jackson called out, "Dungeon Master Level Eight."

A dark, dank-looking castle hallway enveloped her. Gertie held her hands up to find cartoon arms, covered in mesh gauntlets, holding a sword. "Oooh. This is different." She waved the sword in a figure eight. To her right, a character appeared with a face like Jackson's, but he was short like a dwarf and wore a leather outfit, smoking a corn-cob pipe.

She swished her torso to test the effect. "How do we move forward?"

Jackson's voice came out of the dwarf, "Try moving your arms like you're walking. A spatial sensor will pick it up. But don't actually walk. You may hit a wall."

She tried it, and they walked down the dim hall. The stone walls looked so real, with moss growing on them and the lights from the torches cast the correct shadows no matter where she set her gaze.

When she turned her attention away from the walls, gigantic orc in leather battle gear, with muscled green arms, rushed toward her wielding a mace.

Gertie ducked reflexively, holding up her arms to protect herself. "Stop!" She whipped off the headset.

Jackson called out, "Cancel."

"Holy...Jackson, that was amazing."

He took her headset and gloves. "I don't know if I should..."

"Should what?"

His face turned sheepish. "He thinks about you all the time."

"That's his problem. I'm giving him back the money and I don't plan to see him again."

"No, you don't understand. He loves you. I've never seen someone love anyone more."

"His idea of love is bullshit." She shook her head and sighed. "Sorry, normally I don't curse this much...he makes me so mad."

Jackson called out, "Gertie One."

The overhead light dimmed and a projection appeared on the far wall. She was staring at herself, surrounded in her own garden. It was a bird's-eye view, like those taken by drones.

Stunned, she backed away and leaned against the wall to steady herself. "How did he..." There she was, in her yellow housecoat, not the most flattering, her hair tied in a bandana, dirt up to her elbows, pulling weeds. Her lips were moving, singing a song, but there was no sound.

"He sits here on the floor for a few minutes each night before bed."

She couldn't take it any longer. "Turn it off!"

Jackson turned it off and a center light came on.

"I've seen enough."

Jackson shook his head. "No, one more thing. Please indulge me."

"Good grief. What? Did he create a robot in my likeness?"

Jackson blinked and his cheeks turned red. "No. That's…no. Just come on."

She craved another drink. And she felt bad for embarrassing Jackson. "Fine."

Gertie followed Jackson down the stairs and they headed to the north end of the house. He opened a wood paneled door.

"This is Pawpaw's office, where he spends most of his time. Come."

The study had a wall of bookcases, beautiful green toile curtains, and a heavy carved-wood desk with three computer screens. Two empty Snickers wrappers littered the desk, among the messy stacks of paper. The left side monitor had a copy-holder affixed with a single piece of paper—some kind of accounting balance sheet with pencil markings in the margins and the bottom line highlighted.

Jackson handed her the sheet. "This is the reason he's here. He risked everything to buy that bloody real estate investment firm. The family business is on the verge of ruin. Over a thousand employees could be sacked. If he doesn't meet the hard-money loan in thirty days, the effects will be disastrous."

She looked at the number on the bottom. Negative four-hundred and eleven million. "I don't understand."

"He wants to be with you. He doesn't want all this. But he won't hurt the company's employees. Give him a month. Please."

Something caught her eye. A white velvet jewelry box on the fireplace mantle. She picked it up and opened it. It was a huge blue stone ring, big enough to choke a gerbil. *A noose in disguise…*

"Jackson, did he buy this for me?"

"I believe so."

She picked up the ring and held it up to the light. "This is the problem. Thinking he can buy my love." She placed the blue ring back into the box, thought about returning it to the mantle, but with a surge of rage, flung it across the room. It skittered across the rug and disappeared under a sofa. Seeing Jackson's dismay, she instantly felt foolish. "Sorry, I'm leaving."

Clouded in anger, she headed to the quickest exit—the French door to the patio. Jackson called out to her, but she slammed the door behind her and kept walking. The heat outside barely registered on her already hot face. She followed the blue slate path.

After turning the corner, she stopped cold.

The backyard garden was, in a word, stunning. A wild English garden like a fairy tale. With wisteria covered trellises and topiary shaped like hedgehogs and bunnies surrounded by an explosion of long-stemmed pink and white roses. The garden extended to a rock wall by the ocean, with a gate leading to a boat slip.

She ran her hand over the rose petals, mentally tallying all the species of flowers.

Jackson appeared and stood at her shoulder, facing the garden. He handed over her straw bag. "Spectacular, isn't it? You should have seen it before. I wasn't a very good caretaker, letting it become awfully overgrown. But when Pawpaw arrived, he told me to hire a team. Spared no expense."

"Because of me?"

"I believe so."

It was all too much. Did Cudlow fix the garden up in hopes she would live there with him? She wanted to cry. No one had ever created anything so wonderful in her honor. Still, his priorities were so screwed up. These were all empty gestures.

She dug in her wallet and found the check. She handed it to Jackson. "Give this to your grandfather. I used some money for my airfare."

"I can't." He dug his hands in his back pockets.

"Yes, you can and you will." She bored her eyes into his.

Jackson took a seat on a nearby cast-iron garden bench. "Please sit."

Gertie threw up one hand and took a deep breath. She took a seat.

He wrung his hands. "I'm not doing this right. I'm trying to tell you…trying to make you see. And I'm not helping things."

She patted his knee. "This isn't your fault. Don't feel bad."

"He's the *first* one to say how flawed he is. But you need to know." Jackson's voice cracked, "When Grandmaw Winifred died, everything changed."

Gertie froze. What had Cudlow called her on their last night together? Before the kidnapping? *Freddy.* He had assumed she was asleep, when in fact, she was merely quietly confused. *Winifred…that could explain…*

Jackson gazed into the distance. "He locked himself in his study for a month. Then he disappeared. He blamed himself. Blamed the money.

But it wasn't the money. Money is a tool. A thing. So, all that left was himself."

"I'm sorry. The situation must have been hard on you."

"He's been messed up since. Believing he has an on-off switch—like he can only be a greedy bastard or destitute bum. No middle ground. It isn't healthy."

"That's my point. He's being a fool."

"No, hear me out. The best he's been is when he met you. He's getting better. I see it. I hear it in his voice. You should see him, dancing barefoot in the kitchen while he cuts up melons. There's a lightness that wasn't there before. I'm not saying you have to save him, but please, please, give him a chance. I know he can find the right balance."

"What does this have to do with taking the check?"

"I know it's bleeding bonkers. But he doesn't want to be a financial burden to you and he doesn't want to live in fear."

"Fear? Jesus."

"You have to understand. Everyone came with their hand out after Grandmaw died. It was frankly disgusting. The reason he doesn't talk with great-grandmother, my father or uncle anymore. I'm not sure why he gave you the money. Maybe it was a test of sorts. I can't say. You have a right to be mad. But you must know he loves you very much."

"Well, I know one way to deal with his perverted little test." She stood, looped her bag on her shoulder, and said, "Call me a taxi. I'm going to the airport."

Chapter 8

After two layovers, Gertie's flight touched down at Charles de Gaulle Airport at eleven o'clock in the morning local time. Her mouth tasted like month-old milk and she was still wearing the same yoga shorts, although she bought a new t-shirt during her short layover at the Atlanta airport. She hoped her cousin Lisa would be waiting in the arrivals area.

With little sleep and her skin dry from the stale recirculated air, she followed the herd through customs, declared nothing, and followed the crowd downstairs to the ground transportation zone.

Lisa was there, waving wildly with both arms. Her dark hair in flat braids along her scalp and a natural short poof on the bottom. She wore black trousers and a zebra pattern sweater. In fact, everyone in the area wore jackets and long pants. It was mid-May and still chilly. Through the glass windows, rain poured; umbrellas created a black swath along the outdoor taxi line.

"You made it. I wasn't sure. My flight came in an hour ago. How was your trip?" Her younger cousin was talking fast. Excitement beaming from her face like a kid on Christmas morning.

Gertie wrapped her arms around Lisa. "Thank you for coming. I'm so tired. I don't know what I'm doing."

Lisa held Gertie's face. "Cousin, let me look at you. What is going on?"

Her face felt hot and her eyes watered. "I…I wish I knew." A mix of sadness and anger battled inside. The last thing she needed was an emotional breakdown in a crowded terminal. Maybe it was the dryness of her eyes. Maybe lack of sleep. Or maybe she was coming unglued. Probably all three.

"Come, let's get settled. You said you made a hotel reservation?

Where's your luggage?"

"I don't have luggage." Gertie took a deep breath. Bawling in an airport was not a good move. She needed to keep things together for another hour.

"No luggage? So, you got on a plane to Paris and didn't even bring a toothbrush?"

"Like I said, it's a long story." Her mind raced. A toothbrush would be everything right now. And a hot shower. And a change of underwear.

"Birdie, I can't wait to hear it. But come on, we need a taxi. Where are we headed?"

"The Ritz."

Gertie recalled how the agent at the tiny travel agency desk at the Nassau airport looked at her with incredulity. *Unlimited budget? Deluxe Suite? First available departure?* Although, with the last-minute booking, there weren't any first-class seats available on the flights. *But speed meant more…*

Lisa shook her head. "What?"

"No. Wait, first a bank. I need to convert cash to Euros."

"I have euros. First, you need to take a nap and then you can tell me everything." Lisa opened her bag and took out a red long sleeve sweater. "Here, put this on. Can't catch a cold in the most beautiful city in the world."

Gertie put on the sweater and they walked outside. Rain blew sideways, leaving no refuge under the sidewalk canopy. The line for transportation was ridiculous. Gertie rummaged in her embroidered straw bag and pulled out a large bill in US currency. She walked up to the skycap and said, "The Ritz, right away," and handed him the money.

Lisa looked at Gertie, her eyes wide. "Five hundred? Are you crazy?"

Gertie grimaced. "Yes."

The porter spoke rapid French into a radio and within a minute, a shiny black sedan pulled up. The porter shuffled them toward it and held open the rear door. He seemed to convey their destination to the driver.

Gertie slid across the back seat. The seat was cold and she rubbed the rain from her shins for warmth.

Lisa gave her small rolling bag to the driver, who took it around to the trunk. She sat next to Gertie. "Did you win the lottery or something?"

"Ha! Something like that."

"Tsk-tsk-tsk. Well, at this rate, you'll have nothing left in a year."

If only. Gertie threw her head back, eyes closed, and moaned. "A good plan if you ask me."

* * *

Gertie woke to voices in the parlor. She donned one of the fluffy white robes with the words "Ritz Paris" embroidered in gold and opened the antique mirrored pocket doors. The sound of the hotel room door closing piqued her curiosity. "Cuz?"

Lisa walked over holding a bottle. "They sent up a bottle of wine. So nice."

Gertie yawned. "How long was I asleep? What time is it?"

"It's two-fifteen. Are you hungry? A walk might do you good."

"Good idea. Let me fix my hair and we can go. Oh, wait. I don't have anything to wear."

"You can borrow from me. How about we get a quick bite and go shopping?" She chuckled, "I mean, if you are going to spend some of your lottery winnings, this is the best place to do it."

Gertie stretched her back and muttered, "Yeah, that will show him."

"What?"

"Nothing. Call the Concierge, ask about restaurant options. We'll also need a personal shopper who can translate for us."

"Really? We could just explore."

"No. And maybe a driver for the afternoon."

Lisa sat on the velvet sofa by the window. "You really should slow down."

"Why? It's only money."

"You need to tell me what's going on." She sat back and crossed her arms like she was all business.

"Later. I'm starving. I want a steak and chocolate mousse and French bread."

"Fine. Take whatever clothes you need from my bag. Your hair *definitely* needs work."

Gertie wrinkled her nose and jokingly retorted, "Love you."

Lisa snickered. "Use my comb."

Gertie retreated to the bedroom and rifled through Lisa's bag. Unfortunately, Lisa's bras were too small. She admitted defeat and put her original, now smelly, bra back on. Perhaps some Parisian women went without certain support, but she wasn't feeling that free yet. A loose navy V-neck dress did fit, and she added Lisa's red cardigan from earlier.

She used Lisa's toiletries, comb, plus the new toothbrush the hotel gave her when she checked in. It was strange dressing like a refugee in such opulent surroundings. Her straw bag looked out of place and cheap. But all this would change soon enough.

Gertie joined her cousin in the parlor. "I'm ready. Where are we going?"

Lisa rattled off options like she was reading a grocery list. "I spoke with the concierge—Monsieur Belmont—and we narrowed it down to two options. A bite to eat in the lobby bar and then the driver will take us to a commercial shopping center with high street stores. Or we can get lunch at the hotel's restaurant and we can walk to stores like Alexander McQueen, Isabel Marant, Celine, Dior…you get the idea. They are down the street. The personal shopper costs two hundred euros an hour. Are you sure?"

She'd never owned an item of clothing that cost more than $50. If she was going to spend time in Paris, she might as well see how the other half lived. As in, what kind of life Cud had lived after he amassed his millions. A counter experiment to her swimming at night at Hawknest's beach, but now with hopefully less nudity and no run-ins with law enforcement.

Gertie's mind raced. "How about option three? Small bite at the bar and then the designer stores. First underwear and walking shoes. And a raincoat. A bag. Then something fancy to wear to dinner later. And day clothes. And luggage. Well, maybe luggage can wait. Let's head down." She pulled her bag over her shoulder.

"You know, you never said how long we were staying."

"I don't know. Maybe when the money runs out?"

"Gertie! That's terrible. What the hell?"

"Do you want to go or not?"

"Bird, your momma didn't raise you to be no ninnyhammer. She'd be rolling in her grave hearing this talk. You better check yourself."

"Well, I'm leaving."

"Fine." She waved with the back of her hand. "Go do you."

"Don't be angry."

"Cousin, you're being strange. You better tell me what's going on or I'm bouncing." Lisa crossed her arms, setting her jaw in a serious manner.

Gertie didn't know how to answer. Because her plan wasn't much of a plan at all. Simply a knee-jerk reaction to hurt Cudlow. But also hoping a change of scenery would give her perspective. She'd always wanted to visit Paris, but on her teacher's salary, it was never an option. "I don't want to talk about it."

"Fine." Lisa said in a huff. She left the couch and went to the bedroom, slamming the pocket doors together loudly behind her.

Now alone, Gertie faced her distorted image in the antique mirrored panels.

She called out to Lisa, "I'll be back by seven. See you later." Pausing a couple seconds for a response, she was met with silence.

She took her hotel key and secured it in her wallet.

Down at the lobby, Monsieur Belmont waved to her. "Madam, did you decide what you'd like to do?"

"Yes, I'll have something small here first. Were you able to contact a translator?"

"Of course. Mademoiselle Girard is arriving soon."

"Wonderful. Please, ask her to join me at the bar when she arrives. Also, could you make me a dinner reservation for tonight at nine? Your restaurant looks heavenly."

"Perfect. And your cousin? Will she be joining you?"

"I think so." Actually, she hoped so. And she hoped to have a rationale by then to appease Lisa's curiosity about the money.

Gertie went to the bar and ordered a turkey sandwich. Not very Parisian, but she was starving and didn't care.

A few minutes later, a young woman with ebony straight hair, flawless ivory skin, average height and the waist of a teenager, walked up to her. "Madam Brown? I'm Philomène Girard. I'm yours for the afternoon." She extended her hand.

Gertie wiped her right hand with a white cloth napkin and shook her hand. "Bon jour, please call me Gertie."

"Yes, you must also call me Mina."

The woman, likely in her late twenties, took a seat on the bar stool next to her. She wore an ivory jumpsuit, a chunky gold chain necklace and burgundy suede pumps. She had a matching burgundy velvet Dior handbag. "I hear you are interested in some shopping?"

"Yes."

"Any items of interest?" Mina ran her hand through her long hair to smooth it.

"Everything."

"I…everything? I don't…"

"I don't have any luggage…"

The woman's eyes widened. "Oh, I hate it when the airlines lose my luggage. One time…"

"No, I didn't bring any."

"Oh, well, this is different."

"And I'll need a sim card and data plan for my phone."

"Yes, no problem." Mina took out her phone and typed some information in it.

"There's something else. Are you tech savvy?"

"Tech?"

"Could you help me create an Instagram page?"

Mina laughed. "Oh, I understand. To show your family pictures of your adventure in Paris? How nice!"

"Um. Actually," Gertie whispered, "The man in my life is avoiding me. I…" Running away and avoiding Cudlow was her way of turning the tables; playing his game against him. And the angry part of her brain wanted to rub this in his face. Meaning her cousin Lisa was right. She needed to check herself.

Mina's eyes danced and her pert nose wiggled. "Ooh. You want him to see what he is missing? You are a naughty one, eh?"

Gertie chuckled. "Precisely."

Mina patted her hand. "I think we will get along very well. Do not worry. I know the best places."

Gertie nodded. "I'm counting on it."

Chapter 9

His library books were due today. No more stalling, he told himself.

Just go in, smile, and ask her if she wants to go with him for coffee. Or an early dinner. *Was five o'clock too early for dinner?* It wouldn't be early for him, considering he woke before sunrise most days, but he wondered what normal people did. He came prepared with two options. One was coffee at the Java Crescent café and the other was an early dinner at Mama Jo's Barbecue. Both walking distance from the library.

What if she said no?

He entered the library at ten minutes to five, right before closing. As he headed to the counter, he glanced to his left and froze in terror.

Police Chief Tobias was talking with Greta by the computer terminals.

What was he doing there?

With his heart lodged in his throat, he placed the pirate books on the counter and turned to leave before Tobias noticed.

Greta called, "John! Wait."

He froze, like an emotionally stunted mannequin.

Tobias headed toward the door. Johnnie faced the check-out desk, averting his eyes from the Chief, yet he could feel the man's dark eyes sear into his skull. The wood floors shook with the gigantic man's plodding footsteps.

After Tobias left, Greta approached the desk. "Hi, John."

"I...returned..." He shook his head, "Um, what was Chief Tobias doing here?"

"Oh, Joseph reads to the second-grade class every Wednesday. He was helping me put away the chairs."

"He reads to little kids?"

"Yes, they love him. We might film his next reading for YouTube. Did these pirate books help with your story? How is it coming?" She scanned the inside back bar code of the first book in his stack.

"I'm still not sure if I have a solid plot yet." He looked at her, but she was reading something on her checkout terminal. He noticed she didn't have eyeshadow today. In fact, no makeup at all, making her hazel eyes and silky hair all the more beautiful.

"Oh, I forgot. I loaned these outside the system—"

"I was wondering if…if you'd be interested in getting coffee or something?"

"Wow, look at this!" She took a bookmark out of the book on Blackbeard. "Is this yours?"

It was. Gertie gave him an embroidered bookmark every Christmas for the last four years. This one was on the feminine side, with a sparrow sitting on a book, surrounded by pink clouds.

"Yes, my landlady…"

"It's sooo adorable!"

"You can keep it."

"Really? You don't mind?" She turned to put the returned books on a rolling cart behind her.

"No, I have a few." He swallowed hard; a tiny voice in his head told him to give up before she laughed him out of the room. He took off his glasses and told the voice to shut up.

She looked at him perplexed. "What?"

Did he say that aloud? "Not you. Hey, um…you're getting off work soon, right?"

"Yes," She looked at the clock on the wall above the door. "In four minutes."

"How about coffee? Or barbeque? Are you hungry?"

Her eyes widened. "Now? I mean, sure."

"I was thinking about Mama Jo's. Is that okay? We could walk."

Without a beat of hesitation, she smiled. "Yes. Awesome!"

She walked around the main room, shutting down the bank of computer terminals and the overhead lights. At the wall by the door, she lifted the cover for the alarm. "Can you wait outside? I'll be right out."

He stood outside, wondering if he knew how to carry on a conversation with Greta, or if the outing would be a miserable failure.

Talking about the weather would be lame. He could ask her about the short stories she used to write. *Maybe book recommendations?*

Johnnie was lost in his thoughts when Greta bounced outside and said, "Let's go."

Minutes later, sitting at a picnic bench with their cardboard trays of food, his earlier worries vanished. Because Greta was a brilliant conversationalist. At first, she talked about her recent move to St. John, and how her mom had just passed. Then she talked about her masters' in library science and her brief internship at the Library of Congress. She was clearly one of the smartest people he'd ever met. While he listened intently, he became certain that he had nothing to offer her.

"What is your favorite book?" She sipped her bottled root beer through a straw.

"I like adventure stories and thrillers. But I don't have a favorite. What about you?"

"I'm currently reading a history about Genghis Khan. I'm going through all the famous warlords. Last year, I read about British monarchs. But my guilty pleasure is romance stories. I must have read Jane Eyre ten times."

"I don't know that one."

"Hey, I'm sorry. I've been monopolizing the conversation. Tell me about your hobbies."

"I enjoy fishing. When I first moved here, I saw this group of guys spear fishing. I talked to them and they taught me how. Now I try to go once a week."

"What about writing?"

"It's a stupid idea. But my sister keeps saying I should try it."

"It's not stupid. What have you written so far?"

"That's the problem. I write a page and it seems so flat." He wiped barbeque sauce from his mouth. "You know how they say, *write what you know*?"

"Sure," Greta smiled.

"I don't know anything. I mean, I don't have reliable memories of most of my life. And the ones I do have, could be from TV shows or movies. I can't tell them apart."

"You mentioned a poor memory before. Are you okay?"

He didn't want to talk about it or receive sympathy. "I had a brain injury. I'm much better now."

"What happened? A car accident?"

"Something like that." He scratched the scar above his right ear. A first date wasn't the right time to tell her about his hair-brained heroics in Afghanistan, or how damaged it left him. Because he didn't want her pity.

And he couldn't tell her about all the chaos and heartbreak he caused afterward. To make matters worse, last month the news called him the St. Johnnie Killer, just because he found two dead bodies on the beach. Stuff that could happen to anyone. As a news buff, she must have seen it. He felt a headache coming on. "I'd rather not…"

"Sorry, we don't have to talk about it." Greta rested her chin on her hand, "You know, the best part about writing it making up stuff. Don't feel discouraged. In high school, I wrote a short story about a girl who had visions of a deadly plague spread by alien plants; and later, almost everyone on the planet died. My teacher said I was weird. But that is why I love fiction. You can write anything…"

Desperate to change the subject, he said. "I submitted a bid at an on-line auction for a boat a few days ago. A forty-six-foot fishing yacht." He sipped his bottled water.

"Really? Sounds awesome."

"It's a long-shot. But it would be nice to get off this island on weekends."

"You'll need a first mate," Greta grinned.

Probably too much to hope for. "Like I said, I might not get it." He was almost done with his last rib. They were delicious. Part of him was glad the meal was coming to a close. Because his heart had been pounding like a heart attack since they sat down.

Greta bit into her corn on the cob and chewed, "Well, I hope you do. I love the ocean. The solitude, the breeze in my hair."

Johnnie put down the rib bone he'd finished off. "You have beautiful hair." He hadn't meant to blurt that out. *Was he being too forward?*

She put down her corn and smiled at him with her eyes. "Are you flirting with me?"

"Yes, but badly."

Greta giggled. "I think you're doing fine."

"Really? It feels like my nerves are doing backflips into molten lava."

"Ha! Well…" She leaned forward across the table and whispered toward his ear, "I think you're pretty cute."

There was a long silence as he wondered what to say next. Because no one had whispered to him in a sultry voice for as long as he could recall.

He looked at his finished tray. "Um, we should probably get going."

They cleared the table and tossed their trash in the bin.

Greta said, "This was fun."

"Yeah. Thanks for having dinner with me."

She waved, walking backward away from him. "See you around, John."

He waved back and watched her as she walked away, up the sidewalk.

That wasn't so bad, he told himself.

Except for the constant pains in his chest and never knowing what to say.

He let out a deep breath. The sun was going down, and he needed to get home.

Riding his scooter toward Calabash Boom, a realization struck him.

He didn't ask for her phone number!

Classic rookie mistake.

Maybe dating was hopeless, or he was hopeless.

On the bright side, she said he was cute.

But that would change if she knew his entire story.

* * *

Johnnie submitted his on-line bid for the boat a week ago. Not that he expected to win it. Researching the make and year, the nearly four decade old 46-foot Bertram was worth about eighty-thousand. He only had $1500 to play with. Although his bank account showed more, because Gertie wasn't around to deposit his rent checks. He got a post-card from her last week. It had a picture of the Eiffel Tower. She wrote to remind him to water her garden and give away any ripe produce he couldn't use to the food bank.

So, when he opened his email from the Department of Planning and Natural Resources on Friday morning, stating they accepted his bid, he had to read it twice.

He called Robin. "Sis, I got it."

"Hi, got what?"

"The Bertram."

"Really? That's great."

"I can pick it up tomorrow. But I need a place to moor it. And I have to get it certified, registered, plus a decal number from U.S. Customs, and a ton of things."

"God, Johnnie, do you even know how to drive that thing?"

"Of course. I used to operate Marine landing crafts twice the size."

"Okay, but do you *remember* how?"

"It's pretty foolproof. Even for this fool."

"Tell you what, how about Arturo and I go with you on your maiden voyage? Where do you want to go?"

"Well, actually, I promised the first trip to Greta."

"Greta? Oh, Johnnie! The librarian, right?"

"Ow. Don't scream. No. She's a friend. We talk about books."

"But you two are going out?"

"We had dinner two nights ago. That's all. I like her, but I don't know if I can handle a girlfriend."

"Well, I'm happy for you. And I'm still excited. You never know. Look at me and Artie. We were friends—well acquaintances—for a long time. Sometimes you only need a little spark."

"Jumpin' Joe, I'm sorry I even told you."

"Well, pencil us in for the next outing. I can't wait to see it."

Johnnie said goodbye and hung up. *Why couldn't people let him be?* Always focused on his love life. Or non-existent love life.

But the conversation reminded him to go back for a second batch of library books.

And he could find out if Greta was free Sunday for a trip to the British Virgin Islands. He wanted to check out a pirate-themed restaurant on Norman Island and maybe take a hike to check out old pirate coves.

Maybe he could bring Stumpy?

Iguana's need adventure, right?

Sure, why the hell not?

Chapter 10

Dottie sat at her government-issued metal desk in the alcove outside Senator Robin Crosswell's office looking for clues. She scrolled through past news articles searching for anything to help locate the fugitive Thomas Smith, the asshole who kidnapped Gertie last month and made off with millions in bitcoin. The FBI task force called their office yesterday to tell Robin they were disbanding, saying they ran out of leads. She couldn't believe it. And Dottie prided herself on never leaving a task unfinished or a mystery unsolved.

In fairness, the authorities didn't have her resourcefulness or connections. Even so, she scoffed at their lackadaisical efforts.

A possibly related story had caught her attention and nagged at her over the last couple of weeks. She called Janice at the police station.

Dottie wiggled her shoulders with excitement after Janice picked up. "Hey, girl."

"Hey, good morning! What's shaking mama?"

"I'm working on something. You remember that story about the two ornithologists who had their boat stolen last month?"

"Nah. Horny what now?"

"Bird scientists. At LeDuck Island. A man attacked them and stole their boat. Three days after Gertie was kidnapped. Did the police investigate?"

Janice asked, "Why do you care?"

"I have a theory."

"You always have a theory." Janice laughed. "Like when you thought Elvis was alive."

"I swear the guy on the ferry…"

"Now then, what about bird watchers?"

"Did they describe the man that attacked them? The news story doesn't give a description. Simply says a man faking an injury beat them up."

"I could pull the file."

Dottie wiggled her butt in her chair and grinned. "Thanks. Hey, you know what else I found out?"

"No, what?"

"The company behind the murders last month? Guess who bought it."

With agitation, Janice asked, "How would I know?"

"Cudlow."

"What? Does Gertie know?"

"I'm guessing he did it to save her. That's the most romantic thing I've ever heard."

Janice said, "Oh…so that explains why lover boy left her in the middle of the night on business."

"Gertie doesn't know. She would be furious."

"Why? A man comes to your rescue…a billionaire no less? I'm reading a romance novel just like this. He's a baron in Scotland who owns a castle. He falls for the milk maid…and ooh, it's steamy. He does this thing with his tongue…"

"Hold that thought. I have another call. I'll catch you later." Dot hung up with Janice and hit the button for line two. The phone's caller ID read Bahamas.

She put on her game face, cleared her throat, and answered, "Good morning, Senator Crosswell's office. This is Dot McPherson. How may I help you this morning?"

A young man's voice on the other end said, "Um, good morning. My name is Jackson Loughton. Is the Senator available?"

Excitement raced through her veins. With a last name of Loughton, he had to be a relative of Cud's. "Oh, I'm sorry. She's away on St. Thomas in meetings today. Can I relay a message?"

"It's more of a personal matter."

"Great. My specialty."

"Pardon?"

"Lay it on me. Maybe I can help."

"Oh. Well, my grandfather—"

"Cudlow."

With surprise in his voice, he said, "You know him?"

"Sure do. We planned a hostage exchange together last month."

"Oh. Um. Oh, I see. Well, in any case, grandfather is looking for advice from Senator Crosswell about living accommodations on the island. He wants a modest flat. Something discreet."

The wheels churned in Dot's brain as she went over a mental map of the island. "How modest? Parameters! Give me parameters! Location, views, price range, amenities."

"Pawpaw said he requires walls, a sink, a bathtub and a place for a hotplate."

"Hold on. That's all?"

"And walking distance to a grocery store."

"Holy Moly. But I thought he wanted to live with Gertie." With her eyes wide, she held her breath to see if Jackson would dish. She put the volume up two notches on the handset, not wanting to miss anything he said.

"I can't say."

She exhaled. *Foiled.* Needing to regroup, she was determined to be helpful. "Well, I heard a condo in Robin's building is on the market. Same floor plan. A one-bedroom. Might be perfect. I know the agent. Shelly Pirro." She recited the phone number from memory. "Tell her I referred you."

"Thank you. Beg my pardon, what is your name again?"

"Dottie McPherson. If you or Cudlow need anything, don't hesitate to call. I'll hook you up."

"That is so kind. Thank you, Dottie."

"Tell Cudlow not to stay away too long now, you hear?"

"Um, yes. Well, thank you for your time."

"Anytime, sugar. Bye now."

"Goodbye."

Dottie hung up and called Janice right back. "It's me. You won't believe it."

"What happened?"

Dot couldn't contain herself. She scrunched up her face and blurted, "Cudlow is getting his own place to live."

"What? No! What about Gertie? I thought he moved in with her last month."

"I don't know. But can you *imagine*?"

Janice said, "I should call her."

"She's gone, went to Paris."

"Texas?"

"No. France."

"When did that happen? And why didn't she invite us?"

The indignation in Janice's voice made Dot smile. "I think she's on a vision quest."

"Well, with her money, she can do what she pleases."

"Money?"

Janice laughed with a chuckle that seemed mocking. "You don't know? Ha! That's a first."

"What are you talking about?"

"Cudlow gave her ten million dollars. My cousin works at the Carib Bank. Cud signed over his account to her. She's filthy rich now."

"Damn. No wonder she's in Paris."

"If it were me, I'd stay there. You know, I read this novel once where a young Parisian debutante meets a struggling artist who's hung like a horse, and at first they hate each other, because she thinks he stole their family's jewels, but later they make love all night on top of the Eiffel Tower…"

Another call lit up Dottie's phone. Probably work related. "Send me the deets. I got to bounce."

"Sure. Bye, Dottie."

"Bye, Janice."

Chapter 11

I t took most of Saturday for Johnnie to get all the registration and paperwork completed for the Bertram. Each form asked for the name of his vessel. Not feeling creative and in the interest of time, he settled on the name Bert.

Fueling the boat caused a financial hit. The tank ate up nine-hundred dollars in diesel, which he had to put on a credit card. Owning a boat was going to be expensive in ways he hadn't realized. Which meant he had to rethink the whole thing.

No wonder no one else bid on the damned forty-year-old vessel. Besides the fuel, there would be upkeep. It was in great shape now, but unless he was going to start a charter business, it would cost too much for personal use.

He posted Bert on eBay with a twenty-seven-day bidding period, giving him ample time to have a few fun weekends before his dream vanished.

Sunday morning, he drove to Greta's place. She lived in a rented room in Cruz Bay, close to the library. Only, he brought along another passenger.

He knocked on her door.

She opened it as he poised his knuckles to rap again. She wore knee-length shorts and a white cotton eyelet blouse, hiking boots on her feet, and a baseball cap over her long red wavy hair. "John, I'm so excited. Thanks for inviting me." She reached up and kissed his cheek.

He recoiled in shock at her easy affection. "Um, yeah, no problem. Ready?"

She locked her front door. "Ready and willing."

They walked down the stone steps to the road where he had parked his scooter.

She pointed, "What's that? A picnic basket?"

He should have warned her. *Was he a freak for doing this?* "I know this is weird, but I wanted to bring my friend Stumpy."

"Huh?"

The only container he could find to transport the iguana was a wood-slat picnic basket belonging to Gertie. During his brief detour at Hawksnest Beach, he easily coaxed Stumpy inside the basket; but admittedly, the iguana's obedient behavior had more to do with the series of cheese puffs laid down in a perfect path. And Johnnie added some strawberry slices inside the basket as well. He had strapped the basket onto the back of his scooter with a bungee cord.

He unwrapped the elastic stay and opened the basket flap two inches. Stumpy's head popped up, glaring with a side-eye through the narrow opening. "See? He's an iguana."

"I didn't know you had a pet. Cool."

"Really? You don't mind? You'll have to hold his basket until we get to the bay."

"Sure," she smiled.

"Great!" He exhaled in relief because the look on her face told him she didn't consider this unusual.

They arrived at Great Cruz Bay, where he had the boat temporarily moored. From the compartment under the scooter's seat, he retrieved an insulated lunch bag containing three bottled waters, a bag of strawberries, lettuce leaves, and some cheese puffs. Most of the food was for Stumpy, since they planned on eating lunch out. With his inflatable dinghy—another unplanned expense—staged at the marina, he rowed Greta and Stumpy over to Bert, who was fueled, clean and ready to rumble.

Once on board, Johnnie set Stumpy free. The iguana seemed confused at first, running onto the bow, then the stern, then climbed to the roof of the flybridge where he settled down.

Greta took out her phone. "Here, quick." She draped her arm around his shoulder and took a picture. "Smile!"

Her sudden hug made him freeze. He hated his smile. Instead, he pursed his lips into a grin to avoid showing his gummy teeth.

"Got it!" She put her phone away and opened the door to the interior cabin space. "Oh, no way!" Greta ducked through the opening. "It's like a tiny apartment in here." She went further down a set of three steps.

"And there are three bedrooms."

He remained in the living area, knowing how cramped the 'hall' was down below. But after the sounds of cabinets opening and closing, footsteps and some 'oohs' and 'wows', there came a silence.

Was she okay?

He found her in the primary bedroom. Although *room* was too generous a term. Really, it was a tight enclosure with wood cabinets surrounding a queen bed.

She stared at the low ceiling. "You should see this."

"See what?"

Greta patted the mattress, still covered with the blue comforter left from the previous owner. He didn't intend to sleep there, so he hadn't outfitted it with new linens. Sleeping on someone else's bedding gave him the willies. "Um, I don't know."

"I'm not going to bite you, silly. Check out this ceiling."

Johnnie crawled onto the bed and flopped on his back, careful to maintain a foot-wide gap between them. "What should—?" He looked up. "Oh. Cool!"

"See the script in the corner? It's a reproduction of the map from Treasure Island."

"But the map is fictional, right?"

"Right. But wait." She flipped a switch by the bed and the lights went out.

Before he could protest, tiny points of light dotted the ceiling, in the form of constellations.

It was transcendent. Like being in a planetarium, but the closeness of the stars and the motion of the boat made the experience more surreal. "Wow. The auction site had photos, but nothing about this."

He continued to stare, trying to recall the names. Big dipper and little dipper were easy. The others...

Half a minute went by, lying side by side in the dark. Greta gazed upward and whispered. "What are you thinking?"

That was a loaded question. Her proximity made him nervous. He could smell the cherry Chapstick on her lips.

"I...think we should get underway." He bolted up and headed through the cabin, up the stairs, whipping open the hatch door to soak in the daylight and fresh air.

Stumpy was on the deck in front of him, staring like an angry abandoned puppy. *Or maybe it was his imagination?*

Up on the flybridge, he set the GPS navigation system toward Norman's Island. They sat side by side on the two teak and vinyl helm chairs. Greta asked questions about how to operate the boat.

He pointed to the various controls and dials. It was all pretty rudimentary. Like driving a car, almost. When they reached the open ocean, he traded seats with her. "Try it."

She sat behind the wheel. Then shook her head. "Wait, I have something for you." She dug her hand into her shorts pocket and pulled out a gold hoop. "I figured if you were going to write about pirates, you should play the part. Really get into character."

He held up the hoop earring. It was a clip on, about an inch in diameter but chunky. "You think I should wear this?"

"Why not? I mean, come on, try it." She took it from his open palm and steadied his head. "Stand still. This won't hurt."

After she clipped it on his lobe, he touched the backing. It pinched his ear securely. He probably looked crazy. "Does it look crazy?"

She stroked her chin. "I'd say it looks *wicked* handsome."

He scratched his neck. "No, really. I don't want to look stupid."

"Fine, you decide. Check it out in the mirror downstairs."

He turned off the ignition and bounced down the ladder and jogged down the stairs toward the tiny bathroom. The mirror had some rust spots around the metal frame, with greasy smudges. With some toilet paper, he wiped the surface, creating a clean spot. Turning his head at different angles, it was hard to get the full picture, but he had to give it to her. It made him look like Johnny Depp, but without the eye makeup.

He recalled how amazing the Goddess looked with her one earring. Sure, he could wear it on the boat. Though he wasn't confident about going out in public.

Johnnie made his way back up to the flybridge.

He couldn't believe his eyes.

Greta was screaming. "Get off!"

Stumpy had climbed up the back of Greta's chair, a clump of her long red hair in his mouth.

Greta's neck bled from several gashes. She swung her head, trying to dislodge the possessed iguana.

Johnnie rushed up and grabbed Stumpy around his middle. The iguana released Greta and scampered down the chair, off the bridge, down the port side.

"Oh, God, I'm so sorry. Don't move. Let me look."

Greta cried, her face red. Her words came out in pulses between sobs. "I was…just…sitting…here."

Her scalp was bleeding in several spots, plus the gashes on her neck appeared red and inflamed. "Greta, I didn't know…we should turn around."

She gingerly touched the back of her head. Her fingers came back with bloody splotches. She stopped crying, but her breath was still ragged. "It stings. I should probably get a rabies shot. I think. Is he up to date on his shots?"

His head pounded. He had no idea if iguanas carried diseases and what kinds. Another stupid idea of his to bring a wild animal on a boat ride.

"He's not really a pet." Quickly he added, "I can Google. I'll lock him up so he won't bother you again."

"Is there any antiseptic in the bathroom? No, I'll go check. I'm locking myself below." She got up from the chair and grabbed the top of the flybridge ladder.

"Wait, let me go first."

He descended first and waited on the deck, ready to catch her if she faltered.

As she came down, he placed his hand on the small of her back, until she was safely on her two feet. She turned, her red face inches from his, her eyelashes damp. "I'm sorry, maybe animals don't like me…"

"No, don't. It's absolutely not your fault."

She looked like she was ready to cry again.

And he did it. He took her face in his hands and kissed her. A light, quick kiss. Not overly romantic. But not like kissing your cousin, either. He hadn't intended to. It was a reflex. And it felt nice. He felt a tinge of pride for taking the chance.

Her hazel eyes looked confused, searching his. "What was that for?"

"I don't know."

"I can tell a pity kiss."

Johnnie backed away, sputtering. "A…a what?"

"Never mind." She brushed past him and went below deck, shutting the door quickly. He heard the lock turn.

The pit of his stomach ached. He wanted to hit something, or jump overboard, or rip off the rest of Stumpy's tail. Instead, he pulled the hoop earring off, tucked it in his pocket, and blinked his now watery eyes.

So much for a maiden voyage and new adventures.

Stumpy ran along the starboard side toward him, landing at his feet. He put a foot on Johnnie's sneaker and cocked his head. [Treat?]

"No! Get away!"

Stumpy lowered his head and dashed to the corner of the stern, keeping his eye on Johnnie.

Johnnie picked out two strawberries from the lunch bag. He opened the picnic basket lids, dropped them inside, and placed it next to Stumpy. In a fake joyful tone, he called, "Yum time!"

The iguana raced into the basket and Johnnie slammed down the flap, tying it off, testing the fastener for good measure.

It would take twenty minutes to get back.

And it would take all his will power to not chuck the picnic basket with Stumpy inside it into the cold deep sea.

* * *

~Twenty minutes earlier~

Munch. Crunch. Yum.

The were no more cheesy puffs. He beat his head on the wood top, needing to break free. To ask for more.

Small holes between the slats pierced the dark container. Ribbons of air brushed against his dorsal crests.

Where was the round-eyed one taking him?

Some minutes later, his crate jostled. A new human scent, with a hint of flowers but also like lettuce. With a female voice, a cheerful voice.

More riding in the dark on the motor-thing. Then a different sensation. Like floating, but still being carried.

Light seared his eyes when the lid opened. He scrambled out, not recognizing these strange surroundings. Where was the beach? His palm tree?

What should have been soft sand was hard and smooth. The motion of the vessel confused him. But he had to get away. Away from the nasty basket of confinement.

Up. He needed to go up. The only escape. When he reached the top, he realized the strange island was surrounded by water. Only ocean. Nowhere to go. But he could jump...swim. But no...too risky. Even for the Iguana King.

Yum time would solve all. And Johnnie would comfort him.

He searched. Where were the humans? I'm all alone. How could they?

Voices behind the wood door. Happy voices. He sat and stared at the hatch, willing it to open with mental focus.

When the humans emerged, he followed them up to the high landing. The nice man ignored him, too focused on the fire-haired female. The intruder interfering with his cheesy puff quest. He could bite her, claw her, tell her to go away.

Now alone together, the woman greeted him, called his name. Cooing at him like a silly bird.

[I hate you! Leave!] He thumped his short tail on the ground. Jutted his chin in the air.

The human didn't understand him. He climbed her chair.

[This is my tree. He is my friend. You are bad. Go away.]

He clamped onto its hair and pulled; clawed at its pale skin. Holding on at all costs. [Go! The Iguana King commands it!]

The female cried out. His plan was working.

Now Johnnie was back but yelled with anger. This made no sense. He scurried away to consider his options.

Later, he saw his plea worked. The female was locked away.

[Cheesy puff?] he asked his friend. After a minute, he heard the magic words. "Yum time."

Back inside the basket, he savored the strawberries. After eating the last one, he bashed against the top.

Fooled. Trapped.

This must be the red-haired one's fault.

And he would not forget.

Chapter 12

W hen the dinghy touched dry land, Greta announced, "I'm going to take a taxi home."

"Greta, please. It's only a mile and a half. Let me take you. I'll leave Stumpy here."

She stared at the ground. "I'm didn't mean it."

"Mean what?"

"What I said. I was just upset."

"It was dumb of me to bring Stumpy. I'm an idiot."

"Yeah." She looked up and squinted one eye at him. "Not the best decision."

"Like I said, I'm sorry. And I shouldn't have kissed you without asking. That was wrong."

"That wasn't the worst part." She twirled her hair and chewed on the end.

"Come on. Let's get you home."

They got on the Piaggio, but this time, Greta wrapped her arms around his torso, leaning her chin on his shoulder. It felt nice. He let go with one hand and placed his hand over hers.

He thought maybe this would be uncomfortable. But it wasn't. It reminded him of Darla holding his hand in the hospital. Although now it was a happy gesture. It felt nice.

Was he ready for a girlfriend? He hadn't slept with a woman since Miami and that was an alcohol and weed induced lapse of judgement. The hour after the judge approved his divorce with Darla, he began bar hopping into the night. How he ended up at the all-night beach party turned half-orgy, he'll never remember. Plus, he wasn't even sure if he had sex. He recalled making out with a bony woman covered head to toe in anime tattoos. Waking up with his underwear backwards and his shorts in the campfire didn't provide solid clues to what truly happened.

Greta didn't deserve to be with someone as broken as he was. After years of medication, his libido was in the toilet and his anger spells were still no walk in the park. He didn't want to hurt her.

Could he break it to her gently? *What if he told her the truth?*

That would be a longer discussion for another time. When her head wasn't full of bloody scratches.

When he parked in front of her place, they stood on the sidewalk, holding their helmets.

"Maybe we can go out to lunch next time?" she said.

"I like lunch."

"Me, too."

They stood there in an awkward silence. He needed to say something. But his mind blanked. "I hope your scalp is okay."

She touched her head. "It only bled for a few minutes." She handed him her helmet.

Should he give her a hug goodbye? "Um. Good. Good." He shifted his weight from foot to foot.

After some agonizing seconds, Greta announced, "Right. See you around." She headed up the steps.

His thoughts screamed. *Just tell her. Tell her about your accident. Tell her you like her. Tell her not to go!* "Hey."

Six steps above him, she stopped and turned. "Yes?"

"Hey, I…um, I plan to be away for a couple of weeks." These words came from nowhere. Or maybe somewhere, like the chickenshit sector of his idiot brain.

"Oh, yeah?"

"Um, a vacation. Sailing the Caribbean. In the boat." Again, this was news to himself.

"Well, have fun. Maybe you'll find a pirate treasure." She gave him a weak smile and a thumbs up.

"Um, well, I'll call you when I get back."

"Okay, have a nice time." She turned again, but this time jogged up the steps without looking back.

What was wrong with him? Greta was sweet and pretty and smart and understanding…and he still couldn't tell the truth.

And now he had to ask Kemper for two weeks off.

He placed his extra helmet under his seat, donned his own helmet and straddled the Pig. Something in his pocket dug into his thigh. It was the gold hoop earring. Cradling it in his palm, additional regret pierced his chest.

If he could travel the high seas and write an awesome pirate love story over the next two weeks, maybe he could give it to Greta; showing her how he felt and winning her over.

The challenge of it excited him.

Yes, he would live an ocean adventure and write the best damn story ever.

The challenge was on.

* * *

Johnnie returned to the Bertram to retrieve Stumpy. When he arrived, the basket top was busted open with no sign of the iguana. The cheese puff bag was torn, blowing around on the back deck.

Did his friend dive overboard? He'd read that iguanas were decent swimmers. He scanned the top deck. Nothing except a little iguana poo. "Stumpy!"

The door to the quarters was closed. Johnnie shimmied around to the front. A noise, like clattering, rose from below. How did he...?

On the port side, Greta must have opened a window a few inches. Which made sense to get some air in the confined space.

Johnnie went below. Stumpy was running from room to room. He tried to grab him, but the reptile escaped. There were no more treats to offer to get him to stop.

He sat on the cushioned bench by the door and waited. Stumpy would calm down soon and come to his senses. Johnnie reviewed his email on his phone, then began typing a text to Kemper, asking for two weeks off.

Stumpy scampered up onto the bench next to him, holding something in his mouth.

"What do ya got there, Stumps?"

The iguana dropped the object.

It was some kind of gemstone. Johnnie turned on the overhead light. The stone was red, but not faceted. Rough, irregular. Some cloudy spots and some clearer spots. "Where did you get this?"

Stumpy cocked his head. [Treat?]

There were no more treats. "Sorry, I don't have any."

Stumpy bobbed his head up and down. [Yum time?]

"No. Sorry." Johnnie studied the rock. *Was it valuable?*

The iguana blinked at him and took off again.

Not again. He should have grabbed his friend when he had the chance. But he wasn't going to chase him. His phone dinged. Kemper texted back, approving his leave, asking him to give her more notice next time. He wrote back an apology. Next, he thought hard about the supplies he'd need for the long journey.

Stumpy clawed his way back up the sofa bench with another stone in his mouth. He dropped it on Johnnie's lap.

Johnnie stroked the iguana's head with his thumb. "Stumpy, where...? Show me." He got up and headed down to the bedrooms. He peered inside each one. In one of the twin-bed-sized rooms, a small hatch in the floor, maybe the size of a square post-it note, was open, the wood cover askew. Inside were a couple dozen similar rocks.

Stumpy came up beside him and rested his foot on Johnnie's sneaker. [Good, right? Yum?]

"Good, I guess." If someone went to the trouble to conceal these, they had to be worth something.

He pocketed one of the stones and looked for other hatches in the other rooms. On the floors, the walls, the ceilings. He looked behind the stairs, in the cupboards. In the kitchen, he looked behind the drawers and inside the cabinets, the ventilation ducts...everywhere. *Nothing.*

His stomach rumbled. They never got to Norman Island for lunch. Stumpy was waiting by the door.

"Stumpy, come on. Let's go. Yum time. But we need to get home. Come on." He grabbed his friend around his leathery-middle and stroked his head. "We'll start our journey tomorrow night, if we can prepare."

He placed his friend back into the busted picnic basket. The bungee latch had broken, but he used one of his sneaker laces to tie the top.

An hour later, Johnnie and Stumpy arrived home to Calabash Boom. Gertie was still gone, her house dark and the vegetables in the garden were rotting—scattered on the ground, cracked and mushy.

Johnnie had promised her he would care for it. Another failure. Could he impose on one of the neighbors to take over during his journey? Probably not. But Gertie recently received ten million dollars. Losing a few vegetables couldn't be so important now. And maybe the seeds from the rotten tomatoes would create new plants. The circle of life. Seemed plausible. Yes, he'd go with that excuse. Mother nature always knows best.

He unlocked his apartment, closed the door behind him and let Stumpy loose. Johnnie went to the kitchen to find lunch. The choices for lunch were cereal, ham and cheese, microwave rice, an apple, and cheese puffs. He closed the upper cabinet with the snacks, because he would need them on the boat. After cutting up the apple, he placed slices on the floor for Stumpy.

Johnnie looked around his apartment. There was so much to do. So many supplies to get. He hadn't even tested the microwave oven on the boat like he wanted to. In the commotion, he had forgotten.

His phone rang.

"Hey, Robin."

"How did it go? With Greta?"

"You were tracking me?"

"The tracking app showed you came back to shore early. What happened? Did you have engine trouble or something?"

Shit. He'd forgotten they shared locations through their phones. Of course, it made sense at the time. A safety measure for his meeting last month with Thomas Smith to swap the bitcoin for Gertie's return. "No. No mechanical trouble. I don't want to get into it."

"Oh, I'm sorry. Did you break up?"

"We weren't dating."

"I'd call a boat trip a date."

"Well, I was going to take things slow. Take your advice. Be friends. But then I kissed her."

"You did? That's wonderful! Yes!"

He could hear the fist pump in her voice. "No, I…look, I like her. A lot. But I'm going away for a couple of weeks."

"What?" Her tone turned sharp, as if annoyed.

"A vacation. On the boat."

"Wait. Alone?"

"Sure, why do you say it like that?"

The pause on the line couldn't be good. In a more conciliatory tone, she asked, "Won't you be lonely?"

He was already lonely. "No, I have to give up the boat anyway. And I want to have fun first. Visit other islands. Don't be so negative."

"Oh, *I'm* negative?" The concern and high pitch of her voice returned. "What if you get into trouble? What if you capsize? Or you forget to buy fuel? Or get lost? Do you know how terrifying this is?"

"I'm not a complete incompetent."

"I didn't say that."

"It sounds like you are."

Robin sighed. "Look, I worry."

"It will be fine. I'm making a checklist. I'll stay close to shore when I can. Make frequent stops."

More silence. After a few more seconds, she said, "Send me your itinerary. With places and dates and times. Down to the minute. And check in daily. Please. Otherwise, I won't sleep. And you know what happens when I don't sleep."

Johnnie recalled last year when she flew to California for a conference and didn't sleep for two days. She went out drinking with strangers and texted a photo of her bare butt to her assistant Dottie. Not her finest moment. Although she said Dot had started it—whatever that meant. "Sure. I can do that. Stop worrying."

"Remember what happened to dad."

He remembered. One of the early memories he retained. Because it changed the course of their lives. "I'm not dad."

Her voice cracked. "I still blame myself."

"You shouldn't. You did the best you could." After their parents divorced, about twelve years ago, their father, John Senior, moved to St. John to live with his bimbo girlfriend. But when early onset Alzheimer's kicked in, his girlfriend dumped him. Robin left her government job in Miami and moved to the island to take care of him. One fateful night, dad wandered out of the house, stole a row boat from the marina and went missing. The only reason they knew he took the boat was from security cameras. And they found the boat broken on some rocks a week later. When a year passed with no sign of him, they held a small funeral service. Their mother wouldn't come.

"Look, I can't lose you too."

"You won't. I promise."

"If you don't call me every morning, I'll call the Coast Guard. You know I will, so don't get cute."

Johnnie chuckled. "Yes, I know you will."

Robin sighed. "Is there anything I can do to help? How far are you going exactly?"

"I'm only going to Tortuga and back. Look, I have things handled. How about you come see the boat before I shove off? Five o'clock tomorrow afternoon. Meet me at the dock at Great Cruz Bay."

"I'll be there."

They ended the call.

He glanced at Stumpy, now asleep on the worn gray velvet sofa, looking like a prince.

Johnnie began packing, throwing t-shirts and shorts into a black plastic garbage bag. He checked his medication bottle. There were only four pills left. With his laptop, he opened his browser, logged into the pharmacy website and ordered a month's refill. He could pick it up in Cruz Bay tomorrow on his way to the boat.

Johnnie made more lists. And worked on his itinerary for Robin. It was a simple plan. His ultimate destination was Tortuga, an infamous 1800s pirate hangout. On his journey west, he would stop at Vieques and San Juan to visit some historic forts and museums, then Punta Cana for resupply, before arriving at Tortuga.

The outward journey would take four days, he'd spend a day or two on the pirate island, and then two to three days on the return. His plan allowed for a few days to hunker down in a port if the weather turned bad. If he came back early, he'd have time to work on his pirate story before facing Greta.

It was a brilliant plan. *Not bad for short notice.*

And he wouldn't be alone, because Stumpy would be his first mate.

He'd have lots to do on his trip. Fishing for food. Visiting historic sites. Reading. Writing. And watching unobstructed sunrises and sunsets.

Plus, he wanted to come up with a new pirate shanty.

What more could anyone want?

Robin simply worried too much.

Chapter 13

J ohnnie checked the time on his phone. Four o'clock on Sunday and he still had errands to finish. And loading his supplies for his trip on his scooter was more of a hassle and game of Jenga than he'd expected.

Garbage bags of his clothes, food, toiletries, and linens were draped strategically over the back of his scooter seat and crushed down with bungee cords. When he got back from his trip, he'd seriously have to reconsider the idea of getting a car. Because the Flying Pig, laden down with trash bags, looked ridiculous and singularly hazardous.

Plus, he was carrying a basket on his lap containing an extremely confused and upset iguana.

When he arrived at Cruz Bay, he parked his scooter in front of the Marketplace, a three-story square building with tourist shops and open-air walkways around the perimeter. There were a few jewelry stores.

He put down the kickstand, and the scooter leaned to one side, causing the tall mass of bags to shift. The elastic cords strained and the bags oozed under their own weight. The top bag slipped out and fell to the ground. Johnnie would fix it later. He had no time to waste.

The first jewelry store seemed to focus on gold chains and rings. Not many gemstones. The second had a mix of jewelry types and the front window had an assortment of larimar earrings.

He straightened his ball cap and smoothed his olive-green T-shirt as he entered. The air conditioning blasted him and a light melody played over the speakers. The brightly illuminated glass-fronted cases were filled with sparkly watches, necklaces, and rings.

Holding his red rock, he noticed how dull and stupid it looked next to the fine gleaming pieces on display.

But he had to find out.

A woman in a suit jacket, in her fifties, light-skinned with short salt and pepper hair, greeted him with a smile. "Good afternoon, welcome. Can I help you with anything today?"

"Good afternoon. I...I see you sell gemstone jewelry. I had a question."

"Sure, what are you interested in?" She gestured gracefully across the top of the glass case. Her manicure was perfect.

"I have this thing...a gemstone. I'm wondering if you could appraise it?"

The saleswoman's face turned to disappointment. "Our jeweler normally does appraisals. Wait a moment." She went into the back room.

A man in a white dress shirt, a black apron over it, short and wiry, with a crew cut and deep face creases, walked out. "Hi, I'm Terry. What do you have for us today?"

"Um...this." Johnnie opened his palm, revealing the red stone. "What do you think this is?"

"May I?" Terry asked. He reached for the stone; his fingertips had some kind of black stain.

"Sure."

Terry put a loop to his eye, holding the stone at different angles. After a few seconds, he said, "Can't be sure without some tests. Where did you get it?"

He didn't know what to say. *Should he explain Stumpy retrieving it from a secret compartment in a mysterious yacht?* Probably not. "I found it."

"Around here?"

"Yes." Technically true.

"Well, my best guess is red spinel. Going off the visual, of course."

"What's that? Is it valuable?"

"In its polished form, could go for a hundred a carat. Without impurities."

"And like this?"

"I'd say maybe twenty dollars. It's hard to know the yield until it's faceted. But there isn't a big market or demand for spinel. If this were a ruby, then we're talking big money. It would be worth cutting and polishing." He held the stone up to his loop again. "But this, I don't think you'd find anyone interested." The man handed back the stone like it was a lump of coal.

"So, it's worthless."

"Sorry. But looks that way." The jeweler attempted a smile, but it appeared as a lopsided grimace with yellow teeth.

"Well, thanks for looking at it." Johnnie tried on a quick smile to be polite but the awkwardness of the moment made him want to run. Although running would be equally embarrassing. Instead, he stared at the stone.

"Sure, any time." The man walked toward the back room again.

The woman in the suit jacket gave a dismissive smirk. "Is there anything *else* we can do for you today?"

"Um. No. Thanks. I…I'm…bye." He pocketed the red stone, turned and exited the shop.

He shook his head and flipped down his sunglasses as he strode back through the shopping center. *What a failure.* He'd been so excited about finding a pirate treasure. Like in a dumb kid's story.

As he returned to his scooter, he noticed a serious-looking cop standing next to it.

What now? He bit his lip and began counting in his head, 1…2…3…4. *Breathe in, breathe out.* "Hi, Officer, is there a problem?"

"Is this motor bike yours? I need to give you a ticket for public littering."

"Littering?"

"You can't dump trash bags on the ground. The property owner complained."

"These are my belongings. I'll fix it. I'm leaving as soon as I hitch it back on."

The officer glared at him. "Sorry, I started writing the ticket."

"Oh, come on. I was gone for five minutes."

The man wrinkled his brow. "Hey, I remember you. You're the St. Johnnie killer, right? You were in lock-up a month ago."

Not this bullshit again. Johnnie took a deep breath and picked up the trash bag. "Yeah, that was me."

"You're Arturo's girlfriend's brother, right?"

His lungs deflated and his cheek twitched. "For crying out loud!" This came off a little more sarcastic than he intended. "Look, I'm kind of in a rush. I'm leaving for a vacation." He pulled on the bungee to stretch it over the towering stack of squishy black bags. The hook on the bottom of the cord twisted and sprung off, and smacked him across the face.

"Ow. Mother…"

"Hey, I…look at me." The officer put down the ticket pad.

He looked up. "Yes, Officer?"

The officer crossed his arms. "I want to apologize."

Johnnie flipped up his sunglasses. "Really?"

"Yeah, I was the one who hit you in the parking lot. Tobias said you were dangerous. No excuse. But after we learned about Thomas Smith and everything that happened, I've wanted to say I'm sorry."

"So…you won't give me a ticket?"

"No, I still have issue it. Once I start writing, I can't discard it."

Johnnie muttered, staring at the ground. "Jumpin' Jesus. I can't get a fucking break."

The officer handed him the ticket. "Have a nice vacation." He turned and walked away.

Johnnie stuffed the ticket in his back pocket and worked on the problem of securing the bags. Getting angry was no way to start a vacation. A small voice in his brain whispered this was a bad sign. A bad omen. Some kind of disaster must await.

"Shut up!" he screamed.

Two shoppers, one holding an infant, approaching his direction on the sidewalk reared back at his exclamation and quickly crossed the street.

The picnic basket he left on the seat jostled, meaning he had also scared Stumpy.

"I'm sorry, Stumpy." He finished getting everything secure. "We'll head to the boat. Things will be better there." He checked his watch. Four-thirty. Robin would be meeting him soon. If he timed things right, he could get all his supplies on the boat first and then come back to shore to meet her.

It was time to hustle.

Chapter 14

The morning was alive with street noises—commuters zipping by, sidewalks crowded with Parisian's heading to work. Gertie sat alone at an outdoor café drinking her latte. Her chocolate croissant rested half-eaten on a fine china plate. She wore her new floral dress from Valentino, with her white Chanel sneakers and a celadon silk vest from Celine. Around her neck, she wore a long strand of silver pearls; real ones, not the imitation ones she had usually worn to church on Sundays.

Her new cosmetics were a dream to apply, and her skin glowed with the new renewal crème from La Mer. Getting a head-to-toe body wax two days ago, at the suggestion of the salon technician, seemed like a good idea at the time. Although it hurt like the devil. Despite the intensive beauty routine, she stood firm and kept her hair natural. With all her new expensive products, her hair had a new luster.

Her translator slash tour guide, Mina, was fun and knowledgeable, but had too much energy. They needed to slow down. Take breaks. Get off their feet and savor the city.

Today's itinerary included a private tour of the Palace of Versailles. Then a boat ride. Capped off by a sunset picnic at Sacré-Coeur, the highest point in the city. She visited the Louvre yesterday, which took hours, leaving her feet sore from her new gold Prada heels.

Did being rich mean your feet always hurt?

Gertie looked up and saw Mina approaching, her head bobbing with her jaunty walk, her white boucle jacket in stark contrast to the commuters in their black coats.

Mina sat across from Gertie at the bistro table. "Good morning, mon chéri. How did you sleep? Are you ready for another adventure?"

"I decided to wear sneakers today. My feet still hurt."

"Well, you look magnificent. I love your shade of lipstick."

In a rare move, Gertie put on a shimmery royal blue lipstick to match the blue flowers in her dress. The effect was striking. "It's not too odd-looking?"

"With your complexion, you are lucky. You can wear many colors. I love it."

Gertie pulled a compact from her new bag, the $5000 Judith Leiber beaded bag made with pave Austrian crystals in a floral pattern.

She regarded her face. It looked like her, but, at the same time, it didn't. And Lisa wasn't around to be her sounding board. Their fight was quick and decisive. Lisa had said, "I don't know you anymore." And Gertie couldn't argue with that logic.

"Well," Mina said, "finish up your breakfast. I'll order a car for us."

Gertie nodded and bit into her croissant. The shopping was great, but the croissants were divine. Flaky, buttery. Pure heaven.

Mina checked her phone. "Looks like we'll have fine weather. Did you check your Instagram today?"

She swallowed the rest of her pastry and washed it down with the last drops of latte. "No. You updated it last night?"

Mina turned her phone around. "You have four hundred more followers."

Gertie took the phone and scrolled through the images. The pictures were stunning. Like she was twenty years younger. *Amazing what the right lighting could do.* "How do I share this with Cudlow?"

"Oh, see those three dots? Hit those from your phone. Do you want me to?"

Gertie handed her phone to Mina. "Yes. Please."

Yesterday's photo at the hotel bar, under the chandelier, a young handsome man on her arm, would really drive Cudlow nuts. The man, a friend of Mina's, was happy to play along.

"You really hate this man, Cudlow?"

"Hate him? No. Well, yes. I don't really know. I just want him to suffer."

"And he loves you? What did he do that is so wrong?"

"I don't want to get into it."

Mina's eyes widened. "You *do* love him!"

"What?"

"Love and hate are the same thing. Sides of the same coin, as they say. Parisians know all about passion."

"Hmmpf. Passion. I guess that's accurate."

"You should be here with him. Tell him to come. When he sees you like this, he will be ga-ga in love."

A white Mercedes SUV pulled up next to them. The driver got out. "Madame Brown party?"

Mina handed back Gertie's phone. "Yes, that's us."

Gertie paid the check and added a healthy tip, inserting cash in the embossed leather check presenter.

Thirty minutes later, their driver pulled up at the gates of Versailles. Out the side window, Gertie noticed the line for tickets was a quarter-mile long.

Gertie said, "Oh, my. The line looks bad."

Mina squeezed her hand. "That is for the little people. We don't have to wait."

They exited the vehicle. Mina told the driver to be back at one o'clock.

Gertie followed Mina past the queue, to an unmarked door to the right. Inside the small office, a man sat at a gilded table behind a computer screen.

Mina and the man spoke in rapid French. Gertie had no clue what they were saying.

The man consulted a clipboard, then opened a drawer and pulled two lanyards. The card attached said 'VIP'.

"He wants to know if you'd like the indoor tour first, or the garden?"

"The garden first. So we can avoid the noon day sun."

"Ah, very good."

Mina and the man at the desk spoke again in French.

"He says there is a private tour starting now. We can join if you'd like company."

Gertie thought about it. Having additional company would be welcome. Last night, she felt lonely, wanting to go back to the Bahamas and make up with Cudlow. Or back to St. John. Or take a high-speed train to Barcelona to apologize to Lisa in person.

"Yes, let's do that."

"Oh, no. We should have taken photographs at the front gate for your Instagram." Mina clenched her hands. "We must be sure to take great photos in the garden."

They walked directly through the palace and out the back doors. A woman waved to them. She wore a collared shirt with a red name tag; standing next to two glamorous young women in front of a marble statue.

Mina walked up to the guide. "Hello, we are joining your tour."

"Yes, the Brown party? My name is Claudette. Glad you could join us."

Gertie waved hello to the two younger women. Instead of acknowledging her, the two stared at their phones, scrolling.

Gertie said, "I hope we aren't imposing."

"Not at all," Claudette said. "Is this your first time to Versailles?"

"Yes, first time to Paris."

The two glamorous women began taking selfies with the palace in the background. And then Gertie recognized them. They were famous. Or infamous. They had a YouTube channel about fashion and lifestyle that could only be described as vacuous. The one with the long blonde hair and too much plastic surgery—she couldn't recall her name—was in U.S. headlines last year for a fashion shoot in a poor Los Angeles neighborhood, wearing a designer coat with the words, "I'm better than you."

Claudette waved her flag. "Ahem. Follow me." She was obviously trying to get attention of the other guests.

A bit of vomit surged into Gertie's throat. It burned.

Gertie froze, clutched her chest, and whispered to Mina. "I think we should go."

Too loudly for Gertie's taste, Mina replied, "Go? Why? What's wrong."

"I don't feel so good."

"Oh, no. Do you need a doctor? Are you dizzy?"

"I want to go back to the hotel." Her face burned, like she was having a hot flash, although those ceased fifteen years ago. *Was it a panic attack?*

Mina studied her face. "Yes, no problem.

Mina spoke in French with Claudette, ending in an, "Au revoir."

Not long after, they were back in the hired car and heading away.

"How are you feeling?" Mina placed her hand on Gertie's.

"A little better. I think…I think I want to rest today."

"*Absolument.* Do you want anything when you get back? Some aspirin? Some hot tea?"

Gertie sunk her head against the window. Tears came to her eyes. "I have a favor to ask."

"Surely. Anything."

"When we get back, I'll need you to return my purchases."

"Oh, are you sure? Not the white Givenchy! It fits you so nicely."

"Yes, everything. Anything I haven't worn or taken the tags off. It all goes."

Mina studied Gertie's face. "You seem…sad."

Gertie didn't want to talk anymore. She needed to go home. Her actual home. Be in her own garden. Go to her own church. The gardens at Versailles, even at a brief glance, were soulless and stale. And those two young women were awful. But like two powerful mirrors, they made her stomach turn at her own superficial behavior. She couldn't go through with her spite-filled charade any longer.

"And wipe out the Instagram. Now."

"Really? The pictures are so lovely. Don't you want a reminder?"

Gertie shook her head no. She reached for a tissue in her bag and wiped her eyes. The tissue turned black with her mascara.

"I'm going to rest my eyes until we get back."

Mina nodded. "I understand."

* * *

Johnnie and Stumpy arrived in Isabel Segunda on Vieques. It was evening now, about nine o'clock and dark. Their voyage was uneventful. The GPS navigation system worked perfectly and they kept land in sight by hugging the northern coast of St. Thomas before hitting the open water. Stumpy sat in the chair beside him during the ride; either scanning the horizon or sleeping.

It was time to drop anchor, have a quick dinner, read a bit and go to sleep. "Stumps, dinner time."

Johnnie descended the flybridge ladder, while Stumpy slid down the side and wiggled his way into the lower cabin through the window.

"What do you want, boy? We have chicken soup or tuna fish." He'd brought mostly canned goods, unsure of how well the refrigeration worked.

[Yum?]

"Just kidding. Here." He took a handful of collard greens, plus five grapes, and placed them on the counter in front of his friend.

Stumpy chomped down on the grapes first, his eyes closed with glee.

"You know, I probably can't bring you with me to the forts tomorrow."

The iguana didn't look up. Only continuing to savor his grapes.

"But if you can behave, maybe I can walk you through town. Would you like that?"

Stumpy kept eating.

"Hey, I know." He grabbed two grapes and picked up Stumpy. The iguana whipped his short tail violently, wiggling to get free. "Right. I'll wait until you're done." He let him go and gave back the grapes.

Johnnie sat on the sofa bench. "In my story, Grumpy the iguana sits on Captain Cecil's shoulder. We should practice. But you can't dig in your claws, okay?"

Stumpy ignored Johnnie and swallowed another grape.

When Stumpy finished his food, Johnnie picked him up from the counter and placed him on the sofa, rubbing his head with his index finger. "Good boy." The iguana seemed contented.

Slowly, he lifted Stumpy on his shoulder with one hand, while holding out a grape with the other. Like a circus balancing act. "Settle down and you get the grape." When the iguana was steady, Johnnie split the grape in two pieces, giving him half. "Stay."

Stumpy chomped down the grape. Then, in a blur, he leapt like a frog onto Johnnie's outstretched arm, aiming his mouth toward the other half of grape. Razored claws dug into Johnnie's flesh.

"Ow!" Johnnie stood, shaking Stumpy from his arm, dropping the grape. Stumpy righted himself on the floor and ate the fallen nugget.

His arm was bleeding. And it stung. "Stumpy, bad!"

Johnnie descended the three steps toward the bathroom. In the medicine cabinet, the previous owner left behind some random things: two bandages wrapped in yellowed paper; a rusty tweezer; and a trial size bottle of mouthwash.

His own toiletries were still packed at the bottom of a trash bag, along with his clothes. But he only brought a toothbrush, toothpaste, a bar of soap and deodorant. Some hydrogen peroxide would help. One more thing to add to the shopping list.

With some toilet paper, he dabbed some old mouthwash on his cuts, hoping it had some alcohol left. It was better than nothing.

Outside the boat, a siren blared.

He went topside to investigate. A police boat, with flashing lights, was tearing across the harbor toward an immense cruise ship about a half-mile away. The ship had floodlights aimed at the water, like they were searching.

Did someone fall overboard? Was the cruise ship sinking? There was no way to tell.

He climbed to the bridge and watched the scene for a few minutes. More small boats joined the group, aiming their lights into the water like they were searching.

From what Johnnie saw on television, when people fell overboard, it was usually suspicious; sometimes a honeymooning couple where an evil spouse does the other in. Which was really a nasty piece of work if you thought about it. You get married and your husband or wife tosses you? *Who sees that coming?*

In that moment, he was glad he didn't toss Stumpy into the sea after he attacked Greta. Because he was just a dumb animal and didn't know better. And maybe he could teach Stumpy to behave and act right around people. He had to be patient. And wear long sleeves.

He returned to the cabin and found Stumpy asleep. Johnnie finished dinner, cleaned up the kitchen, then put away his clothes in the built-in wood drawers. By ten o'clock, he was exhausted and collapsed on the queen-sized bed. He didn't bother to put on pajamas.

As he drifted off to sleep, he realized he hadn't written his nightly diary entry.

He debated turning on the light and getting it over with.

As his thoughts swam in circles with the gentle rocking of the boat, he made a decision.

It could wait until morning.

Chapter 15

ohnnie woke to find Stumpy sitting on his chest.

[Wake up, Johnnie! The sun is up. Come, look. Yum time!]

The iguana was very excited today.

Johnnie turned on the overhead dome light. He winced and placed a pillow over his face. "Give me a moment…" He drifted back to sleep.

Stumpy bit his toe.

"Ow! Damn it! You can't bite me!" He kicked Stumpy but found only a clump of bedding.

Johnnie heard the iguana scamper away into the galley kitchen, evidenced from the scraping noise of claws on the linoleum floor. [Yummm! Come, follow!]

"No!" He rolled to his side, tossing away the pillow.

Moments later, a dish shattered on the hall floor, disturbing his sleep. Then another clatter.

Johnnie threw off his sheet and ambled with half-closed eyes toward the kitchen. Light poured through the windows. He began plucking grapes, but then tossed the whole bunch on the floor. "Have at it."

Stumpy dashed over and munched away. [Thanks, Johnnie. You're my best friend!]

"Sure. Whatever." He grabbed his phone off the counter and checked the time. It was a little after seven o'clock. He took his phone out of airplane mode. No voice mails. An email from Gertie saying her plane touched down in St. Thomas.

He reached for his pill bottle. Only three left.

Panic tore through his body. He'd forgotten to get pick up his re-fill. In his haste to get the gem appraised and get to his boat on time, his need to stop by the pharmacy for his medication completely slipped his mind. He only had three days left of his pills and his trip would take a minimum of eight.

He needed air. Opening the door, he saw an unexpected lump on the deck. Johnnie rubbed his eyes, wondering if he was dreaming.

But no, he was clearly awake. He took a couple steps toward what seemed to be a large man in a dark clothing curled up in the corner. *Asleep? Dead? Please, for fuck's sake, no.* He couldn't deal with another dead body. Not after last month's troubles.

"Hey!" Johnnie shouted, unwilling to touch the guy.

The man stirred, much to his relief.

"Dude, what are you doing on my boat?"

The man, olive complexion, bald on top, was wearing a damp suit, white dress shirt, and no shoes. He appeared to be in his fifties, and rotund around the middle.

"I'm sorry. I can leave." The intruder pushed himself up from the deck and went to the stern's ladder, turning as if to disembark.

Which was crazy, because they were in the middle of the harbor.

"Wait! Stop! Are you nuts?"

The man threw his leg over the back.

Johnnie ran over and grabbed the man's jacket lapel. "I'm not going to hurt you."

"Sorry. I made a mistake. Let me go."

"Were you the one they were looking for last night?"

The man stopped struggling and looked up, meeting Johnnie's eyes. "Yes."

Johnnie released his jacket. "Tell me who you are and why you jumped and I won't report this."

"Really?"

"Yes."

The man climbed back up. "Do you have any coffee?"

"I have some diet soda. And I can reconstitute some freeze dried eggs for breakfast."

The man extended a handshake. "I'm Mohsen Zandi. People call me Mo."

"I'm John." He brushed his hand across his t-shirt, wondering if he should shake the man's hand. "Come inside. I'll make breakfast."

"Thanks." Mo followed Johnnie inside and took a seat on the bench beside the rectangular wood-laminate table. "Nice boat."

"Yeah. I'm getting rid of it soon." Johnnie took a can of warm diet soda from the non-working refrigerator and tossed it to Mo.

Mo pulled on his wrinkled suit jacket to straighten it. "Well, what do you want to know?"

"You jumped from that cruise ship, right? Were you trying to commit suicide?" Johnnie stirred the water into the powered eggs. They looked awful. Not like real eggs at all. It was a wrong choice. He internally vowed to buy real eggs in town later.

"No. I didn't have a choice but to jump."

"Why?"

"If I tell you, could you take me to the Bahamas?"

"That's kind of far. I don't think I have enough fuel."

"I can pay."

"Plus, I have a job to get back to."

Stumpy came scampering up to Mo. "You have an iguana?"

"Yeah, he's not really a pet. I wanted him to keep me company."

"I could keep you company. People say I'm fun to keep around. I was the activities director."

"On the cruise? You worked for them? Why would you jump?"

Mo laughed. "People take trivia too seriously."

Johnnie put the scrambled egg mixture in the microwave. "What do you mean?"

"It's a long story."

"I've got time."

Mo sighed and gazed out the window to his left. "Alright. If I asked you who led the people of Israel into the promised land, what answer would you give?"

"Do I get to phone a friend?" He couldn't remember many things, although the image of the actor parting the Red Seas in an old movie popped in his head. "No idea."

"Most people say Moses."

"Wasn't he the burning bush guy?"

"Yes. Well, Moses didn't actually cross the Jordan River. Joshua actually led them in."

"Like a trick question?" The microwave beeped. He took out the bowl. The egg mixture still looked soggy, not that he knew how it should look. He put it back in for another thirty seconds.

"The problem was, I was sitting in for the usual trivia guy. And I when I saw the answer sheet knowing it was wrong, I corrected it."

"Meaning?"

"I didn't give points for Moses. And it turns out a team who was on a previous cruise had heard this question before and the official answer then was Moses. They were irate."

"I still don't see the big deal."

"Have you ever been on a cruise?"

"No." He removed the bowl out of the microwave, holding the top edges to avoid burning his hands. The eggs were solid now, but an odd sort of fluorescent yellow that didn't appear in nature.

Mo sighed. "The cruise gives out points to winners. They can trade in their points for swag later. But mostly, the competition between teams gets remarkably aggressive to find out who is the smartest. In this case, a brawl ensued."

"Shit. No kidding." Johnnie had half a mind to toss the eggs in the trash altogether.

"The whole mob wanted me fired. The new HR Director delved into my credentials further. I've been using a fake passport. It says I'm born in Guatemala, but in truth I escaped Iran five years ago. I won't go back."

He showed the bowl to Mo. "Um, take a look at these. Should I toss these eggs?"

"They're fine. I'm starving."

Johnnie looked for forks. *The eggs might not be poison.* "Why do you want to go to the Bahamas?"

"I have a friend there. He can get me a new identity. And then I can go to a country with supportive policies for political refugees. Maybe Canada…"

Johnnie served the eggs on two plates at the small dining table and took a seat across from Mo. "I'd like to help…I'm not sure if I can get you there and get back in time."

"Time for what?" Mo scarfed down his eggs without pause.

"I only have thirteen days and a list of places I need to visit."

Mo's bushy dark eyebrows wiggled like fuzzy caterpillars as he asked, "Need to?" His guest gulped down more eggs, some dribbling from his mouth as he spoke.

"I'm doing research." He poked at the yellow globs pretending to be food, wondering if they would turn sentient and attack his face like an alien.

Mo wiped his mouth and rested his hands on top of his belly. "Ah.

Research. I can help. I have so much useless trivia in my brain. Go ahead. Ask me anything."

"I don't know. See, that's the problem. I don't know what I don't know about pirates. And sea monsters and mermaids. And wooden ships…you get the idea. I'm trying to write a book. Well, maybe just a short story for now."

"A writer. How nice! My cousin was a writer until the Iranian government executed her for heresy."

Johnnie stared. "What?"

"You are lucky to be an American. Do you have any toast? With butter?"

Johnnie shook his head. "Sorry, I don't have any bread."

Mo got up from the bench and opened the refrigerator. "There's no food in here."

"It isn't working. I just won this boat at an auction."

"I'm kind of handy. Do you have any tools?"

"I didn't bring any. But there are old screwdrivers and clamps and stuff in the closet next to the first bedroom."

"First bedroom? How many are there?"

"Three."

"Impressive."

"Like I said, I'm not keeping it."

"How much?" Mo gestured broadly, glancing in a circle.

"For the boat? You want to buy it?"

"I have money saved. In a bank in the Bahamas. How much?"

Johnnie picked up his phone and checked the eBay bids. It was up to only seven thousand. Enough to get his money back but not close to what it was worth. There were still twenty-five days to go.

Johnnie blurted. "Forty-two thousand." The number seemed a good compromise.

Mo laughed. "You are funny." Then Mo's expression turned to stone. He quipped, "Seventeen." He opened and closed the kitchen cabinets, like he was inspecting the property.

"Thirty."

Mo left and went down the steps toward the bedrooms. Johnnie heard doors opening, and 'Ahs' and 'Oh, dears'.

Then Mo strode past him, through the door to the outside deck. Next, he heard footsteps on the bridge.

From above, Mo called, "Twenty. Final offer."

Twenty was pretty decent. And he felt sorry for the guy.

Mo came back inside. "What do you say? Twenty?"

Johnnie washed up the dishes in the kitchen sink. "Deal."

"Wonderful. Now, I will wire you the money when we're ready to swap. Good?" Mo extended his hand.

Johnnie wiped his wet sudsy hand across his shorts before shaking Mo's hand. "Good."

"But you have to keep me hidden. If the authorities take me, our deal is obviously off."

"I assumed so."

Mo clasped his hands together in a begging fashion. "Can I take a shower? Do you have any clean clothes I can borrow?"

"I was…I need to shower first. I have lots on my agenda today." Johnnie looked through the cupboards. He needed to buy more groceries now he had an extra mouth to feed.

"Right, right. You go first. I'll keep your friend company on the boat."

Johnnie had a strange thought. *What if Mo stole his boat while he was in town?*

"If I leave, you won't steal my boat, right?"

"What? No. If you take the keys, I can't, right?"

Johnnie thought. "Yes, of course. Sorry. No offense."

"None taken. I understand. You don't know if I'm a criminal. I could be a mass murderer for all you know."

Johnnie put away the dishes and silverware. "Jeez, don't say that."

"I'm only kidding. Here, look, I'll show you I'm really the activities director." He went outside to the deck and began dancing. And singing. "I know the whole routine. During dance nights, we would do the hustle and the Macarena." He whipped his arms out front, moving his hips. "Hey, Macarena!" He jumped and pivoted ninety-degrees and began the sequence over again.

"Stop! I get it." The guy was pretty fluid for his age and weight. But Mo was way too jovial this early in the morning for Johnnie's liking. Yet, Johnnie inwardly envied Mo's smile, which was big enough to span an ocean.

"Ha. I could teach you how to dance. The ladies love it. Get the stick out of your backside. The women go mad for a pelvic thrust!"

Johnnie shook his head and chuckled. "I'm taking a shower." He went back inside.

Having Mo on the boat was going to be weird. But maybe not as weird as pretending to be a pirate for a week.

Now he had his own personal activities director.

It could be a fun vacation after all.

*　*　*

It was late afternoon when Gertie's flight touched down in St. Thomas. The humidity in the terminal felt welcome, like a warm bath. She had a suitcase this time and her straw bag. No makeup on her face. Designer sneakers on her feet. Her eyes ached from lack of sleep and her head pounded.

She took a taxi to the eastern end of the island to catch the Red Hook ferry to St. John.

On the line to buy ferry tickets, she recognized Johnnie's older sister. Gertie rolled her bag behind her and snuck up on the petite, brown-haired woman, tapping her on the shoulder.

Robin turned. "Gertie! You're back!"

Gertie hugged Robin, so happy to see a familiar, friendly face. "Oh, I'm so glad to be home...you wouldn't believe."

"Well, I'm pissed. Did you hear they called off the hunt for Thomas Smith."

Gertie rolled her eyes. "Well, I wasn't afraid of him then and not afraid now. Men like that only care about money. And he got his."

Robin inched up in the line to fill the gap. "He could come after you again."

Gertie laughed. "I'm too old to give a damn. Plus, Thomas hates my singing."

The Senator looked at her quizzically.

"Long story."

Robin approached the ticket counter and put down her briefcase. "Two please."

Gertie opened her bag and rifled through it. "Let me pay. I have money to burn." But she turned ashen, quickly realizing most of her money was still in Euros.

"Nonsense." Robin paid for the tickets and they walked away from the counter toward the ferry ramp. "Tell me, did you work things out? With Cudlow?" Robin's eyes were wide with excitement.

"No. He wasn't in the Bahamas when I got there. So, I went to Paris."

"Paris? I'm jealous. It's one of my favorite places. You need to tell me everything."

"First, how's Johnnie? Is he taking good care of my place?"

Robin shook her head. "He didn't call you? I told him…"

"Oh no. What now?"

They found an open bench in the middle lower deck of the ferry. "No, I mean. Nothing terrible. He left on vacation last night."

Gertie collapsed the handle on her suitcase and tucked it under the bench. "Well, damn good I came home when I did. That boy…"

Robin darted her eyes slyly. "He might have a girlfriend."

"Who? The stuck-up goddess lady? When did that happen?"

"Goddess? No, the new librarian."

"Whew. Good for him! Hallelujah."

Robin huffed. "He drives me crazy. With practically no planning, he decides to sail to Tortuga. Fucking five hundred miles away. I can only imagine what a disaster this will be." She rolled her eyes. "Plus, he brought the damned iguana."

"Wait, the iguana…you mean Stumpy?"

"I don't know. Probably."

Gertie laughed. "Why am I not surprised?"

"My brother is *weird*."

"Honey, all men are weird."

Robin smiled. "Ain't that the truth."

Chapter 16

A fter visiting several old forts and museums, taking copious pictures, Johnnie's feet burned and ached. Before heading back in his inflatable dinghy, he purchased some shelf-stable milk, more canned soup, a carton of real eggs, two loaves of bread, plus collard greens, peas, and pears for Stumpy.

His ship, Bert, was still in the harbor. Meaning, Mo hadn't hot-wired it to steal it from him.

As he rowed up to the ship, he heard Mo signing in the cabin. It sounded like the Macarena but with different words.

Johnnie lashed the dinghy to the side, crept onto the back deck and leaned next to the door to listen. Mo was, in fact, singing like a baritone, almost shouting:

> Steals from the rich, he's a badass marauder
> Loves a mermaid, Neptune's only daughter
> They rule the seas and try not to slaughter
> HEY, Captain Johnnie!
>
> Blow 'em down hard and cleave in the brisket
> Drinking some rum plus a whole lot of whiskey
> Giant squids always beat me at Frisbee
> HEY, Captain Johnnie!
>
> Silver and gold doubloons are so gaudy
> Fruit roll-ups for dessert if they're naughty
> Manatees sing his song and do laundry
> HEY, Captain Johnnie!
>
> Sea monsters roam and act real surly
> Drink your OJ or you'll die of the scurvy
> Comb your beard daily if you want to look purty
> HEY, Captain...

Johnnie swung open the cabin door holding two grocery bags. "What are you singing? How…?"

Mid-dance, Mo stopped waving his hands in the air. He turned, wearing a broad smile. "Ah, Captain John. Welcome back. Grumpy and I were having a small dance party to pass the time. Did you have a nice day?" He slid a piece of paper out of sight, opening a drawer under the counter and closing it again.

"It was fine." On the sofa bench, his notes for the pirate story were laid out. Unfolded with the creases smoothed. "Did you read my draft?"

"Was that wrong? I was so bored today. But don't be mad. Ha! I need to show you something!"

Johnnie *was* mad. His draft was crap. His scribbles weren't even complete sentences. More of an outline. Mo had a lot of nerve reading it. "What? Show me what?"

"Look in the corner."

There was a large, clear plastic tray in the corner, next to the sofa bench. It had a bowl of water and iguana poop scattered around.

"So?"

"I'm potty training your friend. What's his name? Grumpy? I'm assuming he's the one in your story?"

"His name is Stumpy. How did you—"

"I told you, I have lots of useless knowledge. My recent bunkmate owned an iguana back home. Told me all about how he trained him. Now…we made progress today…he's still pooping up top on the bridge. But he loves fruit roll-ups. It was the closest thing to real fruit I could find."

Stumpy clamored up the steps from the sleeping quarters and dashed through the kitchen and sailed up to the sofa bench, coming to a stop perched on the backrest.

Mo continued, "Oh, and check this out." He sat on the bench, his back to the iguana. "Sit-sit."

Stumpy stepped onto Mo's shoulder, peaceably resting his head downward on Mo's clavicle.

Mo stroked Stumpy's cheek. "Good!"

Johnnie shook his head and leaned on the counter with both arms locked. "What the hell? I was gone for six hours. Jumpin' Jesus."

Mo grinned. He stood and Stumpy remained calm on his shoulder. "There's more. I hope you won't be mad."

Johnnie leaned against the wall with his arms crossed. "What else?" He didn't buffer the sarcasm in his voice. Who was this guy? Superman? *A reptile whisperer?*

Mo opened a drawer in the kitchen and pulled out a piece of paper. "I didn't mention this before…just hear me out." Stumpy leapt from Mo's shoulder and sat on the counter.

"Go ahead." Johnnie took a deep breath, wondering what Mo was so scared of.

"Back in Iran, I was a professor of literature. When I saw your story, I couldn't help myself…" Mo handed him the page.

Johnnie put down his bags and scanned it. "What is this?"

"An outline. You see, you have to use story structure. I kept it simple. I thought it might help."

Johnnie wanted to stay mad. But even at a quick glance, the outline was kind of genius and addressed all the problems he was struggling with. The final battle between Captain Cecil and his arch nemesis—a cruel privateer named Marquis de Smythe—was all laid out. The battle turns for the worse and nearly all hope is lost. In a final plot twist, his mermaid girlfriend, Coral, finds a way to communicate with their earlier foe, the terrifying man-eating amphibious dragon. Coral and the dragon save the day and sink the privateer's ship.

Greta would love it. He loved it.

"Mo, thanks. This looks great."

Mo blushed. "You'll see I left gaps where you can improvise or modify scenes. I'd be happy to brainstorm with you."

"Really? Cool."

"What did you get for dinner? I fixed the refrigerator." He rifled through the bag of groceries on the counter.

"Oh, come on. Now you're just messing with me."

Mo grinned. "There was a loose wire in the back. Anyone could have fixed it."

"Damn. I guess this makes you my first mate."

"Aye, aye, Cap'n!" Mo saluted.

"I'm so tired. I'm having cereal for dinner and crashing. Okay with you?"

"Absolutely." Mo held up the cereal box, running his finger along the nutrition information panel. "Sure, who cares about adult diabetes?"

Johnnie rolled his eyes. "I'm on vacation…"

Mo chuckled. "Hey, I'm game."

A few minutes later, they sat at the small table and slurped their cereal. Stumpy came up behind Johnnie and placed his two front feet on his shoulder.

"Hey, boy." Johnnie picked up a soggy Fruit Loop and offered it to his leathery friend.

Stumpy ate it and began bobbing up and down. Five more loops later, Johnnie said, "Enough. I'll cut you up some collard greens in a minute."

Mo slid out from the bench. "No, you sit. I'll feed our little friend." He called out, "Din-din."

Johnnie watched Stumpy crawl down the bench and go to his poop tray.

Sure enough, as Mo dangled a green leaf, Stumpy squatted and oozed out some blackish-green excrement. Mo then placed the leaves in a plastic cup next to the water dish.

It was uncanny. Stumpy was actually potty trained!

He could get used to having Mo around.

It was really too bad Mo was wanted by the authorities.

Chapter 17

San Juan was only an hour away. The next morning, Johnnie woke up early, had breakfast, and motored on with the sunrise at his back. With Mo in the first mate's chair, Johnnie shouted above the boat's engine. "Mo! I forgot to ask. How did you come up with that song?"

Mo shouted back. "I thought if you could come up with an authentic sounding pirate song for your character, it might help your writing process."

"But it sounds like Macarena."

"Yeah, sometimes it gets stuck in my head. Occupational hazard."

"Could you teach it to me?"

Mo waved his hand dismissively. "Oh, it's silly nonsense rhymes."

"I think my friend Greta would really dig it."

Mo turned his head and grinned. "Ah! I see! A girlfriend? Tell me about her!"

"She's not, like, officially my girlfriend."

"But you like her? Hmm?"

Still shouting above the motor, he said, "She's a really sweet person."

"But you haven't…"

Johnnie took his gaze off the ocean to glance at Mo. His Iranian friend was making a rude gesture with his fingers.

"Ew. Gross, man."

"Captain Johnnie, you need to lighten up. Smile. Laugh. You can't win over Greta if you are so sour all the time."

"I have issues."

Mo chuckled. "Everyone has issues."

"Not like me."

"Ha!" Mo pretended to wipe his eyes with his fists. "Wah, wah.

Nobody understands." In a bitter tone, he muttered, "Pussy."

Johnnie took a hand off the wheel and cut the engine. The boat decelerated, hard. Waves sent the boat at an angle. With the engine off, Johnnie didn't need to shout any more. In a deadpan tone, he leveled his eyes at Mo and asked, "*What* did you call me?" His hands coiled into fists. Maybe his passenger deserved to be thrown overboard.

Mo stared him down. "I called you a pussy. You think your life is hard?" He counted his grievances on his chubby fingers. "My government tortured and killed my father. I haven't seen my family in years. I fled for my life with nothing in my pockets. Do you see me moping and scowling? No! Life is a gift, my friend. And you are too self-absorbed to realize."

Johnnie shouted, spitting, "Look, I know I'm not right in the head!"

"What, depression? I saw your prescription."

Heat rose to his face. He yelled, "I lost everything, too! I had a wife. A military career. Friends. Brothers in arms. A bullet in my head and I lost all of it. My memory. My energy. Not able to feed and dress myself for months. Living in the hospital for a year. Everything I knew. Everything I used to be good at. Fucking *gone*."

Mo's eyes softened; he patted Johnnie's shoulder. "I didn't know." In a solemn tone, he said, "But you are here now."

Johnnie took deep breaths, stunned by his own rage. As he grew still, he stared at the ocean. "I don't know how to move on."

It felt weird telling this to someone he had just met yesterday. But, at the same time, it felt oddly safe. In the middle of the ocean, with no one else around, a floodgate burst.

Mo grimaced. "I'm sorry to tell you, I only know three things that work." He held up three fingers.

Johnnie kept his eyes on the horizon. "Enlighten me."

"First, time helps. Second—in the meantime—you need to fake it until you make it."

"Ha," Johnnie laughed sarcastically. "What's the third thing?"

Mo smiled and winked. "You need to dance, my friend."

Johnnie shook his head. "That sounds dumb."

Mo tapped his temple. "It's not. There's science."

He scoffed. "Science? Right..."

"No, it's true. We store stress in our bodies." Mo thumped his chest. "It piles up. Emotions have a physical component. A very wise woman once sang a song about this."

"Yeah? Who?"

"Taylor Swift! You need to shake it off!" Mo got up and began singing the song, shimmying in a circle around his chair. "Shake it off!"

Johnnie frowned. "Come on. Be serious." But as Mo wiggled, he found it difficult to stay angry.

"That's the problem! Come, you try!" Mo turned on the radio on the bridge console. He landed on a station playing Oye Como Va by Santana and turned up the volume to max.

"We need more space!" Mo declared with a finger in the air. "Come with me!" He headed down the ladder to the back deck. "Come on! The song is half over!"

Johnnie followed Mo down to the back deck.

Mo bopped his shoulders, transferring motion down to his hips and feet. Twirling and waving his arms. "Come. Do it!"

"No." Johnnie crossed his arms defiantly. The beat was enticing though...

"Yes!" Mo pulled him by the arm. "Do it, soldier!"

"Hey, I was a Marine."

"Oh. Sorry. Dance, Marine!"

Johnnie took a deep breath, and shuffled weakly side to side. It felt lame, like he had no idea what he was doing. He listened to music all the time at home, but usually classical to help his brain or sad contemporary songs when he was in a dark mood. There was never any *dancing*.

Mo grabbed his hands. "Come on, shake it out. Move your shoulders...good, now your hips...Yes! Keep going!"

Compared to Mo's ridiculous moves, his own shoulder and hip swaying seems tame and reasonable. If anyone saw them, they wouldn't be able to keep their eyes off Mo. This was safe cover to let go a little, although he confined himself to a small area to avoid Mo's flailing moves.

It didn't take long for Mo to abandon all restraint and break into his own high energy dance routine, whirling like a dervish.

Johnnie found himself smiling as he watched Mo.

His heavy friend pretended to whip an imaginary towel around his head, and then slid it under his crotch, back and forth. During the song's chorus. he grabbed one foot and bounced on the other, hop-dancing in a circle. Which wasn't an easy feat given the swaying motion of the boat.

When the song ended, Mo collapsed onto the side bench. The radio now blared a commercial for auto insurance.

"See, do you feel better?" Mo panted and wiped his brow with the bottom of his shirt.

Johnnie sat down, leaned back and laughed. "It didn't completely suck. But we should keep going." He headed back up the ladder. After turning off the radio, he re-started the engine.

Mo joined him on the bridge and flopped in his seat, breathing hard. He raised a finger in the air, as in victory. "Dancing like no one's watching; it's the best thing besides sex."

Johnnie grimaced. *Sex. Whatever that was.* "I don't remember."

"Oh?" Mo's eyes widened.

"Yeah."

"Well, stick with me, kid. On every cruise, I had women lining up." He motioned his hands in the form of an hourglass.

Johnnie gave him a side eye, then focused on his steering. "Really?"

"I'm not much to look at, but you know what they say…"

He was afraid to ask, but did anyway. "No, what do they say?"

"It's not the size of the boat that matters; it's the motion in the ocean."

* * *

When they dropped anchor and had climbed down to the back deck from the flybridge, before Johnnie opened the cabin door, Mo interrupted. "Wait, I have a request."

"What?"

"I need something to wear other than this shabby suit." Mo grinned and pulled on the lapels on his dark jacket. "Your clothes don't fit my tubby belly, and you probably don't want to see me in my birthday suit."

A truer statement never existed. It was strange enough having Mo on his boat. Even a half-naked Mo would be horrific. "So, what do you want?"

Johnnie opened the cabin door. In front of him, a sight he couldn't believe.

"Stumpy!" Johnnie yelled.

The iguana had found his way into an upper kitchen cabinet, where he had pulled down the supersize bag of cheese puffs, Presently, he was sitting on the counter, gorging on them in a frenzy.

Johnnie dove for the iguana, clutching him. He walked Stumpy outside, dropped him on the back deck and slammed the door shut.

"Jumpin' Johosephat. How did he get in there? I had it locked." Each cabinet had a metal latch to keep items secure in rough seas.

Mo clasped his mouth. "Oh. I may have forgotten to secure it. And…I may have eaten a few puffs last night when I couldn't sleep."

"Well, help me scoop these up. God, I don't want him to get sick."

Mo and Johnnie began scooping up the mess. Iguana dung was mixed in, making the chore both smelly and gross.

Johnnie opened the door under the sink and retrieved the small trash can. "God, this is pretty nasty."

Mo said, "I'm sorry. Well, so much for potty training."

"It was an accident."

When they were done, they both washed their hands thoroughly.

"Now, what can I get for you today?"

Mo gave a sheepish look. "I made a list. With my sizes. If you don't mind. Plus, it would be great if I could have my own phone…"

Johnnie looked at the list. "This looks like a lot."

"I'll repay you. Add whatever it comes to onto the cost of the boat. If I had a phone, I could start wiring you the money."

"Sure. Whatever." Johnnie pocketed the list.

"Make sure the shoes are wide width. Otherwise, don't get them."

"Right." Johnnie pulled one of the red stones from his pocket. "Hey, let me ask you something."

Mo went to the refrigerator and pulled out a diet soda. "What?"

"I found these stones. The jeweler I spoke with said they were mostly worthless. Would it be weird to give them away? You know, to get in character? The pirate captain in my story gives to the poor."

Mo popped the top and took a long sip. "Let me see."

Johnnie handed him the rock.

"They're kind of interesting." Mo held the quarter-size red stone up to the light. "Who would you give them to? And what are they supposed to do with them? I mean, a real pirate would give away coins."

"Yeah," Johnnie took back the stone. "It's dumb."

"I didn't say that. How many do you have?"

"About twenty. I was thinking of handing them out to panhandlers."

"Tell you what. I think giving away the stones is interesting. Like a real pirate treasure. But if you give to the homeless, you should also give them five or ten bucks alongside. Then they won't think you're mocking them. Ha! Remember when Charlie Brown got rocks for Halloween?

Classic."

"I checked my bank account last night. It isn't good."

"Then try it with maybe two or three people. That's more than enough to get a sense of your character and jot down some notes."

They exited the cabin and Johnnie unbundled the inflatable dinghy and affixed the air pump to it. Mo sat on the bench, his arm over the side, basking in the sun.

As the air pump ran, Johnnie asked. "Would it be crazy to buy a cheap pirate hat? See, Greta says dressing the part helps. She got me an earring…"

"Oh, how I wish I could go with you! Yes, go full pirate. More is more, as they say. You need a bandana too, and an eyepatch. And a vest and blousy shirt. The whole deal."

"I don't know…it would attract attention."

"Yes! Precisely! Pirates had swagger! You need to channel your inner Mick Jagger! Ooh, that rhymes. Might add that to your song. But this could be *precisely* what you need."

"What? Why?"

"Playing a part. You could forget all that nonsense about feeling sorry for yourself. Be a brash pirate for a day. You owe it to yourself."

"You make it sound easy. I already look like a doofus with my weird glasses."

"Ha! You think I was always this joyful and full of energy? No! As a cruise director, I had to play a part. And as time went by, it stuck. I embraced the role. When you see the joy you bring to others, it's infectious. And addictive." Mo stood briefly, swirling his hips like a belly dancer, and winked.

Johnnie laughed. "Fine. I'll think about it."

"Yeessss!" Mo raised both palms and spoke like Borat, "High five!"

Johnnie high-fived him back. Turning serious, he frowned. "You know, I had to fib this morning when I submitted my arrival on the app to Border Control; saying I was the only passenger. Which means, you need to stay out of sight."

"Don't worry. I'll behave. Maybe I'll write my own story. An autobiography or maybe a story about a handsome cruise ship lothario who wins an international dance contest."

Johnnie tossed the dinghy into the water and climbed in. The hundred-pound raft was powered only with oars, meaning a good workout to reach shore. As he unhitched from Bert, he wondered if he could pull off the pirate impersonation. It couldn't be any more embarrassing than the time he jumped on the St. John ferry naked. Of course, he wasn't in his right mind then.

He imagined telling the story later to Greta. It would make her smile. Putting down the oars, he retrieved the gold earring and put it on his left ear.

With a grin, he began rowing and humming Macarena. Because now he couldn't get the song out of his head. The real lyrics were unknown to him. Sitting on the center bench, he rowed in time to the song, a long stroke of the paddles through the water with each mumbled verse. On the fourth beat, he rested his arms and called out, "Hey, Macarena!" with the waves muffling his voice. As he neared shore, he gave up humming.

Sure, singing and dancing were fine for some guys like Mo. And he could enjoy both for a short time, but he wasn't a cheerful person and didn't have Mo's confidence.

No, he would never be the life of the party.

And that was more than okay.

Chapter 18

Wandering cruise-ship tourists surrounded the San Juan Customs House, having recently disembarked. The streets were jammed with taxis. Drivers hollered and beeped their horns. In the center of the intersection, a police officer blew his whistle and motioned to vehicles. Gangs of people walked off curbs without looking both ways. The sun overhead was intense, casting the city in a yellow haze with no breeze.

Johnnie had a full itinerary today. The National Park System operated three forts that could make perfect backdrops for his pirate story. A tour was beginning at ten. It was too early in the day for his pirate impersonation. But since he had a few minutes, he stopped at a nearby drug store and picked up some antiseptic, bandages, a bottled water, and two cheap XXL T-shirts in the clearance rack for Mo. One had San Juan written in graphic letters on the front. The other had a picture of beach umbrellas. As he headed for the counter, the aisle to this left caught his eye. The shelves were crammed with souvenirs and children's toys. The black hat drew him over.

It was a cheap thin felt pirate hat, with a bright red feather and a poorly silk-screened skull and cross-bones on the front. Only $3.99. He pulled it off the rack and looked for a mirror. The only mirrors were in the cosmetics section, and he couldn't convince himself to go over there. Instead, he placed it on his head to check the fit. Tight, but manageable. A wave of doubt screamed, "This is too idiotic, even for you." He placed it back on the rack.

He walked back to the counter. There were three people ahead of him and only one cashier.

Holding the plastic shopping basket in one hand, he touched his earring with the other. A compromise popped in his head. *Maybe just a bandana?*

He'd seen a few near the T-shirt section. One in particular intrigued him; black with a repeating print of white skulls. Sort of pirate-ish. But subtler.

Johnnie sighed and left the line, getting the black bandana and returning to the check-out.

Once outside the store, he tied it around his neck and took a sip of his water. He found a bench in the shade. Now that he was back on land, he didn't have to worry about insane roaming charges and he turned on his phone. It took a minute, but then the notifications poured in.

Robin had called twenty-one times.

Shit.

He didn't call her yesterday when he said he would.

With a quick text, he wrote to her, "I'm in San Juan. All is fine. Sorry I forgot. Love you."

The next text message was from Greta, "AAARR you having a good time? Can't wait to hear about it!" She added an eyepatch emoji.

What could he text back that was cute and would make her laugh? He took a selfie of the side of his head, with the earring and bandana, and shot it off to her, with the words, "Channeling my inner pirate" with a smiley face.

He turned off his phone again to save battery. Before he walked to the fort, he explored a few side streets to check out the area. Lots of shopping and restaurants. Upbeat music poured from sidewalk cafes.

Johnnie came across a city park bordered by shade trees with a large fountain in the center. A kettledrum band played. Everyone seemed happy. On pink concrete benches lining the area, couples exchanged sweet gestures, kisses and smiles. Mothers with strollers beside them chatted with each other. Toddlers danced in circles. Four grizzled old men played bocce. And yet, he felt oddly separate from the surrounding joy. Like he had two-dimensional vision, and he was seeing these images like they were on a television or a page in a magazine.

If his protagonist, Captain Cecil, were here, what would he do?

He fished in his pocket and pulled out a five-dollar bill and one of the stones. He placed them in the bucket in front of the kettle drum musicians. One of them called out, "Thank you, sir!"

Johnnie turned to leave and almost tripped over a little girl who was twirling behind him. "Oops!"

The tiny girl, with jet-black pigtails and a yellow dress, pumped her fists and stomped her feet to the drum beat, oblivious to his near collision. She looked up at him, "Woo-woo! Ya-ya!"

He laughed. Like Mo, this girl's dancing was infectious. In response, he called back, "Woo!" He did a quick jig for her and made a funny face.

The girl laughed.

Johnnie estimated the girl was maybe three. He dug in his pocket and handed a red stone to the girl. "For you. Pretty, right?"

She squinted at it, licked it, threw it on the ground. She lurched forward and head-butted him in the knee caps.

Which hurt more than he expected.

He backed away from the assault, turned and strode away. Yet, a pitter patter of feet followed him. The girl was chasing after him at high speed.

He didn't know what to do. *What if she chased him outside the park?* So, he stopped. The girl rammed his knee again with her head.

And it fucking hurt, like being hit with a baseball bat. "Ow!"

The girls' mother dashed over. "I'm sorry. She likes to chase people."

Johnnie rubbed his legs. "No worries. I feel like head butting people sometimes, too." He was kidding, but the woman looked at him like he was insane, or worse, a total creep.

He jogged away while he had a chance. The fortress tour was starting soon. The tour was only an hour long. Perhaps enough time to convince himself to go further with his pirate persona. Work up his swagger.

If he dared.

Maybe he needed a few libations first.

And pirates were always drinking or drunk, right?

After the tour, perhaps he could have a couple rum and cokes. In his head, this sounded fun. But on reflection, he knew alcohol usually gave him headaches. And it was enough of a headache dealing with Mo and Stumpy.

No, nothing was going to give him swagger. That was for his earlier life. When he had muscle definition and energy and normal moods. When he felt like a whole person with a bright future.

He decided to stick with learning historical facts and taking pictures.

The truly safe course.

* * *

~Ten Minutes Earlier~

Dave put his arm around Renaldo as they ducked into the dark industrial-looking bar. "How many more days?"

"Until?" Renaldo asked.

"I'm healed enough for my new passport photos?"

They took two seats at the wood-topped L-shaped bar. "Probably another week. Why? I thought you were happy."

"Sorry. I am. But I like to have options."

"Babe, come on."

"What?"

"If you want to leave, just say so. I won't shed a tear."

Dave hated Ren's martyr act. Instead of responding immediately, he scanned the room, seeing only a few possibly suspicious characters, but nothing he couldn't handle.

When the bartender arrived, Renaldo said, "A mojito, a dirty martini, and two waters."

After the bartender left, Dave whispered in his ear, "Yes, but you'll still miss me."

Renaldo kept his face turned away. "Honey, I *know* you. Don't act like I don't. I know I'm a layover. And it's been fun."

"Well, you know I'm a workaholic."

"You think?" Renaldo tsked. "So, what? You're going to start smashing skulls again and extorting people? Goodness. How do you even find these gigs? Is there, like, an app for that?"

Dave grinned. "Yeah. There is."

"Fuck. Show me."

"What?"

"Are you deaf now? Show me. Show me a listing."

Dave shook his head. In a non-convincing James Bond accent, he said, "If I show you, I'll have to kill you."

Renaldo swatted at him. "Don't be stupid."

"Fine." Dave took out his phone, but hid it below the bar while he called up the listing he had bookmarked. The one he was most intrigued by. He obscured his login name and handed the screen to his boyfriend.

Renaldo moved his lips as he read, then reared back. "Really? El Salvador? A coup leader? Shit."

"See below? Pays a ton. Plus, I would get to select members from their elite military. I've always wanted a true field op."

"Fuck you and fuck your little macho wanna-be militia."

"Hey, you wanted…"

Out of the corner of his eye, a person walked past the front window, on the sidewalk outside.

It couldn't be.

Could it?

Renaldo snapped his fingers. "Hello?"

Dave sucked in a deep breath. "Stay here. I'll be right back." Without waiting for a response, he dashed outside, shielding his eyes from the sun's glare, watching the man with the skull scarf and brown hair walk away. Dave's heart pounded. *Was it Crosswell?*

He had to know. Dave pursued his mark across the street, his hands in fists. Walking as fast as his feet could carry him without breaking into a run, hoping to cut off his target at the next light. His prey turned right at the corner, heading into a park.

With the traffic, he had to wait until the light turned. When it did, Dave dashed across, but headed beneath the trees, where the shade could give him cover.

The asshat—with the weird glasses and the drug store shopping bag—was, in fact, Johnnie. The idiot park maintenance guy who foiled his extortion scheme, then stabbed him and left him to die on that deserted rock island.

There was no mistake.

And in that moment, he longed for his favorite knife. Or his sidearm. But the authorities confiscated his weapons, along with his rented SUV, in St. John last month.

The advertised job in El Salvador was meaningless now.

The universe had made his choice clear.

Time to settle up old scores.

The six-eyed park ranger with the stupid looking earring was going to die.

Chapter 19

ertie woke refreshed in her own comfy bed in Calabash Boom. Birds cawed and chirped outside her bedroom window. She had woken from a mostly blissful dream. She and Cudlow walked along the Champs-Élysées, holding hands with the city lights twinkling above. He kissed her and her knees felt weak, then they were dancing. Her clothing changed into a long flowy white dress and he wore a top hat like Fred Astaire. But then after a few twirls, he transformed again. His hair was long, the way she remembered, twisted in clumpy ropes, wearing his old brown shorts he wore at their first meeting. And she was in her housecoat, holding a handful of rotting lemons.

What did it mean?

She was still angry with him. On the flight home from Paris, she resolved to break things off. Once and for all. No wavering. She'd write him an email, making it plain as day. And she wouldn't be mean; simply explain that she prefers to be alone, which was true. She would say she hoped they could be friends, although at the moment it didn't feel quite true. *Perhaps with time...*

She heard a knock on the front door. Her bedside clock read eight-fifteen. Too early for neighbors to call, unless it was some kind of emergency.

After donning her robe, she opened the door to see an unfamiliar young woman. Dark skinned, thin, wearing a white suit with a gold nametag, *Denise.*

"Ms. Brown?"

"Yes, that's me."

"Hi, I'm with the Tecoma Sands Resort. I have a letter for you from Mr. Loughton." She handed her an envelope. It was large and white; more of a magazine-size envelope. The gold lettering on the front read,

'Ms. Gertrude Brown'.

"What is this?"

Denise smiled. "An invitation."

Gertie placed a hand on her hip. "What kind of invitation?"

"Everything you need to know is inside." With a nod, Denise waved, "Have a nice day, Ms. Brown." She returned to the white van, with the name of the resort on the side, and got into the passenger seat.

Gertie closed the front door and placed the envelope on the dining table.

What was that man up to now?

She had half a mind to chuck it in the trash.

The other half, dying of curiosity, won out. She sat at the table and ripped open the end, without care for the contents inside. Dumping it on its side, another smaller cardboard envelope fell out.

A sheet of paper, typewritten on the resort's stationary, stated:

> Gertie, before you break up with me forever, please meet me in Panama City on June 20th. See the details provided. Love always, Cudlow.

She scratched her chin. *Panama?*

Within the envelope, the instructions explained a charter plane would pick her up on St. Thomas tomorrow and fly her direct. Cudlow had made a hotel room reservation in her name at the Panama Waldorf Astoria.

This was bonkers. If they were breaking up, why choose Panama? Did he have some business there?

What did they have left to talk about? She didn't want to hear his reason for leaving, or why he didn't return her calls all those times. Or about his creepy surveillance movie. She didn't care to hear anything that came out of his mouth. He had no valid reason for giving her the damned money. Soon, she would be rid of the ten-million-dollar account. In a few hours, she had an appointment with an accountant to set up the charity endowments.

Why drag her to a foreign country? The invitation wasn't romantic. Just a power play. To corner her. There couldn't be another reason.

She ripped up the instructions. *Rip. Rip.* Into tiny pieces, like confetti on her dining table. Gertie shouted, "Leave me the fuck alone!"

And then it came to her. The last time she yelled those words. She had aimed them at Sebastian.

Gertie also remembered what her mom had told her, all those decades ago.

It was all about control.

Gertie's ex-husband had abused her through control. Control of the money. Control of her actions. Control over her freedom.

It made sense now. Cudlow made her feel out of control. Which seemed odd because he was hundreds of miles away, avoiding her calls.

She'd been alone for so long. A solitude where she never had to consider anyone else's needs or wishes. What if the money had nothing to do with her anger? Maybe she feared change. And living with another human being. Or worse yet, fear of letting down her guard and letting someone else care for her?

Could it be that simple?

Either way, she had to face him. Tell him how she felt. Get resolution and peace, even if it meant saying goodbye forever.

In the meantime, she would go to church and pray and see her friends, and try for normalcy again.

Her most normal place—her happy place—was her garden.

She walked outside into the sunshine. Her garden was, in a word, deplorable. Once green plants were brown and missing leaves. The garden gnome at the center was face down in the dirt like a drunken sailor. Cracks formed in the soil, looking like decades old asphalt.

Johnnie hadn't tended to it at all. She shouldn't have been surprised. It was her own damned fault for asking him to care for it.

Gertie scooped some dirt in her hands; it was dry like talcum. And most of the plants were falling over, requiring staking, and cutting back to revive them. But the worst part was the decaying produce on the ground. Flies buzzed all over the blackened soft globs scattered among the drooping plants.

Still in her robe, she eased to the ground and sat in the garden. Normally she would sing as she worked. But the destruction in front of her was too sad.

Gertie picked up rotten vegetables and chucked them into the forest beyond. With each heave, she yelled each word, "Fuck...him and his...damn...money. I'll...be...okay. I...don't...*need*...him."

As she picked up another soggy squash, she looked down and wept.

Because she *did* need Cudlow.

Her soul needed him. Like oxygen or sunshine.
And the person she hated the most?
The answer was crystal clear now.
She hated her own damned self.

Chapter 20

M o gathered all the pillows in the bedrooms, including Johnnie's. Oddly, he discovered a bar of pale green soap under John's pillow. His new friend was strange.

He was on a mission to create a cushy recliner on the otherwise stiff bench in the living area of the cabin. Mo drew the curtains halfway, to conceal himself but also allow some light.

The boat was quiet like a tomb. Stumpy was sleeping on the half wall separating the galley kitchen and the living area, his legs dangling on either side.

To fight the silence, he played the ship's FM radio as background, but at a low volume. He was ready to settle in for a long afternoon of quietude and relaxation. Normally, at this hour, he'd be hosting some trivia game or a poolside belly flop contest. With a grin, he counted himself lucky.

A soda and bowl of Fruit Loops would complete the picture. He pulled himself upright and went to the fridge. Only two sodas left. The fridge was likely as old as the boat and showed its age. Its rubber gasket was crumbling in spots. The vinyl coated wire racks showed spots of rust. The shallow molded plastic shelves attached to the door were cracked, and a corner dislodged from the door frame.

He closed the fridge door. Only now it didn't close. He slammed it again, pushed on it. There was a quarter inch gap. One more thing to fix...

Stumpy woke from the commotion of Mo repeatedly slamming the refrigerator door. The lazy iguana eased his lids down again and continued sleeping.

Mo continued to fuss with the door but nothing worked. It wouldn't reseat itself properly. He ripped the plastic door-shelves away.

The problem became obvious.

Five bundled stacks of cash hidden in the door.

Which probably explained why the fridge's wiring was disabled before.

Each wrapper was marked as ten thousand.

What to do?

Put it back? Tell John? Or play Finders-Keepers? Perhaps keep it for himself and use it to buy the boat?

John didn't need the money as much as he did. That was certain.

He had to hide it until he could figure out what to do. He lined the kitchen drawer with it and placed the cutlery tray on top.

With the pesky money gone, he pressed the plastic cover back securely onto the refrigerator door, and the door closed perfectly.

An hour passed while he read a book and later napped on his mound of pillows. The sound of another boat startled him. It was a busy harbor, and it was normal to hear other boats. But this one sounded close and came to a stop, with voices of three men, speaking a combination of Spanish and English, in an agitated manner.

One man shouted, "Go, jump. Take the line. Tie it off."

Mo hid his face behind a curtain and dared to look out through a sliver. A boat, very similar to John's—with a similar black octopus symbol—pulled alongside.

The men looked like they were getting ready to board.

And two of the men had guns drawn.

Drug lords?

They certainly weren't Coast Guard unless the new dress uniform included thick gold chains and face tattoos.

How was he going to survive this?

The living area was a fishbowl. Any attempt to crawl out the windows would be noticed. The windows below were mere portholes, smaller than breadboxes.

Maybe if he timed it right, he could dash outside and throw himself overboard?

Weapons? *What could he use as a weapon?*

There was literally no way out.

A man leapt onto the forward bow, with a loud thud, holding a rope.

Mo locked the cabin door. He remembered the key was still in the ignition on the bridge. If only he could reach it…maybe pull the anchor and run for it?

They would surely shoot him and there was no protection on the bridge.

Unless he could come up with a distraction.

"Sorry, Stumpy. Time to wake up."

This was suicide.

But his only real option.

* * *

Dottie arrived at Gertie's place at noon carrying a bottle of Zinfandel. "Dr. McPherson at your service." She wiggled her shoulders and grinned.

"Come in," Gertie said, still wearing her bathrobe.

"Queen, what are you doing? Why aren't you dressed?" Dottie crossed the room and placed the bottle on the counter. She rummaged in the kitchen drawer.

"I don't know what I'm doing anymore."

"You got that right." Dottie uncorked the wine. "Where are your wine glasses?"

Gertie pointed to the top cabinet over the wall oven and settled on the sofa. The curtains were drawn. The room was bleak.

Dottie poured ample servings in two wine glasses. She brought them over and handed one to Gertie. "Tell Doctor Dottie all about it." She sat on the other end of the sofa, kicked off her shoes and tucked her feet under her.

Gertie's eyes still stung from her earlier breakdown. She didn't know where to start. "I feel like my whole life is upside down."

"Was it so great to begin with?" Dottie sipped her wine. "Mmm, mm. Delish."

"Why did I do it?"

"Do what, sweetpea?"

"Get involved with that man."

"The way you told it, *that man* stoked your fire. Hallelujah! Ain't nothing wrong with getting some at our age."

"Stop. It isn't funny."

"You don't know how to have fun. If I were in your shoes—"

"What? You'd be fine with it?"

"A man who worships me and has millions? Oh, sorry if I don't cry a tear for you."

Gertie guzzled her wine. "You remember Sebastian?"

"That was decades ago. What does he have to do with anything?"

"The divorce was never finalized."

Dottie's jaw dropped. "Girl, are you shitting me?"

"He disappeared. He never signed the divorce papers. Maybe he's dead by now. I don't know."

"Damn."

"Technically, I might still be married to the bastard. Not that I want to get married again."

"Liar." Dottie headed to the kitchen with her glass. "Refill?"

"Bring the damned bottle."

Dottie picked up the wine. "Look, people who have money are different; wired different. If you explain to Cudlow," Dottie brought the bottle over and filled Gertie's glass, "maybe you could work through it." Her eyes widened, "Does he know about your ordeal with your ex? Maybe if he knew about Sebastian and what he did..."

"No. I don't want to tell him. I feel this pit," Gertie pointed to her gut, "right here. Like I could break open any moment and my insides would spill on the ground. I miss Cudlow. But, at the same time, I hate this whole situation. I want it over."

"You are a blessed fool. You can't be so tight. So inflexible. Relationships are about compromise. Ha! Gertie Brown only does things on her own terms. You are a raging bitch, but I still love you."

Gertie sensed a playfulness in Dottie's tone, but also a smattering of truth-telling. "Bitch?"

"If the bitch fits..." Dottie smiled and reached for the wine to top off her own glass.

Gertie gave her a middle finger.

Dottie stuck out her tongue. "I'm starving. It's not right to drink on an empty stomach." She walked into the kitchen and opened the fridge. "Look, sweetie. You called me because I don't sugar coat. You want my advice? Just kiss and make up with him. When he acts an ass, tell him."

Gertie recalled how she tried to tell him, only to get voicemail. Going to meet him in Panama might be her last chance.

Dot pulled out a tray. "Are these brownies?" She pulled back the foil and grabbed a corner and popped a morsel in her mouth. "Yummy." Still chewing, she mumbled, "All men need to be trained and house-broken. Some more than others. It's simple." She walked back with the brownies and placed them on the coffee table.

Gertie sighed and reached for a brownie. "I'm too old for this. Why is he dragging me to Panama? More mysterious bullshit. I just want to die alone in peace."

"You don't mean that."

She hung her head. "I have to figure this out. The flight leaves tomorrow morning."

"Look, be careful." She clapped her hands with each word, "Don't [clap] do [clap] anything [clap] out of spite."

"Too late."

Dottie laughed. "Speaking of, I want to hear about Paris."

"Oh! It was so beautiful. I had half a mind to move there. But I don't know French."

"That's not what *he* said." Dottie giggled.

Gertie laughed, gagging on her brownie. "Oh, shut the fuck up."

"I love you, sweetie." She put down her glass and extended her arms.

Gertie put down her half-eaten brownie and hugged her. She didn't want to let go. "I feel so lost."

Dottie caressed the back of her head. "It's okay. Let it out. I'm here for you momma."

Gertie's lower lip quivered. She sobbed through closed eyes.

* * *

Mo crouched on the sofa bench and held Stumpy close. The position was key, allowing him to remain hidden behind the door when the assailants swung it open. He stroked Stumpy's head and whispered, "I'm sorry, fella. This is our best play."

As he predicted, one of the muscled goons used his gun to break the outside lock. Four shots rang out. The echo blasted his eardrums. The iguana jolted, digging his claws into Mo's chest. Despite the pain, he couldn't let go of his agitated green friend. Mo clamped down on Stumpy's stubby tail with one hand, with his other hand around the iguana's throat.

He looked at Stumpy. With his eyes, he said, "Sorry, boy."

As a short and stocky man entered the dark space, Mo thwacked the guy in the face with Stumpy, releasing the panicked reptile on contact.

The intruder dropped his weapon, screaming, trying to toss the frightened animal off his neck.

Mo dove for the assailant's gun as it skittered across the floor and down the steps to the galley level.

His opponent threw Stumpy to the ground and gave chase.

Mo reached it first, grabbing it at the sunken floor. With the gun in his possession, lying on his back, he aimed at his mark. "Stop!"

The man rushed him.

Mo pulled the trigger.

His opponent went limp, but momentum threw him forward. He landed belly down. Now Mo had a dead man on top of him.

Yells from outside the boat grew louder and approached the doorway. Mo remained still. The man's dead weight had him pinned in the narrow space.

He wondered how many bullets were left. All he needed were two more.

Stumpy waddled across the floor, climbed the bench and took his usual perch on the half wall between the galley and living room; the iguana stared at him with slitted eyes as if saying, "not cool."

The men entered with guns drawn. They immediately noticed their friend face down at the bottom of the three steps. They looked around, wondering what happened.

Mo held his breath and waited until he had a clear shot.

"Ricardo!" the first one shouted. "Are you alright?"

Mustache man stood at the top step, just two feet away, bent at the waist to get a better look.

Mo blasted him, hitting him square in the torso.

His remaining opponent, Big Nose, opened fire, while ducking behind the half wall, shooting wildly without aiming.

Mo felt adequately protected with now *two bodies* on top of him.

Fantastic armor, in fact. But his chest hurt under the weight.

Finally, Big Nose was out of bullets, evidenced by the clicking sounds. He ran away.

A few seconds later, Mo heard the other boat gunning its engine and retreating.

It wasn't easy to see with the jumble of arms across his face, but he discerned Stumpy, who remained on his perch. His head cocked with curiosity.

"Fine help you are," Mo grumbled.

After a minute of extricating himself clumsily, soaked in the other men's blood and his own perspiration, he maneuvered his way to the living area.

One thing was certain. It wasn't safe to remain, because he had the feeling they would come back in larger numbers.

He pulled up the anchor, climbed to the flybridge, and started the engine. There was no sign of the other boat. Mo scanned the horizon. Another cruise ship headed into port. There were many more boats to the west.

He decided.

East.

It was as good a direction as any.

And there was an inlet past the International Airport that might provide suitable cover. It was the best shot to give him time to find Johnnie and explain what happened.

Or he could set sail for open waters and begin his journey alone to the Bahamas.

Johnnie would be upset.

But upset was better than dead.

Chapter 21

afe in the hidden lagoon past the airport, Mo wondered how in Hades he could contact Johnnie. No phone. No tender. He couldn't sail back to the original location for fear of being discovered.

He could use the VHF radio on the flybridge.

Staging Bert near the yacht club was perfect. He could clearly see another shorter yacht departing; a yacht named "The Maid Marion".

He tuned to Channel 9: "Hello? This is the…" To his knowledge, the boat had no name, other than Johnnie calling it Bert. He needed to make something up. "This is the Nauti Iguana calling the Maid Marion."

Only static. The Marion was traveling in the direction of the open ocean.

He tried again. "Maid Marion. Channel 71. Over."

After a few seconds, he heard a woman's voice, "Marion, switching. Over."

Mo changed the channel. "Marion, thank you."

"Do I know you?"

"No, I'm in the Bertram south of the yacht club. Do you see me?" He jumped and waved his arm in the air.

"Yes."

"I need a favor. My cellphone died and I need to contact my captain who is ashore."

Some more static. "Sure, relay when ready."

Mo pumped his fist and wiggled his shoulders. "Yes!"

After relaying the message, Mo heaped thanks on the captain of the Marion. He slumped in the seat on the bridge. He'd give Johnnie two hours. After that, he would hit the high seas.

* * *

Johnnie thought the tour of the fortresses was interesting. He took lots of pictures on his phone. It was close to noon now and he was hungry.

A fast-food restaurant would be prudent to save money. A double cheeseburger was calling his name. Plus, some fries. And a jumbo diet soda with mostly ice.

It was a total tourist move, but he didn't care. He needed to sit and decide what to do next.

Fifteen minutes later, he had his plastic fast food tray and sat at a counter facing a window so he could sidewalk gaze. He chewed large chunks of burger, ketchup drizzling from the corner of his mouth, stuffing fries inside before he completed swallowing. Eating like a barbarian. Which made him wonder about the whole 'pretend to be a pirate' thing. The whole point of writing was to use your imagination. The notion of 'getting into character' made no sense. Because if that were true, hundreds of authors would be bonafide serial killers.

No, he wasn't going to talk pirate or walk bowlegged or wear a silly hat. No way.

He'd still give away some money and more stones. Because that part seemed reasonable.

Johnnie watched some people walk by. Mostly families. A business person or two. He slurped the bottom of his soda, jostling the ice.

A flash of recognition caused Johnnie's heart to stop. He held his breath to process what he saw. It was only a glimpse, but the guy dressed in black on the sidewalk had a familiar build and bandages over his face.

Was it Smith? Was it possible?

No. It couldn't be.

His mind was playing tricks on him.

For all he knew, Smith died on LeDuck island of his wounds, and the birds and crabs pecked away all his flesh, leaving nothing but bones.

Yeah, he was just seeing things.

He bussed his tray and headed outside. The new plan was to give some stones to any homeless he saw on his way back to his dinghy and call it a day. If he got back on the boat early, they could sail most of the way toward Tortuga while there was daylight.

The first indigent he came across was a woman, somewhere between fifty and seventy years old, with a deep tan and wrinkles, wearing a headscarf, lying on a dirty blanket in a side alley next to a bank. Beside her stood a broken-looking shopping cart of her belongings, mostly plastic bags and clothing. She was sleeping and didn't stir when he approached. Johnnie put five dollars in her bucket and placed the red stone next to it. Part of him wanted to give her one of Mo's new clean shirts. But he couldn't risk seeing Mo's bare belly. Instead, he fished out another five-dollar bill.

Johnnie noticed there weren't many homeless in this touristy area of San Juan. Did they try to hide them from the cruise ships? It made sense. Would he have to go further in-land to find people to give to?

He shook his head and wondered what the hell he was doing.

There was a men's discount clothing store ahead. He'd get the rest of Mo's items and head back to the boat.

His Robin Hood themed pirate quest could wait until Tortuga.

* * *

Dave waited outside. The fast-food restaurant was crowded with too many eyes. Not that he had a decent weapon. Only his hands. Which would be fitting re-match.

He wondered if he should let it go. The old him would have. The old Smith would have counted all his millions and moved on. He had planned to retire. What was it again? Rule number 30? *Live long enough to retire.*

Why did this beach keeper irk him so much?

The smart solution would be to put a hit on Johnnie through the dark web. There were chumps and amateurs out there who would do the job for under two thousand. And it would never get traced back to him.

His target exited the restaurant and headed toward more populated areas, in the direction of the cruise ships.

Did dingle-head come here on a cruise? *Typical.*

As he followed a block behind, he came across a construction site. A broken piece of steel pipe, jagged on one end, caught his notice. About eighteen inches long. It would do the job.

He dusted it off and held it low behind his right leg as he continued on.

But Johnnie was gone.

Anger tore through his chest. How could he let this happen?

It was close to one p.m. He said he'd meet Renaldo at the movie theater at 1:30 to see the latest Disney film. Dave began typing a message, "I'll be there soon," when he saw Johnnie pop out from a narrow alley a hundred feet away.

He deleted the message to Renaldo.

What was Johnnie doing in the alley?

Taking a piss? Meeting with someone? Or was he lost?

Dave hurried up to the alley. He scanned the situation. Only some blue plastic trash cans and a homeless woman. But the red-pink rock looked interesting. Did meathead give that to her? The woman was snoring.

He snatched the rock and went back to the sidewalk where he could view it in the light.

It looked like a ruby. There were ways to confirm. He turned his attention down the street. No sign of Johnnie.

Many times, over his career, he transported assets by way of precious stones. They were small, easy to hide, and sometimes worth hundreds of thousands. In fact, he knew an excellent black-market jeweler in town who could appraise the stone.

At the corner, he chucked the pipe on the ground and flagged down a taxi. He gave the driver the address.

Fifteen minutes later, he stood outside the nondescript building with the solid black windowless door. He pressed the intercom.

"It's Smith." He gazed up at the small camera to his upper right.

A voice said, "I can't see your face completely."

"I had an accident. Code word Emerald Dawn."

The door buzzed and he pushed it open.

Down the dimly lit narrow hall, he walked thirty paces and knocked on the door to the left.

It flew open.

"Smith! There was word you were dead or captured." The young Latina woman with black long hair and nose ring, wearing a white canvas apron, gestured for him to enter.

He grinned, "News of my death was intentional. I'm Jones now."

"What do you have?" She held out her right hand, her other hand on her narrow hips.

"Nice to see you too, Paz." He laughed and handed her the stone. "I need to know what this is."

She held it up to the fluorescent tube lights on the ceiling. "Hmm. Interesting."

"Can you check it out?"

"Sure. Take a seat."

He looked around the cramped gemology lab. A metal folding chair in the corner—tucked between a flat grinding wheel and a chest-high steel jewelry vault—was the only seat available.

Paz flumped down on her rolling white stool and gazed at the stone under her microscope, turning it under a beam of light. Then she took out a device with a pen-like probe attached with a cord and watched the needle move on the dial.

"What is that?"

"Tests thermal conductivity. The reading indicates ruby. The color is Pidgeon Blood. Can't tell you the exact value until it's cut. The yield could be ten carats. Worth more than a quarter million after faceting.

"What?"

"Yeah, you shouldn't take less than fifty-K. Are you looking for a buyer? I'll take twenty percent." She flashed her brown eyes at him and smiled.

"Whoa." Dave shook his head in shock. "What a numb-skull!"

"Man, I think twenty percent is fair!"

"Oh, not you." He stood to leave. "I might be back."

"Sure." She put the gem in a small red velvet drawstring pouch and handed it back to him. "Hours are Monday through Friday, noon to five. I've had to cut back. No more night hours. We got robbed last month."

He took the pouch and pocketed it. "Really, who would do such a thing?"

"They wore masks, but I think I know. The Garcia Madre Clan. You know them?"

"You mean Ricardo?"

"Like I said, I'm not sure. And it's best not to make a stink. Gotta preserve secrecy. Hey, you used the old password before, but I recognized your voice. The new one is Captain Morganite."

"Got it. See you around." He walked to the door and she buzzed him out.

Back down the hall, he waited at the exit door until it buzzed.

As he stepped onto the hot sidewalk, he checked the time, 1:24. He'd be late to the movie by at least fifteen minutes and Renaldo was going to be ticked off. He walked to the corner and hailed another taxi.

"Center Plaza Theater, stat."

He looked out the side window as the taxi pulled away from the curb. *How many of these stones did Johnnie have?* It was worth looking into.

Maybe he could steal the rest and kill Johnnie in a single op.

What was the downside?

Nothing.

Dave smirked, wondering if he should skip the movie and track his prey while the trail was hot.

But he would need to track the idiot's phone.

His buddy in the CIA could get Johnnie's phone number in thirty seconds.

"Driver, take me home instead." He gave the driver the address.

Yes, he'd have his revenge.

And it would taste so sweet.

* * *

Johnnie scratched the scar about his ear.

His memory was poor, but not *that* bad.

As he bobbed up in down in his inflatable dinghy in the bay, he wondered how he could lose a 46-foot-long yacht.

Did Mo steal it after all? After the first day, he left the keys on the bridge in a show of trust for Mo.

Maybe his faith in mankind was misplaced.

In his mind, he went through his options. Head back to shore, rent a hotel room and take a plane home the next day? Spend a couple hours paddling around, scouring the harbor and coastline for his missing boat? Call the Coast Guard and have them track down Mo like the dirty rat he was?

He didn't want to overreact. But the more he thought about it, the more his head felt aflame with thoughts of revenge and hate. Because it meant Mo stole Stumpy as well. *Who does that?*

Johnnie turned on his cell phone. Calling the authorities was the right thing to do.

A missed call from a number he didn't recognize. He played the voice mail.

"John, my name is Kara and you don't know me, but I was told to give you a message. Your friend on the Nauti Iguana said to meet him near the San Juan Yacht Club by three o'clock. Otherwise, he has to leave."

He played the message over again.

"Huh?" Johnnie scratched his chin. *Where was the Yacht Club?* He did a map search. Almost eight miles! A long-ass way to row. Why didn't he spring for a small gas motor for his tender?

But this made no sense. He called the number back.

"Hello, this is John. You left a message for me."

"Hi, yes. Your friend sounded upset."

"He's upset? Could you radio him and tell him he has to come get me? It's too far to row."

"Hold on."

Johnnie waited.

"Okay, I have the phone held up to the radio. Tell him yourself."

"Mo? What the hell?"

Through high-pitched static, Mo said, "We were attacked. Over."

"What?"

"We need to get the hell out of here. Over."

"I don't understand."

"Are you at our last anchor point? Over."

"Yes, come back here now!"

"Roger. On my way. Over."

Kara's voice came on, "Are you squared away?"

"Yes. Thank you."

"Great. Take care now."

Johnnie hung up. Why was Mo acting so weird? What did he mean by *attacked*?

His phone battery was down to twenty percent. The weather app showed a storm coming in from the south, plus a maritime alert of high seas tonight between eight and two. *Great.*

Johnnie stared into the water. Two manatees swam by.

They didn't look remotely like mermaids. With dull gray wrinkled skin, chubby noses, and whiskers, they looked like slow-motion walruses, floating around as if they smoked too much weed.

Sitting under the hot sun, with nothing to do but wait, he told struck up a conversation. "Sorry dudes. Not my type."

One of them winked and smiled at him. He heard a voice say, "You aren't my type either."

Which didn't seem right.

Was he hallucinating? Was the sun baking his brain? His thoughts turned to his medication. Had he taken it this morning? He couldn't remember. With the dance lesson and talk about Mick Jagger earlier, he'd probably forgotten to take his pill. And the morning before, he remembered counting out his remaining pills, but then he found Mo on the back deck.

His eyes went wide. He'd forgotten his medication two mornings in a row. Meaning, he couldn't forget again. He had to take a dose the moment he got back to the ship. He rocked back and forth, chanting, "Don't forget...don't forget...don't forget."

Twenty minutes later, Bert came into view. Mo was at the helm but he wasn't a good pilot, because the boat was on a collision course with his dinghy. Johnnie picked up the oars and rowed to avoid disaster.

"Mo! Take it easy!"

From the bridge, Mo called, "Sorry! How do you stop this thing?"

Really? "Try reverse!"

Bert drifted past Johnnie by over two ship lengths before it stopped.

Johnnie called sarcastically, "Yeah, no problem. Stay where you are." He picked up the oars and paddled over.

Mo was waiting for him on the deck. "Come on! We need to go."

Johnnie threw his line to Mo to pull him in close. He climbed onto the back ladder. "What the hell?"

Mo pulled the dinghy up on the back, crowding them against the far wall. "Deflate this thing. We need to get underway."

He grabbed Mo's shirt collar. "Why are you acting like this?"

Mo's eyes narrowed. "Fine." He pushed open the cabin door, grabbed Johnnie's arm and tugged him inside.

"What?"

Mo pushed him toward the galley. "See?"

"Holy shit!"

"Three men attacked the boat. One of them got away. I have a strong hunch they'll be back."

"These two are dead?"

"Yes."

"Why? What did they want?"

Mo shook his head. "Silly me. I should have asked the armed men storming our ship what they wanted first."

"We should call the Coast Guard."

"And tell them *what* exactly?"

Mo had a point. Greta had told him the news story about the drug cartel pirates. He didn't need to be caught up in another international crime investigation. Last time he was arrested merely for finding a dead person.

Johnnie sat on the bench and rubbed his face, trying to come to grips with the situation in front of him. *Was a relaxing vacation too much to ask for?* Because now he firmly believed he was cursed. "It was self-defense, right?"

Mo sat beside him. "Going back to Iran would be a death sentence. I can't talk to the authorities."

He looked around. There were bullet holes in the door, woodwork and windows. The scene was messed up. "Where's Stumpy? Is he okay?"

"He's fine. On the bridge soaking in the sun."

"Whew."

"John, the boat the attackers used…it had a similar mark. The black octopus."

"I'm making a wild guess. Drug cartel?"

"That makes sense. Wait." Mo jumped up and pulled open a drawer in the kitchen, bracing himself on the half-wall to not step on a dead body. He retrieved a rectangular looking item and held it up. "I found this in the refrigerator."

A stack of money. Johnnie stared at it. "Jumpin' Jesus."

Mo put the money on the table and pulled on Johnnie's arm, bringing him to a stand. "Do you get the picture now? They'll come back."

Johnnie took a deep breath, staring at the wad of cash. "So now what?"

Mo replied deadpan, "We get the hell out of San Juan."

Chapter 22

Johnnie climbed to the flybridge. Mo followed.

"Where to?"

"North. The Bahamas. You can drop me off and then head home."

"Sorry. Too far. A storm is coming. If we head east, we could be back on St. John in four or five hours. Then you can take the boat wherever."

Mo's head sank. "Yes, that would be prudent."

"Exactly. I'll sign over the title, we can split the cash you found. Call it even."

"Sure."

"John, if I'm to sail by myself later, I could use some practice, while you are here to train me in navigation."

He scratched his chin. "True. Come on."

"But first, we should get to open water. Where the pirates won't find us."

"Good idea. Navigating is easy. See this chart plotter? Works like a cell phone. Let me power it up."

Johnnie hit the on button. He hit it again. The screen remained dark.

"That's weird. It was working before."

"Maybe a bullet hit some wiring?" Mo offered with a shrug.

"Could be. Damn. These things cost hundreds."

"Well, it's more my problem now."

Johnnie sighed. "Damn. We'll have to go old school. As long as you know your starting point and end point, you can plot a course using ded reckoning."

They went over the process which involved drawing lines on a chart, using magnetic north, and a compass rose to determine the angle of the desired course, and calculating your speed and travel time to figure out when to turn.

Mo scratched his head. "This looks complicated."

"It doesn't have to be. Do what I did. Take a course that keeps land in sight. Hug the coast here, then along Vieques, head east. Soon after, you'll see St. Thomas." Johnnie pinched the bridge of his nose. "Ow."

"Are you alright, skipper?"

"I have a headache. I hate the idea of heading back when I haven't written any of my story for Greta. And we still need to dump these guys somewhere."

"You know, we should probably head away from shore. Somewhere in very deep water."

"Agree. Let's complete that first. I'll drive."

Johnnie steered the boat due north at full throttle.

Mo said, "Hey, I'm sorry."

"Why? It isn't your fault."

"Yeah, but I feel like trouble is following me. Like I'm cursed."

"You feel cursed? Ha. I'm the cursed one."

They sailed in silence. No radio. Stumpy climbed down and sat on the front of the boat, his face into the breeze.

After forty minutes, Johnnie cut the engine. "I think this is far enough."

They went down below and lifted the first body out. The blood had congealed, but there was a thick pool on the floor in the kitchen.

Johnnie pulled the man by the arms across the living area.

Mo said, "Stop!"

"What?"

"We should check his pockets."

Johnnie dropped the dead man's arms. "Hell no."

"Why? Aren't you curious to see who they are? Where they come from?"

"Believe me, nothing good will come from it. Pick up his legs and come on. Now!"

"Jeez, testy."

They opened the cabin door and dragged the first man overboard. The trail of reddish black blood was grotesque and slippery. The second body was a little heavier, but they dropped him over the side after some effort.

"We need to clean this up," Mo said. "Let me get some sponges from the closet." He went down to get them.

A drop of rain pelted Johnnie in the eye. "Oh, damn."

The sky to west was black, a downpour was coming. *Fast.*

On the horizon, another white yacht appeared.

"Mo?"

Johnnie stared at the oncoming boat. It seemed to be sailing directly toward them. Although over a mile away. This seemed odd, because they hadn't seen another vessel in the last thirty minutes. "Mo?" His voice sharper now.

"MO!"

He poked his head back through the door. "What?"

"Look."

"Oh, no. Do you have binoculars?"

"Up on the bridge. In the box under the center dash."

"Wait here." Mo climbed up. A few seconds later. "I can't tell. But it looks similar to yours. It's got to be them."

Johnnie climbed to the flybridge. "We should get moving."

Mo took the second-mate's chair. "Which direction?"

"Fuck if I know."

"We could head into the storm."

"Don't be dumb."

"They might not follow us. It's our best option."

Johnnie stood and stomped his feet, banging his palms on the wheel. "Fuck! Fuck! Fuck!"

"Yelling won't solve this." Mo said, his hand on John's shoulder.

He stopped flailing. "I know. My stomach is doing backflips. I used to never get seasick, even in the roughest seas. But now…"

"You need to get yourself together."

A wave of new panic came over him. "Jumpin' Joe. I forgot my meds again. I'll be right back."

"You know what? Why don't you go down and relax? Maybe look around for things we can use to fight. I'll drive."

Relax and find weapons? Johnnie climbed down the ladder. "I'm going to grab Stumpy first."

Down below, he opened a side window and called, "Stumpy, yum time!" He held out a piece of pear. The drops of rain were coming faster; they splashed off the hull into the room.

The iguana scampered along the fiberglass surface, losing his footing here and there, zigzagging toward the window. He ducked only his head inside, snatched the pear and ran away again, up the window to the flybridge.

"Stupid reptile."

Johnnie figured Stumpy would come in when it rained hard enough and he closed the window.

The engine roared to life and the whine vibrated through the cabin. He opened the kitchen drawer with his pills and took one. He took a seasickness pill as well.

Mission accomplished. At least one mission.

Driving through the now heightened swells felt like slamming a car into a pothole on repeat. He held onto the kitchen counter to steady himself.

The idea of heading into the storm was terrifying. Though not as terrifying as armed drug lords. And if he wanted to see Robin, Gertie, Cud, and Greta again, it was their best option.

Johnnie headed towards the cabin door to join Mo up top. He lost his footing when the ship dipped hard, tried to right himself only to slip on the trail of blood. He faltered, staggered into the door and slammed into it face first. Lying on the floor, his consciousness drifted.

* * *

Johnnie woke to Mo yelling outside.

He pushed himself off the floor. A swell sent his shoulder careening sideways into the wood-paneled wall. Johnnie grabbed the edge of the table and held on.

When he opened the cabin door, a wave crashed over the side and drenched his clothes.

"What?" he screamed toward the bridge; the raging storm swallowed his words.

Mo yelled something indistinguishable.

Stumpy darted between his feet into the cabin.

He climbed the slick aluminum ladder to the bridge, his clothes stuck to him, the wind in his face. Every move had to be calculated. Gripping whatever fixed object or surface was available to him. Once on top, the ship leaned to the side at the bottom of a swell. Johnnie dove for the first mate's chair, gripping it, hugging it to him.

Mo was wearing a life vest. "We need a plan! Did you find any weapons? Put on your life vest."

Johnnie surveyed the scene. It was dark as night. Except for the lights on their own boat. In the distance, the pirate ship was still pursuing.

Perhaps only a few minutes had gone by. But soon, it would truly be nightfall. He took the spare life vest from under the control panel and fit it over his head.

Wondering aloud, Johnnie said, "How did they find us in the middle of the ocean?" Not waiting for an answer, he said, "There has to be a transmitter."

He looked at the switches on the dashboard. "Mo! Goddamnit." He switched off the button labeled VHF band.

Mo yelled, "Hold on!"

A wave the height of a tractor-trailer crashed over the bow.

Johnnie fell and wrapped his arms around the support of the captain's chair. Salt water drenched him; he sputtered and spit to clear his throat.

As he stood, he kept a firm grasp of the chair back. "When you turned on the radio station...you must have turned on the location transmittal system."

Mo yelled, "Sorry!"

"We can't keep running. Shut it down."

"Are you crazy?"

"No. It could work."

"What could work?"

"A story Greta told me about the capture of Calico Jack's pirate ship. We turn off all the lights. They won't find us in the dark."

Mo cut the engine. "What then?"

"Then we attack."

"With what?"

"I don't know yet."

"Oh, brilliant plan, captain."

"We need to sink their ship."

The wind howled and another tall wave approached. "Hold on!" Mo yelled.

After the wave passed, Johnnie looked behind them. The pirate ship seemed to have slowed down. But it could be his imagination. Distances were so deceptive at sea.

"Shit." Johnnie couldn't believe his eyes. The pursuing ship's light also went out. Like it vanished into thin air.

Mo grabbed Johnnie's shoulder. "What are they doing?"

"Maybe they will think we capsized and will leave us alone."

Mo wiped spray from his face. "Or maybe *they* capsized or lost power?"

"I don't like this."

"One way to find out." Mo returned to the captain's chair and engaged the engine. "Go turn off the lights in the cabin, break the running lights if you have to. Maybe we can sail away and stay hidden."

Their ship advanced through the water. Johnnie went down the ladder to manage the light situation.

In the distance, the lights of the pirate ship came back on.

Which meant they were screwed. Like a mouse being chased by a cat with submachine guns.

He dashed around the cabin, turning off any sources of light. Seawater—an inch deep—filled the floor of the lower bunk rooms. Johnnie found a rusty hammer in the tool closet and went to the stern to smash the rear light. Hitting the small target while bouncing across the waves and holding on for dear life was like threading a needle while walking on a tightrope. *Not easy.* But he did it on the fourth swing.

Johnnie went topside with Mo and scanned Bert. Only a dim green glow from the dials on the bridge. He ripped the bottom portion of his soaked t-shirt and draped it over the lights.

Mo asked, "Are we good?"

"We should change course. Just in case."

"East?"

"Weren't we going east?"

"Um, yes. I meant, to the right."

"Sure." Johnnie had no idea where they were. Direction had no meaning. Getting away was the only consideration. "Do you want me to drive now?"

"Yes. My nerves are shot."

"Mine, too."

They switched places. Mo asked, "How is Stumpy?"

"Asleep. No help at all." When he was turning off the lights, the iguana was sleeping on his bed, without a care.

Mo laughed and said something unintelligible.

"What?"

Mo gestured at him to look forward.

Another gigantic wave. Johnnie gripped the steering wheel with all his strength to hang on.

The storm was intensifying, if that was even possible.

For the next twenty minutes, the ship took a pounding and lightning danced across the sky in terrifying jagged ribbons. Thunder roared across the dark expanse.

Mo said, "I don't see them."

Johnnie slowed the engine and stood to look. No sign of their previous pursuers.

The engine made a loud booming noise and the vibration ceased.

"No!" Johnnie screamed. "No! No! NO!" He slammed his palms on the wheel.

"What happened?"

He turned the ignition key on and off. *No change.*

Drenched, cold, and now with no engine power, the situation was bleak. Battery power be gone soon. "We need to call a Mayday."

"Are you sure?"

"Yes!" Johnnie turned on the VHF band and picked up the radio receiver and tuned to the correct channel. "Mayday. Mayday. This is the Bert 1500. We're at…" He took his thumb off the transmit button. "Shit."

Johnnie remembered the navigation system was down. He scraped water from his eyes. His phone would have GPS coordinates, but it was inside the cabin. He grappled his way back down the ladder; a jolt of lightning took his attention and he bumped his chin on a rung as the boat lurched upward.

Once inside the cabin, Stumpy was awake, sitting by his food bowl, which was upside down.

His phone was plugged in where he left it on the starboard window ledge. As the GPS map slowly came up, he had to check it again. They weren't even close to home.

Where had Mo taken them?

Due north. The middle of nowhere. He stared at the blue dot. No land for miles.

On a sheet of his notebook paper, he scrawled the coordinates in large letters to read them easily in the wind and rain once topside.

Back at the radio on the bridge, he called, "Mayday. Mayday," and relayed the coordinates, wiping his eyes constantly. The ink ran off the soaked page.

A voice responded, but he couldn't make out what it said with the roar of the ocean and claps of thunder. He hoped they would come. Because they were far outside US territorial waters by quite a distance.

Johnnie scanned the area. Still no sign of their pursuers. No lights, no visible ships.

The boat fell into a deep trough and listed hard to the side. A wave swamped the back and pulled the boat further over.

Mo yelled, "Brace yourself."

It was too late.

They headed sideways toward the water's surface. The boat capsized.

The waves pulled him under with the force of a car careening off a cliff. He held his breath and paddled with all his might to reach the surface.

Even if he didn't drown right away, the end was near.

And it rightly pissed him off.

* * *

No purchase. Nothing to climb. Only water. Where was Johnnie? Where was the large Cheesy man? His legs kicked and kicked. A plastic floaty thing. Get to it!

Stumpy gripped the narrow bit of jetsam with his claws. So tight he thought the narrow points would break. Another splash, whirling him under.

Back to the surface. Johnnie was calling. Arms reaching.

Then his friend was gone again.

Lightning pierced his eyes. Thunder made him quake.

The Iguana King cannot die.

Must not die.

He scowled at the next wave, but it didn't stop. It smashed him down. Spinning, upside down, he couldn't see.

Hands on his torso. Cheesy man!

He gripped the big human's forearm. Climbed to his chest. A better perch.

The man called, "Sit-sit."

And he sat.

They rolled on and on. The rain pelting them, the waves punishing them.

Cheesy man held on to him and he felt appreciation.

Live another day.

Another day for cheesy puffs.

And live another day as Iguana King.

Chapter 23

J ohnnie broke the surface, buoyant with his life preserver, but the five-foot waves waterboarded him repeatedly with each crest and trough. Like falling down an elevator shaft. Not that he'd experienced it.

"Mo!"

The wind wailed and water drummed, muffling his shouts.

A bolt of lightning illuminated the sky. In that sliver of light, the flash of an orange life vest appeared. But it disappeared the next instant in the darkness.

Just breathe, his mind chanted. It was all he could manage. The ocean was like an insane rollercoaster operated by a psychopathic killer clown. And he couldn't get off.

Time passed, as if in suspended animation, where minutes seemed like hours and hours seemed like days.

The storm eventually subsided, but now it was night. The ocean calmed and the stars appeared.

A memory came to him. Swimming in formation in Marine basic training. Coming in silent, precise. To take the shore and overtake the opposing force with stealth in a war game exercise. How old was he? *Twenty?* A lifetime ago.

The adrenaline in his body eased, leaving nothing but sheer exhaustion. The foam-core lid of his cooler floated nearby. He swam for it, captured it, then rested his arms and head across it.

He drifted to sleep.

* * *

Dottie read the copy of the police report Janice had slipped to her. *LeDuck Island.*

It made no sense. No one went there. It was a deserted bit of rock. A wildlife preserve.

The ornithologists described their attacker as a tall man wearing black trousers with a chest wound and sinister eyes. It had to be Smith. The timeline fit.

But how did he get there?

Did Arturo find him and mess him up? *Probably not.*

Did Smith have other enemies on St. John?

There was only one answer: Johnnie.

Robin had mentioned that Johnnie liked to go fishing at the beach at John's Folly. A beach directly across from LeDuck Island. *Did they have a quarrel? Did Johnnie wound Smith?*

It certainly wasn't Gertie.

She recalled how the hitman acted so belligerent with Johnnie that afternoon in the trailhead parking lot. There was genuine anger. Which meant Smith had a score to settle with John. Otherwise, why would Smith stick around after he got the ransom money?

Before that, Johnnie had hit Smith with a shovel, messing up his face. More than enough reason for revenge.

A man like that always seeks a re-match.

She made some photocopies of Smith's picture from the newspaper. Even printed stills from the security camera footage of Smith's visit to their office last month. It was time to put her network into action.

Dottie called Jupiter first. He operated the passenger ferry.

"Good evening, Dottie."

"Good evening, Joop."

"What's happening?"

"I'm still trying to find the murderer."

"Of course you are," he chuckled. "What can I do to help?"

"If I bring you some photos tomorrow, can you keep a look out? Smith probably looks different now. But if you see someone of his size, weight, coloring, could you give me a shout? Pass the message to the folks on the other shifts?"

"Ha! The FBI gave me his picture weeks ago. I still have it. But yes, we'll call."

"Thanks, Jupiter."

"Anything for you. And if I see Elvis, I'll call you too."

Dot laughed. "You'd better."

They ended the call. Her next calls were to the car rental agencies. Or more specifically, only two of them. The ones which had black SUVs in their inventory. Because a man like that has certain tastes and rarely changes.

She leaned back in her chair to consider other moves. What if Smith rents a taxi? Or arrives by private boat? The answer had to be more traps.

There were several webcams on the island, but mostly recording pretty beach views. Those were useless.

Maybe she needed to wire up Johnnie's place with some hidden cameras and motion sensors. Gertie's house too. Would that be going too far? *Gertie was so private...* Dot opened her browser and looked up laws about spying. And some technology options. Nothing too expensive.

After an hour of searching the web, she came up with another idea.

Even felons need to eat. But they don't hang around in restaurants.

After Smith escaped, she remembered a conversation she'd had with the owner of the resort Smith stayed at. *Several empty packets of protein shake powder in the trash.*

She called Mr. Bravos from Calabash Market.

"Good evening, Mario. It's Dottie."

"Good evening, Dot. How are you?"

"Oh, I'm good. Did the FBI ever give you a picture of the killer?"

"What, the guy who dropped those bodies at the beach last month?"

"Yeah."

"No. I only saw his picture on the news."

"Well, he's like six-foot-three and wears black all the time. And he probably has a new face now. Drinks lots of protein shakes. If you see anyone who fits that description, could you call me?"

"Why can't you let the authorities handle this?"

She giggled, "You know why."

He chuckled and teased, "Because you have to get in everyone's business. That's why."

"You know it!"

"Yes, I'll call. Have a good night now."

"Good night, Mario."

* * *

Gertie's flight touched down in Panama on time. She had packed light, not intending to stay long. Although she brought a change of clothes and a toothbrush, not wanting to repeat her disaster in Paris. Just confront Cudlow one last time. End their relationship like civilized adults. Maybe kiss him on the cheek.

She wore her favorite dress. The one she bought in Paris, chiffon with a floral pattern with butterflies. On her feet, white espadrilles. Her hair was fashioned in a tight low bun, and she wore her old strand of long fake pearls.

After passing through Customs, she reviewed her instructions. A driver would meet her near the luggage carousels.

Descending the escalator among the throng of arrivals, she shook her head, wondering why Cudlow wanted the drama of this distant meet up. Still, her curiosity burned. The speech she refined and recorded mentally during the flight echoed through her thoughts. Once delivered, she could have peace.

On cue, at the bottom of the stairs, a driver held up a sign, "Ms. G. Brown."

In almost no time, she was seated in the back of a car, being whisked to the hotel.

The hotel was gorgeous. Light piano music played in the lobby; a magnificent space adorned with marble floors and plush furniture. She drew in a long breath and headed to the front desk.

They gave her a key to a condo suite on the twenty-first floor.

With her electronic key, she entered the room. The views were stunning. The room was spacious and modern in hues of creams and golds. On a rectangular dining table, a vase of pink roses. She opened the attached card.

"Meet me for dinner tonight at eight at the hotel restaurant.
Love, Cudlow."

It was four o'clock now. Why was he making her wait to get this over with?

This was bullshit.

She dialed the hotel operator. "Cudlow Loughton's room please."

They connected her and she heard ringing.

Then his voice, "Hello?"

"What room are you in?"

"Gertie? Is that you?"

"Who else were you expecting?"

"I'm in 21011. But I can come to you…"

She hung up the phone, grabbed her key and headed out.

His room was five doors down. She knocked.

He opened the door. And his appearance shocked her. The last time she saw him, he was still wearing Johnnie's t-shirts and his own cut-off trousers. Now, he was wearing a suit—a perfectly tailored suit—with a gold silk tie, and gleaming dress shoes. His hair was closely cropped, unlike his previous mop top style. His complexion was paler, his face smoother.

"Gertie, my Gertie!" he exclaimed. He threw his arms around her in a hug. "I'm so glad you made it." He released her.

"Hold on." She backed up. "What is this?" She gestured to his attire.

"These are just clothes. I'm still me. But yes, I can appreciate it would be a shock."

"I...yes."

"Come in. Come in. Take a seat. We have so much to talk about." His green eyes danced like there was nothing wrong. Like he wanted to exchange muffin recipes or talk about the weather.

She walked up to him, sticking her finger in his shoulder. "You! You don't get to do this."

He backed into the room.

She followed him, slamming the door behind them.

"Do what?" he asked.

"Act like...fuck...act like we're friends."

"Oh, I would never presume."

"Really? You assumed I would come here, at your beck and call."

"You should sit." He walked past the divider for the bedroom area, toward the sofa.

She followed, inhaling deeply. "Sit? I'm so mad at you I could spit."

He smiled, "Think of the furnishings."

"This isn't funny," she scowled.

"I've missed you so," he said, still smiling, but his eyes showed concern.

She stared at the floor. "I only came to say goodbye."

He exhaled; his body stiffened. "I understand."

She met his gaze, her eyes wide. "You do?"

"Yes, it was rotten of me to give you the blasted money. Jackson told me what you said. So, yes, I understand."

She shook her head. "Why did you bring me here? Are you just mind-fucking me?"

"I was going to explain over dinner. Are you hungry? I'm ravenous."

"Tell me, damn it."

He took a deep breath, his eyes darting as if wondering what to say. "I have a proposition." He wrung his hands.

Was he proposing? She surveyed the room, deciding where to sit. Because she was feeling faint. The sofa was the closest. Gertie wanted a drink badly. But she stood her ground and closed her eyes. "What?"

He placed his hands on her shoulders. "I want to see some damned tortoises."

She opened her eyes. "What are you talking about?" Had he completely lost his mind?

"Go a journey with me to the Galapagos. Five nights. A short cruise tour of the islands. Before you walk away forever and before I give up my fortune again—for good this time—I want to go on this trip and enjoy it with the person I love most. Even if we are only friends."

Now she really needed a drink. She couldn't think of a response.

He knitted his brows and leaned to the side to examine her face. "Are you all right?"

She wasn't sure. Somehow, a marriage proposal would have been easier to handle. "Why the Galapagos?"

"It's a long story. One I'll tell you another time. If you accept." He went to the refrigerator and pulled out a bottle of wine. "Can I pour you one?"

"Yes." She wandered around his hotel room. It was a carbon copy of hers, with a bedroom area separated by geometric wood panels, a living room with a small u-shaped kitchen. A bank of windows overlooked the balcony.

He poured the wine in two glasses and handed her one.

She took a sip and stared at the ceiling, trying to compose herself. For what, she didn't know.

He loosened his tie and sipped his wine. "Do you feel better?"

She returned her barely-touched glass to the kitchen counter. "No."

"The cruise leaves tomorrow afternoon. You can give me your answer in the morning. But I'm departing, regardless."

She spun away from the kitchen and narrowed her eyes at him. "I only came here for answers. And now you are running away again. You…you are a piece of shit."

"Yes, well, I'm rightly working on that." He finished the rest of his drink.

"I need something stronger." She opened the fridge door and found a small bottle of Jim Beam whisky.

"Hey, stop."

She held up the bottle. "Don't what?"

"If your answer is no, I understand, but perhaps you should leave."

"This! This is what I'm saying." She unscrewed the cap and took a swig. "Ah." The hard liquor felt good on her tongue. Gertie trained her eyes on him and circled him, feeling like a wild animal. All the things she'd rehearsed, all her rational thoughts, flew out the window. Choking down tears, she chose anger, shouting in a voice she didn't recognize. "You! You threw us away." She took another sip. "Threw me away. Where the hell do you get off?"

"Gertie, you are scaring me. Stop it. Stand still." He grabbed her hand, taking the bottle away from her. "Why are you acting like this?"

She pulled on his gold tie, bringing their faces inches apart. In a low voice, tears welling, she whispered, "You make me crazy."

His eyes softened. In a level tone, he said. "I love you, Gertie. All I wanted was for us to be happy."

And there they were, Cudlow's eyes. The same ones that made her weak in the knees. A flood-gate opened. The first tear oozed down her cheek. "Really?" She let go of his tie.

"More than anything." He caressed the droplet from her cheek with his thumb.

Gertie sniffed, "Me too." She dropped her head and closed her eyes, dizzy from a wave of grief she didn't know she had.

His lips met hers. Soft yet electric. His hand behind her neck, the other around her waist pulling her close.

She kissed him back. "I've missed you so much."

He stopped kissing her, met her eyes, and smiled. A smile like the old Cud, the silly one who made her laugh and feel at ease. With irresistible dimples that made her forget she'd ever been angry.

They sat on the couch holding hands and he asked her about her trip to Paris. She gave him the highlights. Night was falling and the room became dark.

"I wish I could have gone with you," he said.

"Me too."

After a long period of silence, Gertie said, "I gave away the money."

He pecked her on the cheek. "It was always up to you."

Part of her wanted to know why he did it. But their reunion felt so wonderful. And Cudlow's cologne with hints of lavender, plus his silky-smooth skin from a close shave, sent her senses into overdrive. In that moment, she wanted him more than she knew possible. Gertie nuzzled his neck and whispered, "Yes, let's go see some damned tortoises."

Chapter 24

With one eye squinting, Johnnie knew it was morning. The sun beat his neck and forearms, burning his skin raw. His mouth was dry like it was stuffed with baby powder.

Seagulls screeched. And more sounds. Sounds that didn't belong. Like the low droning baritone of a ship's horn and faint calypso music.

He turned to look. On the horizon, an island, small and flat, with a docked cruise ship.

Johnnie sighed with relief and kicked his cold, rubbery feeling legs toward civilization.

As he drew near, water slides, a zipline, a beach with striped cabanas and a bevy of tented shops with colorful signs came into view.

He had a choice to make. Swim toward the dock and the cruise ship, or make landfall on the beach, among the sunbathers. His stomach ached with hunger; his throat burned with longing for fresh water.

The most direct route to land was the best choice. A sign above the beach read, "Perfect Day at Manatee Bay," confirming his assumption the island was owned by a cruise line.

Stepping onto the semi-firm sand in the shallow water brought intense joy. He gave thoughts of gratitude to the heavens to be alive and safe.

A kid wearing a pink flamingo inflatable tube bounced in the water in front of him. A large man floated by wearing sunglasses and a speedo.

His own attire was laughable. A soggy stretched out T-shirt and his jean shorts plastered to his legs. His sneakers and glasses must have dislodged in his violent trajectory off the Bertram.

On the beach, a man in an official-looking polo shirt and white name tag handed out towels to customers. Johnnie exited the water and headed straight toward him, taking two towels and dropping to the hot sand.

He dried his body and placed the towel over his face, appreciating the protection from the sun and tried to figure out his next move.

Water. Must drink water.

He wrapped the towels around himself like a mummy and walked along the concrete path to a food vendor's cart.

Six dollars for a liter of spring water. Ridiculous.

And he had zero dollars. He checked his pockets. No money, no stones, no identification. Only some wet lint.

It was a dumb move not to have his wallet on him when the weather turned bad. A credit card would be everything now.

He kept walking along the path, looking for a rest room. Happy couples and families strolled by. The cruise goers all wore colorful wristbands, likely their identification as registered guests.

At the men's room, he waved his hands under the motion sensor on the faucet. Each activation only gave him a handful before he had to begin the process again. And the water tasted terrible. Like desalinated sea water, but still with a hint of salt. *Not good.*

He had to face facts. Talking with someone in charge was his best option. Explain his ship wreck. Call Robin. Maybe they would drop him at the next island with an airport so he could get home.

But who should he talk to?

Back outside, he saw an employee selling cotton candy and ice cream at a thatch-covered square booth. Maybe he could point him to the right person...

Johnnie stopped cold and stared.

He walked up to the 'employee'.

"Mo?"

The rotund man behind the counter, with the crisp white-collared shirt, adorned with a pink flower lei, and a name tag of "George" clasped his hands to his ruddy cheeks. "You're alive!"

Johnnie shook his head. "How? I thought you drowned. When did you get here?"

Mo leaned forward, "Shh. Two hours ago. And you?"

"Just arrived. I need water. Do you have any?"

Mo reached into a cooler behind him and handed Johnnie a bottle, wet with condensate. "On the house."

Johnnie rolled his eyes. "Oh. Thanks. What the fuck, Mo?" He gestured at Mo's attire.

"Shush. Not so loud," Mo whispered. "You're probably wondering why I'm working here."

"Yeah, no shit, Sherlock."

"I used to work for this cruise line, about five years ago. I still remember the passcodes to the employee locker room. I'm trying to blend in. Maybe stowaway on the ship. Not sure yet. Maybe bribe someone." Mo gestured Johnnie to come around the side. Then he lifted his shirt. "See?"

The stack of bills, the fifty-Gs, was wrapped in clear plastic and duct taped to his round belly.

"Jumping Joe, when did you do that?"

"When you were napping on the floor. The seas were getting rougher. Some of it got soaked, but it's still viable currency."

"What about me?"

Mo stroked his chin. "You're a bonafide U.S. citizen. Ask a manager to call the Coast Guard. They can arrange to get you home."

"So, this is goodbye?"

"Best for both of us." Mo tsked. "Don't look sad. Hey, I have some good news."

Johnnie gulped down some water. It was crisp and cold. Worth more than fifty-grand to him at the moment. "What? What could possibly be good about this situation?"

"Look behind me. In the tree to my right."

"What?" He looked around, not sure what Mo meant.

"Your buddy is hanging out, keeping me company." Mo pointed.

Johnnie squinted.

Stumpy!

In the row of eight-foot-high bushes behind Mo's refreshment stand, the iguana lay resting on a tall twisted branch.

"Oh, my God. How did he survive?"

Mo grinned. "Iguanas are pretty good swimmers. Not long after the boat went under, he floated by on a seat cushion. I grabbed him and we stayed together the whole time."

Johnnie walked under the branch. "Hey, Stumpy!" Without his glasses, his vision wasn't optimal, but it was clearly Stumpy with his short tail.

The iguana gave him a side-eye and blinked. [Hi, Johnnie]

"How are you buddy?"

[Tired. It wasn't a fun ride.]

"I know. Sorry, fella."

[Mo gave me pistachio ice cream.]

"He did?"

Stumpy closed his eyes as if drifting to sleep.

Mo was busy serving a family some popcorn and sodas. When he was through, Johnnie asked, "Should I let him stay here? He looks happy."

Mo shook his head. "No. Never. This is a terrible place. You should take him back to his home."

"Why is this place terrible?"

"These cruise ship islands are ecological nightmares. Which is why they were cheap available real estate. Everything here is fake, artificial. Stumpy would die from malnutrition and there aren't any other iguanas."

"Well, who should I see about getting out of here?"

Mo pointed to his right. "Try the excursions desk. They have telephone and internet. See, a few feet that way."

Johnnie stood on a rock to reach Stumpy. He placed him on his shoulder. "Sit-sit." The iguana held on.

"Goodbye, Mo. I hope you get to the Bahamas if that's what you want. If you do, and need more help, maybe my friend Cudlow can help. He's a wealthy old salt."

"Wait. Cudlow Loughton?"

Johnnie stared. "You know him?"

"Only by reputation. I read his book maybe fifteen years ago."

"He has a book?"

Mo gave him an incredulous look. "Only one of the best books on entrepreneurship I've ever read. Inspirational. Got a bootleg copy while I was in Iran. Followed his career in magazines. But then he seemed to disappear."

"Shit. I guess I shouldn't be surprised. Anyway, look him up. Drop my name."

"Thanks, I might do that. In fact, I know I will. Cudlow Loughton!" Mo looked entranced.

Johnnie shook Mo's hand. "Take care of yourself."

"I will. And Johnnie?"

"Yes?"

Mo dug into his pocket and pulled out a red stone. "I grabbed this too. I imagine it's worth more than you think, given how the pirates chased us."

"Thanks." Johnnie pocketed the stone and walked towards the excursions tent.

Mo called out, "And one more thing."

Johnnie turned in place.

Mo smiled. "Always remember to dance!"

Chapter 25

Gertie woke to find Cudlow gone.

It was morning. Although the curtains were drawn tight, thin ribbons of light outlined the windows. The bedside clock read 8:14.

She pulled the top sheet off and wrapped it around her like a toga.

A note in the kitchen from Cudlow said to order room service and he'd be back by ten.

She looked for her dress, expecting it to be in a heap on the floor. Her thoughts danced back to the night before and she hugged herself. Her toes curled into the tan carpet.

They were going to the Galapagos. But more importantly, they were back together.

After looking under furniture and around the room, she found her dress in the closet, hung with care. Her shoes side by side directly below.

Where could he have gone? It was a Sunday morning.

She donned her dress and borrowed Cud's toothbrush, then found her room key on a side table and headed back to her original hotel room.

On the short walk, she wondered how she was supposed to go on a five-night cruise with no other clothes.

When she walked in, the first thing she noticed was a stack of white glossy boxes on the dining table. Second, she saw a rolling suitcase sitting in the corner.

A note on the top was typewritten.

"Dear Ms. Brown. Pawpaw asked me to get you a few things. I hope you like them. Have a wonderful time. Looking forward to meeting again soon. Love, Jackson."

She opened the first box. A pair of tan leather hiking boots. The next box had an assortment of cotton short-sleeve shirts and Bermuda shorts in jewel tones. The third box contained underwear, two nightgowns, socks…pretty typical stuff. But the fourth box was lined in pink tissue paper with a gold sticker she recognized immediately. It was the white Givenchy dress like the one she had bought and returned in Paris. *How did Jackson get it?*

Gertie hugged the dress and held it up to herself in front of the mirror by the door. She felt like Cinderella, although a seventy-year-old Cinderella with varicose veins and crow's feet. Even so, she couldn't wait to show Cudlow.

After a quick shower, she put on shorts and a shirt and tried on her new hiking boots. A good fit. Now presentable, she longed for a large coffee from the café downstairs.

She headed to the elevator. When the doors opened, to her surprise, Cudlow stepped out. Instead of a suit, he wore red Hawaiian print board shorts and a "Don't Hassle Me, I'm on Vacation" T-shirt. Designer leather-strapped flip-flops on his feet. He looked almost like the old Cudlow, but with short hair and matching footwear.

He embraced her and kissed her cheek. "I see you found the items Jackson procured. I hope you don't mind. I was eager to get our adventure started."

"How did he…?" She stammered. "The dress?"

He chuckled. "Jackson followed you on the Insta-thing app. The cruise has a formal night. He called the shop in Paris to get the dress details and find out your sizes. He's such a bright lad."

She smiled. "Yes, it was one of my favorites."

Cudlow gave a coy look. "Mine as well."

With a yawn, she declared, "I need coffee."

"Wonderful. Did you eat? We should go have breakfast."

He held out his arm.

In that moment, she couldn't be happier. She put her arms around his waist and kissed him. A deep kiss lasting a full minute. People got on the elevator, giving them a wide berth. She didn't care.

The elevator dinged again and the doors opened. Two boys in their early teens said, "Ewww. Gross."

Gertie released Cud. "Right. Coffee."

He chuckled. "Yes, let's."

They got on the elevator and the two teens exited, waving their hands, shooing them away. "You can have it."

Alone now, as the elevator descended, Cudlow giggled and swished his hips in a silly dance.

Which made her giggle.

And soon, they were laughing so hard, tears streamed down their faces.

It felt so good.

Like they were two crazy teenagers in love.

* * *

At the customer service hut, a short woman with a sing-song voice named Alice happily agreed to help Johnnie contact his sister. He didn't remember Robin's number, but Alice looked up the number of her government office. He dialed and Robin answered on the second ring.

"Hello?"

"Robin, it's me."

"Johnnie? Oh, sweet Jesus! The Coast Guard called me last night. Are you okay?"

"I'm okay. The boat is gone. I washed up on one of those crazy cruise ship islands."

Robin huffed. "Thank God. I've been on the phone all night. A whole armada is out looking for you."

"Really?"

"The news of your Mayday hit the news in San Juan. After the storm cleared, boat owners set out to help."

"Wow."

"I called Cudlow."

"You did?"

"He was up most of the night also."

"Jumpin' Jesus."

"We need to get you home."

"I don't have my passport. I don't have anything. No ID. No wallet."

"Don't worry. I'll have the State Department fax your passport information. Just sit tight."

"Thanks, here, the customer relations director for the cruise line wants to talk to you." He handed the phone to Alice.

It helped to have a sister in government. And a billionaire best friend. Although he hated relying on them again to get him out of this jam. It made him feel like a child. An incompetent. A liability.

Which made him wonder what Greta could ever see in him.

Johnnie sat on the guest chair across from Alice, wondering what to do with himself. The cruise was leaving again in two hours. If he didn't get squared away with some transportation, what would happen to him?

Alice moved the phone from her ear and said, "We have some things to work out. Why don't you go have some fun? Come back in an hour?"

"Can I get something to eat?"

"Hold on." She dug in her desk drawer. "Here is a gift card for fifty dollars. Get whatever you want."

He took the card and put it in his pocket, the same one carrying the red mystery rock. "Thanks, Alice."

Stumpy, who had been hanging out under his chair for the last few minutes, was gone. *Great.*

Johnnie asked Alice, "Have you seen my pet Stumpy?"

She looked at him like he was asking her something dirty.

He explained, "No, the iguana."

She shook her head.

"No problem." He walked outside. The aroma from the Pirate's Grill, behind the entrance to the zip line, made his stomach growl. As he walked outside the customer service building, he noticed Stumpy on the path fifty feet ahead. His iguana friend was in a stand-off with two young women, one holding a stick in his face.

The one with the stick, a red head wearing a gauzy sequin cover-up, swatted at Stumpy. The other woman, a brunette in a white bikini, huddled behind and yelled, "Go away! Shoo! Hit him!"

The iguana circled them, then lunged.

Johnnie ran up to the scene. He grabbed Stumpy around his torso and picked him up before they could lunge again. "Stop! You two should be ashamed."

Bikini girl shouted, "Look, mister, he attacked *us*. I thought he was going to bite my friend Sheena."

He shook his head. "Don't worry, we're leaving." He placed Stumpy on his shoulder and said, "sit-sit." Then he strode to the restaurant.

At the bar, he placed Stumpy on the wooden stool next to his.

The bartender said, "No pets."

Johnnie narrowed his eyes at the bartender sporting a top knot and pointy beard. After nearly losing Stumpy, there was no way he was leaving him again. "He's *staying*. I'd like a pina colada with two slices of pineapple and a grilled chicken sandwich with extra lettuce and tomatoes."

"Sure. But, hey, if anyone complains about your stinky lizard, you'll need to take your order to go."

Johnnie scowled. "Fine."

A few minutes later, Johnnie happily fed Stumpy some of his pineapple from his pina colada.

[Thanks, Johnnie.]

"Anytime."

[What about Mo?]

"He's not coming with us."

[I like him.]

"I like him, too."

The bartender gave him a strange look.

Johnnie bared his teeth at him, "You got something to say?"

Pointy beard shook his head and walked to the other end of the bar, wiping down the wood top with a rag.

[More? Yum?] Stumpy leaned across the divide in their stools, placing his front foot on Johnnie's thigh.

When Johnnie's sandwich arrived, he took off the lettuce, wiped off most of the mayonnaise, and gave it to Stumpy. He stroked Stumpy's dorsal crests lovingly. "It will all be all right."

[Yes, head rubs are the BEST!] Stumpy blinked his eyes with contentment.

Over the loud-speakers, a woman's voice announced, "John Crosswell to the Excursions Office. John Crosswell, Excursions Office."

Johnnie handed the gift card to the bartender. "Keep the change." He stuffed a handful of fries in his mouth and lifted Stumpy onto his shoulder.

He hurried, weaving his way through the crowded path. At the office, Alice was standing there, waiting for him.

Breathing hard, Stumpy still on his shoulder, he gasped, "Did you receive my passport info?"

"Yes, and better."

"What?"

"A helicopter is arriving in ten minutes for you."

"The Coast Guard?"

"No. A private one. Come, the landing pad is on the other end of the island. I'll take you over in one of the carts."

He'd wondered why there was a golf cart parked next to the building. "Where will the helicopter take me?"

"Apparently anywhere you want to go." She handed him a piece of paper. A copy of the photo page of his passport.

"Wow." The picture was grainy, but it was better than nothing. He folded it and put it in his back pocket.

Another woman, older, wearing a white uniform with gold striped epaulettes, entered the office and extended a handshake. "Mr. Crosswell? I'm Captain Lovejoy. The Staff Captain. The Captain and the entire crew extend their warmest welcome. You've been through quite an ordeal. Do you want to see our Medical Officer?"

He shook her hand. "Um, thanks. But I just want to get home. I feel fine."

"That is wonderful to hear. Before you go, we were wondering if you'd pose for a quick picture? For our newsletter?"

He didn't feel like he had much a choice in the matter. Alice had a camera in her hand, like a weird magic trick.

They stood in front of the cruise ship's emblem in the office, and he tried his best to smile in a way that didn't look dumb. Because on one hand, he was happy to be alive, and on the other, he was still pissed at nearly dying and losing his boat. Having his picture in a newsletter for strangers to gawk at would only add salt to his wounded pride. But he was leaving soon. He could be polite.

Alice shook her head. "Could you put down the iguana for the picture?"

He set Stumpy down on Alice's desk. He told his friend to stay. But as Johnnie improved his posture and posed for the photo, Stumpy took a poop on the desk and knocked over Alice's soda; streams of fizzy liquid fell off the side onto the floor.

Johnnie took a tissue from her desk and tried to clean off the excrement, but it only spread to more across her desk blotter.

Alice huffed. "How about you hold him?"

"Right." He abandoned his attempt at cleaning and held Stumpy low, so he'd be out of the photo.

After the picture, Alice walked to the front door and held it for him with a strained smile. "Ready?"

Johnnie placed Stumpy back on his shoulder. "Ready as ever."

Chapter 26

lice came to a stop at the helo pad.

A man in a flight suit approached them. He held out his hand. "Mr. Crosswell? Mr. Loughton sent me to come get you."

"Cudlow?"

"No, Jackson."

"Oh."

Alice waved, "Take care now, Mr. Crosswell!" She sped away like her hair was on fire.

The pilot said, "I'm Ned. Where would you like to go? Back to St. John?"

Johnnie held onto Stumpy—still on his shoulder—to steady him. "We can go anywhere?"

"Yes, you have my services for the day."

"Can I bring a friend?"

The pilot shrugged. "That's entirely up to you."

Johnnie lifted Stumpy off his shoulder and handed the iguana to Ned. "Can you put him in a safe place in the helicopter? I'll be right back."

"Sir?" Ned took Stumpy, but seemed unsure how to hold him, shifting the squirmy reptile in his arms to find the right grip.

"I need to get someone."

"Um. I'll wait."

Johnnie ran down the sinuous stone path which hurt his bare feet. He kept his sights on the zip line in the distance to orient himself.

He jogged for ten minutes, sweat pouring down his back. His feet felt raw. The pina colada, with all the alcohol and sugar, had been a wrong choice. A little vomit burned his throat.

"Mo! I mean, George!"

Mo was counting out change to a customer. "You're back!"

"I have a ride. Come with me."

He whispered, "I can't. The authorities…"

"No, it's fine. We'll drop you at the Bahamas. Directly to Cudlow's place. Come on."

Mo looked side to side, noticing the line of five customers. "Are you positive?"

"Stumpy insisted."

Mo laughed. "Well, he is the brains of our operation."

Johnnie laughed. "Come on. The helicopter's waiting."

Mo said to the next customer in line, "Sorry. We're closed." He took off his apron and lei and threw them on the ground. He said to Johnnie, with a wide grin, "Let's blow this popsicle store."

They jogged together down the path.

Johnnie said, "I think the saying is popsicle *stand*."

"Are you sure?"

"Pretty sure."

Mo wheezed, "Thank you…" he held his side as he jogged, "for helping me again."

"You'd do the same for me." He stepped on a sharp pebble. He dusted off his foot and continued jogging.

Mo said, "I almost didn't come back."

"What's that?"

"After the druglords first attacked. I considered leaving without you."

Johnnie gave him a quick glance. "But you didn't."

"I'm not always very nice." Mo stopped jogging. He bent at the waist, panting for air.

Johnnie stopped. "You've been nice to me."

"I cut the power cord to the ship's navigation system."

Johnnie shouted, "What? Why?"

"Because if we went to St. John, there was a greater chance of my getting caught. So, instead, I steered north to the Bahamas. Meaning, I deceived you. I don't deserve your friendship."

"Whoa." Johnnie didn't know what to make of this confession.

"You have every right to be mad."

Still stunned, Johnnie kept his gaze on the ground. "Thank you for telling me."

Mo waved his hand dismissively, while bent at the waist gasping for air. "Go on. Get out of here. I'll be fine."

Johnnie crossed his arms. "Mo, come with me. I forgive you."

"You sure?"

He wasn't sure why he forgave Mo, but on balance, he enjoyed having Mo around. "Yes, now, come on!"

The pair began jogging again, but at a slower pace.

When they got to the helicopter, Ned opened the rear door for them. "Buckle in tight. Where are we headed?"

"Nassau. The Bahamas."

Ned nodded. "Sure." He slammed the door shut and twisted the handle.

In no time, they had their headsets on and lifted off.

The view of the theme park from above was comical. Yes, perhaps it was best Stumpy was coming with them. Although he wondered if iguanas liked to zipline. And he could certainly imagine his friend enjoying the lazy river.

Johnnie laid his head against the backrest and closed his eyes. With the aid of their headsets, he said to Mo, "That was a real adventure."

Mo said, "Yes. One you can tell Greta about."

"I've been thinking about that."

"And?"

"I think she can do better. Although, I'm not looking forward to telling her."

"What?"

"I'm not boyfriend material."

"John, you can't be serious."

"Look at me. I'm always screwing up. I bought a drug boat, almost got us killed. I'm an idiot."

"Do you love her?"

"I don't know. Not that it matters."

"I think you do love her."

"I like her. And I liked kissing her. But relationships are too difficult. And I'd probably do something dumb like yell at her when I didn't mean to. So many days I don't want to get out of bed. She doesn't deserve to deal with my shit."

"Look, don't decide now. You've been through a lot in the last twenty-four hours. Keep an open mind. And an open heart."

Johnnie looked out the side window at the tiny waves below. Yesterday, the waves were the size of refrigerators or tractor-trailers.

Now they seemed insignificant.

Maybe life was all about perspective.

"Sure, Mo. I'll try."

* * *

Pilot Ned said over the headset, "We're arriving soon. Does your guest have his passport?"

Johnnie jolted awake. "Um. I don't think so."

Ned shook his head. "Is Mr. Loughton expecting him?"

"No."

Mo chimed in, "Is there a way around this?" He unfastened a wad of the cash from under his shirt and flipped it in the air. "I have money."

Ned said, "Put your money away, sir. You look like our company's accountant. Your name is now Jason. Got it? When we touch down, you go straight to the hangar and head to the men's room. Wait for me there."

Mo said, "Got it. Thank you."

Ned mumbled something with his headset off.

A few minutes later, they touched down on a helo site in Nassau, next to the water but surrounded by commercial buildings. The whining of the blades slowed. Ned said, "Mr. Loughton is sending a car. It will be out front shortly."

Ned exited and opened the side door. Mo jumped out, his head down, and strode to the hangar fifty feet away. Ned didn't make eye contact, keeping his head tilted to the ground. *See no evil.*

The sun was setting. Surrounding buildings cast long shadows across the pavement.

Johnnie asked, "Now what?"

"Come with me."

Johnnie followed the pilot. They entered an office and did some paperwork. John recited his passport number and expiration date from the fax. Then they walked to the waiting room.

Ned said, "The driver will get you here. Stay out of trouble now." He walked away.

Johnnie sat and waited. The air conditioning sent a chill up his spine. *Where was Mo?*

He picked up a Plane and Pilot magazine dated six months ago. The cover highlighted a feature article titled, "Surviving a Water Crash". *Interesting stuff.*

Fifteen minutes passed. The outside door opened. The man in the collared shirt said, "Crosswell?"

"That's me."

"I'm Daniel. I heard about your adventure. I'll take you to Jackson."

"Thank you." Johnnie looked around. Still no sign of Mo. Perhaps it was best this way.

Captain Ned came striding into the waiting room holding a white cardboard box, the size of a standard office file box. He handed it to Johnnie. "Take this."

Johnnie scratched his head. "What is it?"

"You forgot your iguana." A red slash mark on the Ned's forearm looked eerily familiar.

Sure enough, the box jostled and Stumpy was banging his head against the top.

Before Johnnie could utter a 'Thank you', Pilot Ned had his hand on the glass door and exited.

Johnnie followed the driver to the sidewalk. The car was black and sleek—an immaculate 1960s Mercedes with rounded fenders, round headlights and beautiful chrome grille. Johnnie sat up front with Daniel. "Wow. Nice car."

"I was told it originally belonged to a famous movie actress. I'll tell you; it is a beast to maintain. His grandson Jackson has his own car, a Prius. Anyway, ol' Bess doesn't get out much. In fact, she was in storage the past ten years, until Mr. Loughton returned."

"I've never met Jackson before. Where's Cud?"

"He's on holiday."

"Really?"

Daniel said, "He was working long hours for the last month. I doubt he will return."

"Where did he go?"

"I'm sure Jackson will explain."

Johnnie looked out the window. They passed the Atlantis Resort, but kept going. The area turned more residential. If you considered mansions residential. The car pulled up to an iron gate. Beyond it, the house looked like an 1800s beach cottage on steroids. It had a wood shingled roof, double terrace the length of the house, two chimneys, and an expansive front yard surrounded by mature palm trees.

A young man stood on the front steps and waved.

Johnnie said to Daniel, "Thanks for the ride." After exiting the fancy car, he walked up to the man on the steps. "Hi. Um. Thanks for rescuing me."

"Johnnie, so nice to meet you. I'm Jackson. Pawpaw has said wonderful things."

"He did?"

"Come inside. You must be exhausted."

The young man smiled so warmly and acted like this was no big deal. Like he took in strange men all the time.

"I've had better days."

Jackson held the front door. "After you."

He expected the house to be expensive looking. But there was a charm and lightness about it. *How could Cud ever leave this?*

A horn blared outside. Johnnie backtracked and found Daniel holding the white box containing Stumpy.

"Don't forget your friend."

Heat rose to Johnnie's cheeks. "Thanks." He carried the box into the house.

Jackson ushered him to the kitchen and turned on the overhead recessed lights. "Can I get you a beverage?"

Johnnie placed the box on the counter. "Bathroom?"

"Oh, right. I'm such a sod. Down this hall, to the left."

"Great. Don't open this." He pointed to the box. "I'll be right back. Maybe some water?"

Johnnie found the half-bath, next to the laundry room. In the driftwood-framed vanity mirror, his face was red, with blisters on his nose. Still traces of salt at his hairline and his earlobes.

He wasn't gone long. When he returned to the kitchen, a glass of water on the counter greeted him, and Stumpy's box was still intact and silent, but no sign of Jackson.

"Hello?"

From the living room, he heard Jackson yell, "Go away or I'll call the authorities!"

A figure in the darkness rapped on the window.

Johnnie jogged to investigate. "What's going on?"

"A trespasser."

Johnnie looked out the back-door window. It was Mo! "Put your phone away. I know him."

"You do?"

Jackson opened the door. "What's going on?"

Mo entered and brushed past Jackson; he hugged Johnnie. "Ta-da! Hello again, my Pirate King!" Mo smooched his right cheek before he could protest.

Johnnie pushed him away and wiped saliva from his face. "What happened to you? Where did you go earlier?"

Mo put his finger to his lips. "Shh. Better not to discuss."

"Jackson, this is my friend, Mo."

Mo extended his hand.

Jackson scratched his head. "Is he a friend of Pawpaw's?"

"You mean Cudlow Loughton?" Mo grinned. "Not yet. But I hope to be. Is he here? I'm a huge fan." Mo peered around the room.

Jackson turned to Johnnie and frowned. "You need to explain…"

"He was shipwrecked with me." Johnnie blurted. "And he may or may not be a fugitive from the law."

Mo laughed. "Johnnie makes it sound worse than it is."

Jackson closed the door. "I'm going to have to call Paw."

Mo said, "Can we have dinner first? It's been a long day."

"Sure," Jackson rolled his eyes, "why in blazes not?"

The sarcasm wasn't lost on Johnnie. "I'm sorry."

Jackson put his hand on Johnnie's shoulder. "I'll tell you what. I can ignore whatever legal troubles your friend is in…for a price."

"What price?" Johnnie wondered if Jackson wanted money. *Mo had the ill-gotten fifty grand…*

"First, you need to tell me all about my grandfather's life on St. John. The old bugger has lied to me for the last decade. I want the truth."

"Okay."

"Second, I want all the details about his new friend, Ms. Brown. She's your landlord, correct?

"Yes."

"She came to visit a few weeks ago and, well, I want a clearer picture of what's going on between them."

"Ha! Not sure I know either. Anything else?"

"One last thing. I need your solid opinion on Paw's mental health and ability to care for himself going forward. I'm terribly worried for him."

"Sorry, man. I'm the last one to comment on someone's mental health."

"Oh, why's that?"

"It's a long story."

Chapter 27

ertie and Cudlow boarded the cruise ship. It was more like a small ocean liner, with a passenger capacity of only a hundred guests. Two porters carried their luggage.

Once past the ramp, a steward offered flutes of champagne from a silver tray. Gertie took one and sipped it on the way to their cabin.

They went up an elevator to the third deck. Light rock music played throughout the vessel. The first porter opened a door. "Mr. Loughton, this is your cabin."

Behind her, the second porter said, "Ms. Brown, this way." He opened a different door, next to Cud's.

"Cudlow?"

"Yes, dear?"

"You booked us separate cabins?"

"Well, yes. Like I said, I didn't want to presume."

Gertie chewed on her thumbnail. "Wow."

Cud said, "You're welcome to join me. But don't feel obligated."

She followed her steward inside her room and closed the door.

The steward said, "My name is Danny. Would you like me to unpack your things? Can I order room service for you?"

A plate of cookies and chocolates lay on a table by the sliding door. The room was spacious. Ridiculously large for a single person. "No, I'm fine. I think I'll take a brief nap."

Danny said, "Yes, as you wish. The itinerary is next to the television. The mini-bar is by the closet." He took her empty champagne flute. "Should I put on the do not disturb sign?"

"Yes, please."

Danny exited and the door closed with a loud click.

She dove onto the bed face down. Maybe she brought this on herself.

Their relationship was far from solid. If she were in Cudlow's shoes, she would have done the same.

Instantly, she regretted the decision to go on this trip.

She heard a knock on the side-door adjoining their suites.

Gertie pushed herself off the bed and unlocked the door. "Hi."

"Hello."

"What now?" Her question was a loaded one. Because, in reality, she wanted to know where their relationship was heading, not what activity on the itinerary they should attend.

"Well, in fifteen minutes, there's a briefing in the auditorium about the different islands and tours. Do you want to go with me?"

Holy shit. Again, he was acting like everything was fine. And that being next-door neighbors was completely normal.

"I think we need to talk."

"Let's go down to the restaurants. I hear they have a wonderful sushi bar."

"Okay."

They walked downstairs, examined a floor plan, and found the restaurant. They were seated immediately. Cudlow ordered water, she ordered a white wine.

After they put in their food order, Gertie said, "I have questions."

"I'm an open book. Ask anything." He took the white napkin off the table and placed it on his lap.

"Why the Galapagos?"

He took a deep breath. "In truth, Winifred, my departed wife, always wanted to go. But I never made the time."

"I'm sorry." She reached across the table, placing her hand on his.

He looked like he might cry. "Well, I want no more regrets in life."

The next questions were tougher. She waited until he composed himself.

Finally, he looked up and asked, "What else?"

"What are your plans after this? Are you coming back to St. John?"

"Yes. I plan to. But I won't be living on the beach anymore."

She wasn't sure what to make of this proclamation. "Where will you live?"

"I've been chatting with Dottie. She found a small place for me in Cruz Bay. A condo in Robin's building is available."

"Wait...you've been talking to Dottie?"

"She's quite a resource."

"Mother f…"

"Why, what's wrong?"

"You tell Dottie your plans before you tell me?"

"Nothing is decided yet. And, the last I checked, you weren't speaking with me."

She drew in a long breath. This was not what she wanted. She needed to stop getting so angry and get a hold of herself. In a softer tone, she asked, "What about your fortune?"

He reclined in his chair and took a sip of water. "After this trip, I'm going to lead a normal life. Jackson is giving me a stipend of seventy-thousand a year. More than enough for a small place and necessities."

"I see." She played with her fork.

"You look unsure."

She shut her eyes. "What about us?"

"I don't know."

"What do you mean?"

"We should discuss this another time."

"I'm not good with ambiguity."

"I've noticed. Gertie, my beautiful Gertie, we have five days to figure things out." He took her hand and kissed the top of it. "Maybe we can start over."

"Start over?"

"Yes, where I'm not a homeless lunatic or a reclusive billionaire. Let's assume we just met. Right at this exact moment. And I'm a normal person who lives in a regular home, who wears clean clothes and bathes indoors."

Gertie laughed. "You are far from normal."

With a serious look, he said, "And you, my dear, take my breath away."

She smiled. "We could go back upstairs…"

Cudlow sighed. "Gertie, I've been thinking about this."

"Yes?"

"I think we should slow down. Put aside, as they say, the delights of the flesh. From the start, we've never had a real courtship. Honestly, I'm not complaining. Being with you is like heaven. But we haven't worked on the relationship side of things."

Gertie had to admit he had a point. Maybe some platonic time together would strengthen them. Ease the constant conflict. But the other night was so magical. "Not even a cuddle?"

"Cuddling is allowed. Clothes on. Humor me. It's only five days."

"Fine. I'll keep my filthy hands to myself." She said this playfully, but a tinge of frustration snuck through.

He smiled and cleared his throat. With an earnest look, he said, "So, nice to meet you, young lady," Cud leaned forward. "What brings you on this cruise?"

This seemed silly, but the twinkle in his eyes told her to play along. She had to think of a normal reason to visit the Galapagos. "I've always loved wildlife and nature. And you?" *This conversation was already boring…*

"I've wasted too much of my life not appreciating the world's splendor. Now, tell me, what are some of your hobbies?"

Gertie laughed. "I like needlepoint and gardening. And some strong dick."

Cudlow belly laughed. "You are so bad."

She beamed and batted her eyes. "Sorry. I'm still giddy from last night."

"Well, those memories will have to tide you over. I'm not your meat puppet, you know."

Gertie covered her mouth with her napkin to muffle laughter.

The server came by and brought them their first course.

After the server departed, she smiled. "I'm going to call you MP the rest of the trip."

He chuckled. "See, this is nice. To laugh. To not be so serious."

She nodded. "Do you want to go dancing tonight? The sign in the elevator said it's disco night."

"Gertie, I would love that."

They ate their dinner and talked about their favorite disco songs. Afterward, they walked hand in hand to the upper deck and watched Panama City fade into the distance. There were kisses and hugs and sweet gazes as they watched the sunset.

Later they got soft serve ice-cream and went to a music trivia contest, where they lost badly, and laughed afterward, not knowing much about modern rock. After an hour at the disco, Cudlow yawned. "Gertie, I need to get some sleep. Johnnie was shipwrecked last night and I've been awake for thirty-six hours."

"You should have told me! Is he all right? What happened?"

"He's fine. Some sunburn and dehydration, but he's in good spirits now. Somehow, he sailed into a dreadful storm. I arranged transportation; he's with Jackson now."

This explained why he checked his phone every so often throughout the day. "He went to the Bahamas?"

"Yes. A long story. I'll tell you over breakfast in the morning. You know, from the pain in my spine, I expect it might rain tomorrow. Goodnight, love." He kissed her goodnight with a short respectable peck on the cheek.

Gertie opened the door to her cabin, reluctant to close it and end their wonderful day. But he walked straight away. The slam of his door from the air pressure imbalance in the hallway signaled a finality that made her heart sink.

She leaned her ear against their common wall, hoping to hear his voice. But detected only sounds of water running briefly before complete silence.

It was time for bed. *Alone.*

She brushed her teeth, washed the makeup off her face, and put on her pajamas. She moved the towel animal—an elephant—off her bed and pulled back the comforter.

In the dark, she wondered what life would be like with a normal boyfriend. It was all she wanted.

Or was it?

There were plenty of perfectly normal men in her church. Many tried to court her in the past. *Why Cudlow?* Was she just feeling her age and lonely? Or was she enthralled by his sincerity, sparkling green eyes, and hot British accent?

The first time she saw him, she knew he was homeless. But he also seemed so happy. An effusive positivity which made her curious. *Had she unconsciously favored the power imbalance? Letting him in because she never dreamt he could hurt her?*

If so, she needed to examine her own psyche. It would explain so much.

The next four days were going to be the ultimate test.

Chapter 28

ave snapped his fingers. "Turn that up," he called to the bartender, gesturing to the television screen behind the bar, mounted to the brick wall.

Renaldo said, "When did you start caring about the news?"

Dave slammed his mojito glass on the bar. "Shit, it's him."

His boyfriend sipped his martini. "Who?"

"Look."

Ren waved his hand in a circle. "Some guy got lost at sea. Big deal."

Dave felt every hair on his neck stand up. "It's Johnnie."

"You mean the brain-damaged loser who stabbed you?"

"Yep."

"Too bad they found him."

Dave tapped his fingers on the bar, thinking. "Depends."

Ren stared at him. "Oh, no, sweetie. Don't tell me."

"He has to pay."

"Pfft, what are you going to do? Kill him?"

"Shh."

Ren rolled his eyes and grabbed a free pretzel from the shallow wicker basket on the bar. "I thought you wanted to play Rambo with your khaki-mafioso."

"It could wait."

"You have some messed up priorities. Honestly, I don't know why I haven't given up on you."

Dave didn't understand it either. "You don't understand."

"So, explain it to me."

With heat in his cheeks, he growled, "No one's laid a hand on me in ten years. At least no one I allowed to live afterward."

"You could have died. You said he only stabbed you once and then went out of his way to not let you drown."

173

"What? I'm supposed to be grateful to that little shit?" He slammed his drink again, but this time, he chipped the bottom of the glass. "Fuck."

"Why not? You are always fucking glass half empty. Look on the bright side. You came away with more money than you would've on your last gig. Enough to retire. And Johnnie didn't kill you or turn you into the police."

"You're unbelievable," he grunted.

"Ha. And you have anger problems." Renaldo patted Dave on the shoulder. "I'm going to get a manicure. Want to come with?"

"No, thanks."

"Stop brooding. If you are going to act crazy, don't bother coming home." Ren pulled some cash from his wallet and placed it on the bar.

"Fine."

Ren zipped up his sequin fanny pack and crossed his arms. "Fine?"

"Yeah, this was never going to work."

"Yeah? Well fuck you and fuck your stupid bruised ego." Renaldo gave him a middle finger and stormed out.

Dave took the stone out of his pocket. He should cash it in. Use the money to get new identification and some cool weapons.

Would it be enough to walk up to Johnnie on the beach and shoot him point blank? A quick death seemed too generous.

But bad guys in the movies always failed because of elaborate schemes that allowed their subjects to escape. He wouldn't make those mistakes. *Definitely shoot him in both legs first. Then a little torture, like electric shocks. Then drag him behind his vehicle until his skin tore off.*

The more he thought about it, the fun wasn't the killing; it was inflicting suffering.

And for maximum suffering, there had to be life.

Yes, mutilation was the goal.

And he would strive to be inventive.

Dave grabbed a cocktail napkin and asked the bartender, "Can I borrow a pen?"

The bartender handed him a ball-point pen. "Don't steal it."

"Yeah, yeah." Dave glared at the bartender until he walked away.

He clicked the pen. In bold letters he wrote, "A Hundred Ways to Torture Your Enemy."

A fine new title. And a different direction from the previous how-to book he'd envisioned.

The Crosswell moron would be his guinea pig.

It was only right.

* * *

On the second day of the cruise, Gertie and Cudlow returned from their first excursion and walked up the gangplank holding hands.

"I had a good time today," Cud said. He scratched his upper arm where a mosquito had left a large welt. "Although I could do without those blood-sucking monsters."

"Momma used to say, means you are made of honey." Her large brown eyes met his and she squeezed his hand. "You lived on the beach all those years. How did you deal with the insects?"

A valid question. One he hadn't thought much about. "Maybe my less than pristine odor kept them at bay?" He shook his head and laughed. "Ha! I suppose this means I'm domesticated now!" Cudlow decided to change the subject. "What was your favorite part of today's tour?"

"Those Marine iguanas were spectacular. So colorful."

"They say May is one of the best months to visit. Too bad about the rain."

Gertie smiled, "Rain? I didn't feel a drop."

Cudlow kissed the back of her hand. "I'm glad you're enjoying this."

They took the elevator to the third deck and walked to their rooms.

He said, "How about we change into dry clothes and get a pre-dinner cocktail?"

"Cudlow, I…"

"Yes, dear?" He waved his key card on the lock and opened the door a few inches.

"I'm a little tired."

He drew in a breath. "Yes, it was a long hike today."

"And I've been thinking…" Her face was serious.

Serious talk had no place in the hallway. "Should we sit down for this?"

"Yes."

He held his door open for her. "Come in. Whiskey?"

"Absolutely."

She sat on the sofa and unlaced her hiking boots while he poured their drinks.

He sat on the other side of the L-shaped sofa and took a sip. Bracing himself mentally, he placed his glass on the coffee table. "Speak freely."

She downed her glass in three gulps.

This could not be good, he thought.

She cleared her throat. "Something has been bothering me."

He waited, examining her face for clues.

"Why did you give me the money?"

"Oh, that. I apologize." Definitely a subject he didn't want to discuss. "We're having a delightful time. Can't we forget it and move on?"

"No."

He stared at her face. She looked like she might cry.

"Oh, no, no!" He scooted over and hugged her. "Don't be sad."

She pushed him away. "Tell me. The truth."

He moved back to his original spot on the sofa and clasped his hands below his knees. It was best to get it over with. "Two reasons."

Gertie rubbed her temples. "Keep going."

"First, I wasn't sure what would happen to my fortune after the takeover. It was a way to protect a nest egg for what I hoped would be our future together."

She let out an exasperated huff. "You could have said so."

"And I thought if you were financially secure, it would alleviate any tension from our last quarrel. You were so angry when I brought up my fortune. I know you said it doesn't matter to you..." He knew he was entering a minefield, wondering if he should turn back. "It seemed the obvious choice to remove money from the equation...."

She shook her head and beat the seat cushion with her fist. "Shit. It was a test."

"No. What?"

"That's what Jackson said."

"He said that?"

"Yes."

"No, not like that at all. I thought if my having money was an issue..."

"Go on."

He didn't know how to phrase this. Because she was right, maybe it was a test. "I think we should leave this here."

Gertie stood with her arms crossed. In a raised voice, she said, "You are a chickenshit asshole. You wondered if I'd still be with you."

"Shh! Stop."

She shouted, "You figured I'd take my payday and kick you to the curb."

He closed his eyes. Tears welled and his neck felt hot. His lips quivered. "Gertie, you don't understand."

"Fucking say it."

He stood. "Damn it! STOP!"

Her jaw trembled; her eyes wide.

Cud hadn't meant to scare her. But his rage was real. With fisted hands, he barked, "People have been looking at me with disgust and pity for the last decade. Treating me as sub-human. Acting like I was rubbish to be discarded."

He strode to the kitchen with his glass to refill it, this time with water. "If you were going to discard me, I wanted to get it bloody well over with." He heard the anger in his voice, but didn't regret it. Because it was the truth. A tremendous weight on his shoulders lifted.

Gertie sat back down. In a measured tone, she asked, "Why would you think I would do that?"

He kept his gaze on the floor, his hands gripping the kitchen counter. "Why *wouldn't* I think that?" He took a long gulp of water.

"What?"

His face was hot now and throat still felt tight. But he had to tell her what had weighed on him. Facing her, he said, "You've NEVER, NOT ONCE, told me you love me."

Gertie's mouth dropped open. "I haven't?"

With his eyes closed, he took a pause. "No."

She was silent, which only confirmed his fears.

In a softer tone, he asked, "What? It never occurred to you?"

"I don't know what to say."

"There!" He pointed. "There it is. The truth. You don't love me."

"I…I don't know."

He didn't want to hear anymore. Couldn't hear anymore. Cud strode to the door and held it open. "I think it's best if you leave."

"Seriously?"

He nodded.

She didn't meet his gaze as she walked out.

They didn't speak another word.

Chapter 29

G ertie padded over to her room in her hiking socks, holding her boots. Once inside, she dropped them to the floor, as in a daze. Feeling both stunned and confused, she went to her balcony and sat on the chaise, hugging her knees.

I'm a complete asshole, she thought.

Could she simply apologize?

It wouldn't do any good until she knew her true feelings.

Did she love Cudlow?

What was love anyway?

In truth, they barely knew each other. She did some mental math. They'd only met 7 weeks ago. And they had spent most of that time apart.

Did she *want* to love him? And would that be enough?

But what if she hurt him further? Not willing to give up her independence?

I don't deserve to be here.

She left the balcony, took her key, and headed into the hall, still in her socks, in search of the customer service desk.

The line was five-deep and she rocked on her heels, anxious for those in front of her to hurry up. When it was her turn, she took a deep breath and skipped the pleasantries. "I want to leave the ship."

The woman behind the counter stopped typing at her terminal. "Good afternoon. Are you ill? A family emergency?"

"No. Can I depart at the next island?"

"Are you sure? We can't force you to return to the ship, but there aren't any transportation options at our next port."

"When is the next stop with an airport?"

"Not until we return to Baltra Island." The woman pointed to the map on the desk showing the route and daily stops.

Gertie's heart sank. "At the end of the cruise."

"Correct."

Gertie winced. "Thank you." She walked in a daze to the center lobby and collapsed into a blue velvet club chair to think.

A voice on the loudspeaker announced, "The Captain's champagne reception begins at six o'clock in the Darwin Center."

A woman in the chair next to her turned. "Are you going?"

"I don't know what I'm doing."

"I'm Sara. I'm traveling by myself. How about you?" She was dark skinned, short and round, maybe in her forties, with black-framed oval glasses, wearing black pants and a pink sequin tank top.

"I'm Gertrude. And I'm not sure."

"Well, join me for champagne while you figure it out. Come on." Sara stood.

Gertie looked down at her own clothes, damp shorts and dirty socks. "Maybe I should change."

Sara chuckled. "Yes, get some footwear. See you soon."

Ten minutes later, Gertie arrived to the reception wearing her floral dress, her hair slicked back in a bun, and her faux pearls. Back at her room earlier, she had tried to be quiet as a mouse, so Cudlow wouldn't hear. She didn't want to face him again. Not until she knew what to say.

Sara was standing in a group with another couple. Sara noticed her arrival and waved her over. "Gertrude, right? Meet the Campbells. Laura and Mark. They've been my adoptive family on the trip."

The couple were in their fifties and looked like they were from Iowa. Both blond and featureless.

"Hi, nice to meet you."

Laura asked, "Where are you from, Gertrude?"

"Call me Gertie. I live in the Virgin Islands."

Laura gushed, "How nice! I love it there. In fact, Mark and I got engaged there twenty years ago."

Gertie gave a weak smile. Making small talk with strangers required a mental energy she didn't have. "That's nice."

Sara took Gertie's arm. "Hey, are you all right? Want to sit?"

Gertie looked around the room. The pianist played a jaunty melody. Mostly couples were chatting with other couples. The Captain stood in the middle of the room telling some kind of funny story because the crowd around him erupted into laughter every few seconds.

"Sara, thanks for inviting me. But I think I'm going to head back to my room."

Sara turned to the Campbells, "We're going to take a walk. See you later."

She ushered Gertie to a side door. "Let's get you some fresh air. You look green." Out on the deck, she asked, "Are you sea sick?"

"No."

Sara placed her hand on Gertie's shoulder. "People tell me I'm an excellent listener."

"Why are you being so nice to me?" Gertie held onto the rail and stared at the waves.

"Girlfriend, have you noticed we're the only home girls on this bread truck? Sisters need to stick together."

Gertie smiled, "Yeah, not much melanin on this cruise."

"So, why the long face?"

She turned her back to the rail. "Man trouble."

"Your boyfriend seems nice. Sorry, I saw you both at dinner last night. You looked happy."

"It's complicated."

Sara smiled. "Ain't is always?"

"You really want to hear this?"

"Queen, I'm LIVING to hear it. I can't take one more white person talking about the stock market or their new Range Rover."

Gertie chuckled. "Are you hungry? I can tell you about it over dinner. But not the main dining room. I don't want to run into him."

"The wine bar has good tapas."

Gertie smiled. "Sure. Lead on."

* * *

Four hours later, Sara and Gertie were sitting on the floor of Sara's cabin, drinking fruity daiquiris and laughing. A row of empty glasses with straws and tiny paper umbrellas lined the wall next to the door.

"Gurrl, you need to tell him how you feeeeel," Sara said, lying on her back, shoes off, pointing her finger in the air as if making a royal proclamation.

"I like him. He makes me feel like a teenager…I just don't want to be serious." Gertie leaned against the dresser, her head drooping to the side, gesturing with her palm. "That old fool told Johnnie he wants to marry me. After two days. What's up with that?"

"He luuuvves you. And he can put DOWN. What's the problem again?" She pressed her shoulders up to face Gertie, then flopped back, resting her hands on her stomach.

Gertie picked a strawberry seed from her gums and flicked it on the floor. *Not classy.* But she didn't care. Her mind too numb from alcohol. She wondered what time it was. And how long they had been drinking. But she had to focus. *What was the problem again?* Recalling her reunion with Cud, she giggled. "He is a SEXY BEAST!" Chuckling, she added, "That's my point. We're having [hic] fun. Why RUIN it with love?"

"Look, tell him you love him. You know you do. And go live with him in his frickin' estate in the Bahamas. Like a boss. A BOSS!" Sara rolled to her stomach. "And get that coochie coochie!" She giggled and started humping the floor.

Gertie rolled onto the floor sideways with a thud, laughing so hard her eyes watered. Her drink spilled on to the beige rug. "Damn! [hic]"

Sara got up and pulled on Gertie's arm, helping right her. "You! Go! Get it, Sister!" Sara let go of Gertie's arm and fell backwards on her bed, her feet still on the floor, her arms waving in the air. "For the rest of us. Live the fuckin' dream!"

"Shhh!" Gertie got off the floor, arms and legs like noodles, and lay down next to Sara, mirroring her posture. "He called me Freddy. His dead wife. And he lived on a beach. He might be insane. I'm so [hic] tired. I want my old life. Diggin' in my garden. [hic] Doing my needlepoint."

Her eyes closed, Sara whispered, "Oh, fuck crafts. You know what I wouldn't do for a pokey-poke on the regular? You're just stupid talking now."

"Maybe."

Sara rolled to her side and looked Gertie in the eye. "The truth. Would you rather…have this man or your dumb vegetables?"

"Ugh," Gertie shook her head. A sleep-deprived shiver brought gooseflesh to her bare arms, "I have to choose?"

"Shit, girl, yaaas." Sara poked Gertie's cheek, as if she was fascinated by an alien life form.

"That's not *fair.* I've [hic] been with my garden for years. Years…"

"Oooh. Sheeet. That's the damn answer. You have to tell him. Give respect. No more pokey…" Sara closed her eyes.

Soon after, Gertie heard snoring.

Time to head home.

Gertie sat up on the edge of Sara's bed in an abrupt yet false sense of energy, causing her head to swim. She tried to concentrate. *Now stand up*, she willed her legs.

She rose up a couple of inches. *Nope. Not happening.* She flopped back down, again horizontal, and whipped an arm back to grab a pillow. She tucked it under her neck, then tried to sleep on her side. Instead, she and the pillow toppled onto the floor. Gertie embraced her new found position on the floor, curled up, and drifted to sleep.

Chapter 30

erv sat behind the wheel of his Park Service truck and ate his sandwich. A book titled, "Training Your Pet for Movie Roles" was propped open on the steering wheel.

Ranger Taylor knocked on his window. "Hey, whatcha reading?"

He tucked the book away on the seat next to him. "Um, nothing. What can I do for you?"

"Didn't you get a call? There's a fight over at Maho Bay. Ranger Rick is there but he wants backup. Come on." She walked around the truck and got in the passenger seat. "Drive."

"Yeah, right." He placed his sandwich on top of the book to shield it.

On the drive, Taylor picked up the book, "You have a pet?"

He needed a good lie. "I, no, um, found this next to the trash. Figured it would be fun to read during lunch. Hey, did you know people have trained their cats to paint?"

"Paint what?"

"Like, works of art."

"Sounds ridiculous."

"I guess." Merv kept his eyes on the road.

Taylor said, "I had an uncle who trained his dachshund to say I love you. But to me, it sounded like *wub-wub-wub*."

"Ha. Do you have any pets?"

"Growing up, we had turtles. Little guys, named Tiny and Tim, but we overfed them and they died. I think I was six."

"You know…Johnnie feeds this iguana at Hawksnest. I told him to quit it."

"Johnnie is weird."

"Yeah, I guess."

Taylor grunted, "I don't know what Kemper sees in him."

Merv took the turn toward Maho Bay. "What do you mean, *sees in him*?"

"I think she has a crush on him. I mean, pathetic, am I right?"

"Wait, what?"

"She's always saying stuff like, *Johnnie's so special* and she was practically all over him at happy hour a couple weeks ago. If you ask me, she needs to learn to be without a boyfriend for a hot minute."

As they entered the beach parking lot, Taylor pointed toward the entrance, "Look! Shit."

Merv parked and shut off the engine. He didn't recall Kemper flirting with Johnnie at happy hour.

Taylor exited the vehicle and ran toward the beach. Ranger Rick was straddling a guy on the sand, yelling, "Don't get up." Rick had zip ties in his hand.

Merv scratched his chin and watched the scene. He should really be helping. But the thought of Kemper with Johnnie left him stunned. It was bad enough Johnnie took the damned iguana and his extra income. But if he took his woman Kemper? He tried not to think of what he would do. Besides, Johnnie was some sort of eunuch. *Maybe he didn't even like girls.* And Kemper had such a big heart. Maybe she liked Johnnie the way someone likes an injured puppy. Still, it stuck in his craw.

Through the truck window, he heard Taylor yell, "Merv, get over here!"

Ranger Rick and Taylor were on the sand, faced off with a second unruly dude wielding a broken bottle at their faces.

Another day in paradise.

Merv got out of the pickup and stalked over to the warring trio. "Sir, put down the bottle." He pulled his sidearm out and trained it on the guy. "Hey, look at me."

The man with the bottle, with his wild eyes and hair, was clearly on some type of amphetamine.

[BLAM] Merv blasted his gun in the air.

That got everyone's attention. A flock of birds erupted from the tree tops, flying off in a screeching formation.

While the wild man was distracted, Taylor yelled, "Aaaaa!" and tackled the druggie asshole. Soon enough, bottle man was in cuffs. Local police arrived a minute later.

Taylor yelled, "Merv! What's wrong with you? You need to have our backs."

Merv leaned against a palm tree. "I backed you up."

"After I yelled at you. What the hell, man?"

"Sorry, it won't happen again."

He watched as Rick and Taylor handed the two men off to the police.

A young dusty-green iguana was resting in a low tree to his right. He sauntered over and offered it a dried apricot from a bag he kept in his pants pocket. The iguana snatched it and scampered away.

He would call this one Olive. The book said to start training animals when they are young.

The big bright green iguana at Hawksnest—the one he named Kelly—was as dumb as a doorknob and liked to bite. Kelly would come for treats after prolonged coaxing but never mastered the art of the stealing. Unlike Stumpy, who was the most clever and stealthy thief he'd ever seen.

It wasn't clear if Stumpy or Johnnie would return.

And he needed a backup plan.

* * *

Where was she?

Cudlow had knocked on Gertie's door at ten last night. No answer. After a fitful night with almost no sleep, he knocked again. It was now five in the morning and Gertie hadn't come back to her room all night. He'd searched all the common areas. It was a smaller ship; only a hundred meters long with eight decks and only six were open to guests. Up and down the stairwells, the fitness center, library, lounges, even the medical center, he visited each three times.

At seven, he came across her room steward. After much pleading, the steward checked her room. It hadn't been disturbed since his turn down the night before, confirming his worry. Her perfectly intact towel animal, a chimpanzee, gazed at him from his perch on the end of her bed, mocking his concern.

Cudlow made another circuit of every deck, this time going from bottom to top. He had her paged and waited at the guest services desk for a half hour, trying to convince himself she was fine. But if that were true, it meant she slept somewhere else. He wondered if it was with the tall server with the high cheekbones who had complimented her the other day. *Was she trying to torment him again?*

He only wanted to know she was safe and regretted being so cross with her.

Did she accidently fall overboard? Should he insist the crew do a cabin-by-cabin search? The time was now eight.

Perhaps he needed to give her space. The day's excursion was starting at nine and his stomach insisted he get a quick bite to eat first.

Cudlow went to the dining room. At their usual table, Gertie was drinking coffee, wearing her floral dress, her hair messy.

He strode to the table and didn't mask the alarm in his voice. "You didn't sleep in your room last night."

She held her head. "Not so loud."

He took the opposite chair. "I was worried." He touched her arm.

"No, you were jealous." She picked up his hand and removed it.

His eyes narrowed. "No, Gertie. I was worried. I wanted to apologize."

"Don't." She sipped her coffee without making eye contact.

"Don't what?"

"Apologize." She put down her cup. In a quiet voice, she said, "It's my fault."

"Are you okay?"

"I had a few drinks and an interesting talk with a new friend."

"And?"

"You should move on."

The breath left his body. "No. Don't do this."

"You were right. I don't want a serious relationship. I'm too set in my ways. I like you. Maybe I love you, I don't know because I don't know what that means. When I was in my twenties, I thought I knew. But it was so fucked up…"

He waited for her to continue, hoping for an opening to plead his case.

She rested her hand on her cheek. "To tell you the truth, I don't know anything about you. And you don't know me either."

"Gertie, I see you. I see everything about you." Did he dare tell her about her aura? *No.*

She waved a hand at him. "I don't even know what you're talking about. And look at you. You're not remotely the same person I met last month."

Speaking slowly, Cud met her eyes. "I think you are scared. And I understand. There is a powerful force here. It scares me too." He tried to catch her hand again. She declined. "Which is why we need to start over and slow things down."

"I don't think I'll change my mind. Maybe we could have one of those casual relationships…I think they call it friends with benefits?"

He couldn't believe she could be so callous to consider such an arrangement. This couldn't be the real Gertie. "I've told you this before. And I'm being deadly serious. I won't let you use me and discard me whenever it suits you. I have feelings."

"Yes," she gestured with a circular palm motion, "you have ALL the feelings."

"Don't mock me."

She sipped her coffee again. "Can we admit we're both too old to live happily ever after?"

"No. I don't accept that." Cudlow let out a long breath, knowing it was now or never. "In fact, if you would just marry me, we could get past all this nonsense."

"What?" She put down the china cup.

"Marry me. The Captain can officiate. Tonight. You have that beautiful white dress. And we can live wherever you want and however you want. We could live in Paris. Or my home in Nassau. Or New Zealand. In a palace or a modest flat. I don't care as long as we're together."

Gertie laughed. Then she froze. "Oh, you're being serious."

"I know for a fact you love me. Even if you won't say it. Take yesterday." *Should he tell her?* He didn't want to mention the aura stuff, but it was his best argument. The reason for his certitude. "It doesn't take supernatural powers to see, when you're with me, you light up pale blue like the morning sky."

He placed his hands over hers. "Marry me, Freddy. I promise we'll have a wonderful life."

She pulled her hand away. "Do you even hear yourself? My name is Gertrude."

"Oh, what did I say?"

"You called me Freddy…again."

"I'm so sorry. I know who you are. I…"

"You still love your wife."

His insides felt hollowed out. "Of course. I'll always love her. But my love for her doesn't diminish my feelings for you. I promise it won't happen again. Marry me. Tonight. We can move past all this. You'll see."

"Why does this feel like an ultimatum?"

She had a point. He felt as if his heart had left his chest and jumped overboard. "It is."

"And the other option?"

What were his other options? Live on St. John, miserable without her? His next words flowed with a sense of defeat. "I'll move back to the Bahamas and you'll never see me again."

Gertie tapped her fingers against her chin, her eyes flickering as if deep in thought.

He looked at his watch. A full minute passed.

Cudlow pushed back his chair and said, "Have a nice day." He left the dining room.

Chapter 31

ohnnie held the phone away from his ear as Robin yelled, "When are you coming home?"

He put her on speaker. "I don't know."

"What are you *doing* there?"

"Helping a friend. Can't go into it. Hey, did you know Cud's grandson has this awesome virtual reality game? It's badass."

"You're playing video games? Get your hiney home now! Are you even taking your meds?"

Johnnie searched his memory. He'd been at Cud's place in the Bahamas for three days, plus the day at sea. Four days since he took his last pill. "Oh, yeah. I forgot."

"Do I have to call Dr. Phillips again?"

"No! I mean, I'm fine."

"You always say that."

In truth, he was feeling great. He'd woken up with morning wood for the first time in three years. But he couldn't tell Robin this kind of stuff. That would be supremely gross. "I mean it. I feel like a new person."

Robin sighed. "Are you afraid to face Greta?"

"What?"

"I spoke to her."

"What? When?"

"Three days ago. When you didn't call me. I thought perhaps you'd called her. I needed to know if you were okay. So, I visited the library."

"You had no right—"

"She's a sweet person. I'm proud of you. I like her much better than Darla. And her red hair reminds me of mom's when she was younger…"

"Jumpin' Joe, what did you talk about?"

"She wanted to know all about you."

"Oh, fuck. What did you tell her?"

"Everything. We went for coffee. Chatted for a good hour."

The blood drained from face. Words refused to form. "Ugh."

"She misses you."

"Really?"

"Yes."

"Hey, I'll catch up with you later."

"Wait, don't—"

He hung up and went to the game room. Johnnie handed Jackson his phone back. "I want to be the orc this time."

Mo said, "Dang. I guess I'll be the elf king."

Jackson smiled. "I'll be the dwarf, but only if we can travel to the snow kingdom this time."

"Sure," Johnnie said.

A short time later, Hugh, the butler, knocked on the door, "Jackson, a man from Customs and Immigration is here for Mr. Crosswell."

Mo whipped off his headset. "Oh no! Where can I hide?" He opened the door, brushed past Hugh and headed to his bedroom.

Johnnie went downstairs. In the living room, a serious looking middle-aged man held a clipboard. He wore a cap with an emblem on it.

"Hello?"

"Are you Mr. Crosswell? My name is Inspector Barnes." The man didn't offer a handshake.

Johnnie put his hand away. "Yes, is everything all right?"

"Well, that depends. The paperwork from your pilot was flagged."

He blinked. "Flagged?"

"You had a passenger on board without the requisite documentation."

"Oh."

"So, you are aware of the laws violated?"

"Mister, we were shipwrecked and I promised him—"

The man laughed. "You promised him?"

"Really, he saved my life. We were being chased by pirates. They would have killed us."

"*An iguana* saved you from pirates?"

Johnnie froze. "Um. Yeeess?"

"This must be a smart fellow. Is he here? On the premises?"

Johnnie blinked. The inspector was asking about Stumpy. After a pause to collect himself, he said, "Last I saw him, he was in the garden, sunning himself."

"Well, sir, you can't let a wild animal roam free here. There could be diseases. The laws demand we capture him and euthanize…"

"What? You can't kill Stumpy!"

"Or, we can keep him at Animal Control, caged, until you return him to his land of origin. There is a fine, incidentally."

"Yes, we'll leave. Right away."

"Can you retrieve this *Stumpy* creature now?"

Johnnie nodded. "Follow me."

They walked out the French doors to the garden. Stumpy was sitting on the wrought-iron bench, next to his plate of lettuce.

Johnnie picked up Stumpy, placed him on his shoulder and said, "Sit-sit."

Barnes eyes widened. "A tame old thing."

"Sometimes."

"Well, I need to take him with me. I have a cage in the back of my van."

Jackson jogged outside. "John, is everything all right?"

With fear in his voice, Johnnie said, "They want to take Stumpy."

Barnes said, "Sorry, we must enforce our animal control laws."

Jackson walked up to Barnes. "Surely, you might be open to an accommodation?"

"I don't know what you mean."

"Perhaps a charitable donation?"

"Do you mean to bribe me? I hope that is not your intention. The punishment for bribery…"

Jackson held up his hands. "You know, Loughton Enterprises pays its fair share of local taxes. I was wondering, if you'd consider a favor? For example, if John and Stumpy were to get on a flight, in say two hours, could you see fit to let it go with a warning? John is a wounded warrior and just survived a harrowing ship wreck. We can arrange private transport right away."

Barnes looked at Stumpy. "Fine. I want a report the moment the iguana leaves the island, understand?"

"Yes, we understand." Jackson clapped Johnnie on his free shoulder.

Barnes wrote something on his folder. "The next time I won't be lenient."

Johnnie nodded.

The inspector headed to the front door. "I'll let myself out."

After they heard the front door close, Jackson whispered, "Mo almost jumped off the second-floor balcony. It was all I could do to pull him inside."

Johnnie raced up the stairs. "George! They wanted Stumpy!" He whipped open Mo's door. "Where are you?" He entered the bathroom. Through the translucent shower curtain, it was obvious Mo's sizable form was behind it. "Dude, not the best hiding spot."

Mo pulled back the curtain. "I panicked."

"It was animal control. I have to leave and take Stumpy with me. Right away." He held open the bathroom door.

Mo walked past him and sat on the four-poster bed. "I want to stay here."

"What will you do?"

"Jackson said the new company they acquired will create three new theme parks. Last night, after you went to sleep, I gave him lots of ideas. Hospitality and fun being my specialty and all."

"What about your immigration issues?"

"Jackson said he'd help me petition for political refugee status. He and Cudlow know a few lawyers who can help."

"That's awesome."

"Yeah, and I have you to thank."

"I didn't do anything. Cudlow did—"

"No, you were the one who helped me escape. You brought me here. You're my guardian angel."

"Ugh. Let's not get sentimental."

Mo stood up, smiled and hit him on the shoulder. "I think Greta will feel the same."

"Hey, um, Mo? About Greta, I'm not sure what to do."

"How so?"

"This morning? I was able to, you know…"

"No, what?"

"You know."

"I'm sorry, what?"

Johnnie made a hand movement.

"OH!" Mo grinned. "Fantastico! See? More reason to sweep her off her feet."

"No, that's the problem. I'm off my meds. I can hammer nails now, but in a couple days, I'll either be a raving lunatic or back on my pills and comatose."

"You need to talk to your doctor. I can't help you there."

"I guess."

"Just tell Greta; when the time comes. There are many ways to be intimate."

He shook his head. "I can't remember, no really."

"See, being honest is the best policy. Women love honesty."

Johnnie laughed. "Sure, *George.*"

Mo gave him a bear hug. "Hey, who knows? When I get a new legal passport, I'll come visit. Deal?"

Johnnie smiled. "Deal." He went to his bedroom. There wasn't much to pack. Only the clothes he washed ashore in, and those were best left to the garbage. He'd been wearing a mix of Jackson's and Cud's clothes for the last three days, depending on which fit best.

Looking around his room, he decided all he needed was Stumpy.

And a box to store him for the flight.

And some snacks.

Because leaving his new friends Mo and Jackson was sad, but a trip without snacks would be even sadder.

Chapter 32

G ertie sat in the dining room, staring into space. She finished her orange juice still trying to sort out what happened. She remembered what Sara said. *Go live the dream.*

Perhaps that was easier for an outsider to say.

She went back to her cabin and took a well needed shower. In white Bermuda shorts and a cobalt blue tank top, she went in search of the ship's chapel.

The space was small but had leaded glass windows looking out onto the ship's aft. A dark space with only six rows of pews and a non-denominational altar. The room was eerily quiet. So quiet, the only perceptible sound was not a sound, but the vibration of the ship's engines.

God surely wouldn't know the answer to her problem, or better yet, He would help her figure it out on her own.

She prayed on it, asking in her mind: *What is love? Why can't I trust?* and *How will I live without him?*

She remembered the time they'd first met. How despite his crazy hair and long beard, his appreciation for life exuded through his eyes like sparklers on the Fourth of July. A wild, pure spirit unlike any she'd seen before. And later, with his beard removed and hair tamed, when she could see his face and how ruggedly handsome he was, it took her breath away.

But back then, he was a simpler man with a simpler life.

If she chose to leave him, could she really go back to her garden and act like everything was the same?

A woman came into the chapel, tall with long brown hair and broad shoulders, wearing a pastel pink sundress.

"Good morning," Gertie said.

"Good morning," the woman whispered back in a slightly deep voice, taking a seat in a row in the back to the left.

Gertie chuckled. "You don't have to whisper. It's only us."

"I see." The woman got up and took a seat in the pew across the aisle from Gertie. "Are you Catholic?"

"No, Protestant. You?"

"I was raised Catholic. I left the church, but I still talk to the big guy."

Gertie smiled. "How are you enjoying the cruise?"

"It's wonderful. Are you traveling by yourself?"

She chuckled. "That's a tough question. Part of the reason I'm sitting here. He just asked me to marry him."

The woman crossed the aisle to sit next to Gertie and held out her hand. "I'm Charlotte."

Gertie scooted over to make room on the bench. "I'm Gertie. Nice to meet you."

Charlotte said, "I want to hear all about it."

Gertie scratched her head. "I didn't give him an answer."

"Really? Do you love him?"

"I don't know what love is...I'm so confused."

"But you're thinking about it?"

"We haven't known each other long. It happened so suddenly. And when we're together, I lose all reason. Other times, I question everything." A tear came to her eye and she blinked it away. "I've been alone for decades. It never bothered me. But when he went away for a month, it felt like I died inside."

"Is he a good person?"

"Yes. The sweetest."

"Does he make your heart sing?"

"It's not that simple."

"Honey, you know what I would do for *one minute* of true love?"

"Don't say that. You'll find someone."

"That's what straight cis-folks always say. Believe me, when you find happiness, you need to grab it with both fists. Understand?"

"What if it doesn't last?"

"Gertie, right? Nothing lasts. We're all gonna leave this earth one way or another. Which is why you should get your hiney out of this tomb and go to him."

Gertie nodded. "Maybe you're right. Everyone keeps telling me the same thing."

"You know what they say. Messengers come in all forms."

"Thank you, Charlotte. I guess I have my answer."

Her new friend stood and smoothed her pink skirt. "Yes, you go find your lover boy." She winked before making her exit.

Gertie crossed herself and sighed. To the heavens she said, "I hope you know what you're doing."

She headed to Cud's cabin and knocked on the door.

He answered, "Yes?"

"Yes."

His head reared back. "Yes? As in…"

Gertie nodded and brought her face in close, resting her forehead against his. She whispered, "I'll marry you."

Cudlow laughed and whispered. "Maybe I've changed my mind."

She pursed her lips and feigned exasperation. "No, you haven't."

In a kidding tone, he said, "Oh, well, like you said, we barely know each other…"

She took his hand and led him inside. "Well, we can fix that."

She kissed him, wrapping her arms around his waist. He twirled her around. Sun streamed through the open balcony doors and a gray seagull cawed at them from the wood railing outside.

They swayed back and forth, in a slow cheek to cheek dance. Gertie whispered, "I'll ask you a question and then you ask."

"Hold that thought." Cudlow jogged to the window and closed the curtains to remove the distraction of the obnoxious bird. He dug around in his nightstand and sat on the bed. "Come here."

She sat next to him.

He opened the small white box. "Let's make this official."

Did he plan this from the beginning? "You brought it with you?"

"I hoped." He took the blue diamond ring out of the box and slipped it on her finger.

"It's beautiful." She held it up to the light. The hunk of stone no longer felt like a bribe or a noose.

He kissed her neck and asked, "What's my favorite color?"

She guessed the obvious, "Blue?"

"No, green," he chuckled. "Your turn."

Her turn to ask a question. *Not that the answer mattered.* But there was a question she was curious about. "Where did you get your name?"

His eyes went wide. "Oh, it's a long story."

She kissed his cheek. "I'll take the short version."

"Our family's forebearers lived in the town of Cudlow, off the coast of West Sussex. The town disappeared into the sea in the late 1500s. Completely washed away by the sands of time. Father loved history. But as a child I always wondered if the name was cursed. Like I might disappear, too."

"That's awful." She caressed his cheek. With a chuckle, she added, "But still better than Gertrude."

"I love your name. My turn." He scratched his chin. "What kind of music do you like?"

"You've heard me singing." She poked him in the chest. "What music do *you* enjoy?"

He chuckled. "Celtic chanting songs."

"Really?" She raised an eyebrow.

Cudlow bopped her on the nose. "No, silly. I like Bob Marley."

She loved his smile. But she needed to ask a serious question. *One that mattered.* "Where do you want to live?"

Between his fairy kisses, he whispered, "Anywhere, my love."

She waggled her finger at him. "No, wrong answer. You have to be specific."

He worked on taking off his shirt. "Can we…live in my house in the Bahamas?" He freed his arms but his head was stuck. With his voice muffled by fabric, he said, "The garden could really benefit from your skills." He freed himself from the shirt and tossed it on the floor. "Jackson said you liked the kitchen…"

The time for questions was over. The rest of their lives lay ahead of them, and it buoyed her soul. "Yes. Bahamas. Whatever. Now shut up and kiss me."

Cudlow beamed, his eyes like emeralds. He held her hand and kissed it. "I love you, Birdie."

There was one more thing she had to face. Time for some real truth. She nestled down next to him, resting her head on his shoulder, gazing into his sweet eyes.

Gertie stilled herself before taking the leap. "Cudlow, I love you, too."

And she meant it with all her heart.

Chapter 33

T he helicopter pilot never introduced himself, but Johnnie was happy to ride in silence. Stumpy was quiet in his perforated cardboard box on the seat next to his. When the island's lights came into view, he let out a sigh and wondered if he should visit Greta. It was close to eight o'clock at night. But it felt like midnight. He desperately needed to put on his own pajamas and sleep.

The helicopter touched down on the St. John vehicle ferry dock. Robin's car was waiting.

He removed his harness and took off his headset as the blades slowed. The pilot came around and opened his door.

Johnnie bounced out and headed to Robin. She jogged toward him with her arms outstretched.

In a hug that felt like a tackle, Robin said, "I'm so glad you're home."

He scratched the scar above his ear. "Good to be home."

"Are you hungry? Do you want to come to my place for dinner? We'd love to hear all about it."

"I'm really tired. Can you take me back to my scooter?"

"No."

"What do you mean, no?"

"You've been gone for days and I need to know if you are alright. Let me look at you." She held his shoulders. "How are you feeling? Any dizzy spells? Headaches? Were you injured in the accident?"

He hated when she fussed. In a flat tone, he said, "Look into my eyes. I'm fine."

An approaching figure took their attention. The pilot walked up to Johnnie. "You forgot this."

Johnnie took the cardboard box. "Oh. Right. Sorry."

The pilot walked away.

Robin asked, "What's in there?"

"Stumpy."

"Jesus, Christ. I thought you were dead." She slapped him on the chest. "Dumb butthead." Despite her playful tone, her eyes were tearful.

"I'm sorry for making you worry."

"Please, come for dinner. Spend some time with me. Tell me what happened."

There were too many disasters to recount and he was too tired to explain. "No, you should enjoy your time with Arturo."

"Don't be a putz. I only have one brother."

Johnnie retreated. "I don't want to talk about it." He tucked the box under his arm and began walking. It was only a twenty-minute walk to the spot he left the Piaggio.

He heard her panting behind him. She grabbed his arm, her eyes flashing with anger. "Goddamnit, what's gotten into you?"

"Me?"

"Yes."

He matched her anger with his own, refusing to back down. "Oh, I don't know. You talk to Greta behind my back? And tell her things, private things? Treating me like I'm a child? Never trusting me to take care of myself? You aren't mom. I don't need you to smother me."

"Smother you?"

"You act like you can solve all my problems, but you can't. And I'm tired of you interfering."

Robin jutted her chin. "What? I'm not supposed to care? Not supposed to help? Fuck you. And fuck your stupid iguana. What are you? Ten? Fine. Go sulk alone in your dumb apartment and ignore anyone who's ever cared about you. I'm done." She took a pill bottle out of her suit jacket pocket and shoved it in his face. "Here." She turned and walked back to her car.

He stared at the bottle. She had picked up his prescription. But he was still angry. Johnnie tucked the bottle in his pocket, turned and continued walking north while holding Stumpy's box.

As he strode down the road, he muttered her cutting words with teeth bared. *Fuck your stupid iguana…What are you? Ten?…I'm done.*

A small voice in his head suggested he might be overreacting. Which meant he needed his meds after all.

But no, she needed to back off.

And he could get his shit together on his own.

* * *

An hour later, after dropping Stumpy at Hawksnest Beach, Johnnie arrived at his garage apartment in Calabash Boom. Gertie's house was dark, as was his place. His spare key to his apartment, one of many hidden in the surrounding landscape, was still under the white rock to the left of his door.

Once inside, he flipped on the overhead light.

The living room and kitchen looked the same. His bed was a mess with scattered belongings he had considered taking with him, but didn't have space to carry. No phone, no Stumpy, no Mo, no Cud, no Gertie, no Robin. He opened his laptop. At least he had internet.

Johnnie opened up a chat window and contacted Greta. "I'm home."

After a few seconds, the dots along the bottom rippled. She was typing. "I'm so relieved. I missed you. How are you?"

He typed back, "Tired. Going to bed. Just wanted to say hi."

Greta typed, "Hi :) Sweet dreams, Captain John."

He closed his laptop. With a sweep of his arm, he brushed all the junk on his bed onto the floor, crawled toward his pillow and face-planted onto it.

The silence was deafening.

His mind went in a million directions.

Johnnie pulled a new blank journal from the drawer of his bedside table and took off the cellophane wrapper. On the first page, he wrote the date at the top, then began to write.

Dear Diary,

I'm home. But it doesn't feel like home. I said awful things to Robin tonight. I meant them at the time, but now I feel rotten. Why can't she trust me more?

I miss Mo. He is good at making me smile. But he'll have a good life now.

In the shipwreck, I lost all my notes for the story I was going to tell Greta. And I don't remember the pirate song Mo made up. I don't deserve to be with someone as nice as her. If Robin told her about everything, Greta probably only likes me because of pity. And that hurts more than rejection.

My nerves feel shot. I can tell I need my meds. Driving home, I kept imagining monsters coming out of the shadows. And when I brushed my teeth, my reflection in the window scared the shit out of me. Like someone was watching from outside.

Mo said I should talk to Dr. Phillips about my libido issues. Lou is cool, but I'd still feel embarrassed. Maybe a guy like me doesn't deserve true happiness.

See you in the morning, Diary. Remind me to get groceries and a new phone.

Love, Johnnie

Chapter 34

C udlow rang the concierge at the first morning light. "Yes, hello? I'm wondering if you can help me."

"Yes, Mr. Loughton. What can we do for you today?"

"I'm wondering if the Captain performs wedding ceremonies?"

"Yes. Why do you ask?"

"Well, I'm wondering if he could perform a ceremony tonight?"

"Congratulations. I'll have to get back to you. His schedule is quite busy and this is considerably short notice. In the meantime, perhaps you and your betrothed could fill out some forms at the front desk?"

"Oh, yes. Right away. Thank you."

Gertie looked at him as he put the receiver down. "Well?"

"They're looking into it."

"Should we call Jackson and Johnnie?"

"Not quite yet. Let's see if they can accommodate us first."

"Yes, you're right."

"We need to fill out some information. Get dressed."

"Information?" Gertie got out of bed and put on Cudlow's bathrobe.

"I imagine some routine details."

"Right." Gertie looked preoccupied as she walked into the bathroom and shut the door.

Cudlow got dressed and while Gertie was showering, he opened the bottle of complimentary champagne which had been sitting on the credenza next to the television since they boarded. There were only short round lowball glasses available, but it didn't matter. He was marrying the woman he loved—perhaps tonight—and his life would again be complete.

The phone rang. The concierge explained the Captain had a small window of twenty minutes at eight o'clock and could marry them at the reception center if they opted for a simple and quick ceremony. Cudlow responded, "Yes, perfect."

After he hung up, he knocked on the bathroom door. The water wasn't running anymore. "Gertie, eight o'clock. But they said we need to fill out the forms by noon. We need to get down there."

She opened the door, wrapped in a towel. "Are you sure? Maybe we should wait until we get home. Get married in a church."

Cudlow said, "Is that what you want? Or are you getting cold feet? Because if you are having second thoughts…"

"No. I…yes, let's get married tonight."

"Good! Wonderful."

Gertie got dressed and they hurried to guest services. A woman named Margery gave them a form to fill out and made additional copies of their passports. At a small table, Cudlow began filling in his details. Gertie peered over his shoulder. "Your middle name is Eldrid?"

"Yes. What's your middle name?"

"Jean. Don't ask."

Cudlow read the next part of the form, which seemed a bit tricky. "Oh, my. It says if I'm a widow, I need to produce a death certificate. You were never married, correct?"

"Um." Gertie shook her head, "Er. No."

"I wonder if Jackson can send a copy of Freddie's certificate. Let me ring him." He took out his phone and stepped away from the table, pacing the lobby by the front desk and clasping his other ear to block the music over the PA system.

Jackson answered, "Hello, Pawpaw, how is the cruise?"

"Well, splendid actually. How is Johnnie?"

"He's well. He went home. I need to talk to you when you get back. He brought a visitor. But it can wait."

He couldn't contain himself anymore, "Jackson! We're getting married. Gertie and I are exchanging vows tonight!"

After a pause, Jackson said, "That's wonderful." In a faint voice, as if talking to someone else, he said, "They're getting married." He cleared his throat. "Hugh says congratulations."

"But first, I need your help. Could you find Grandmaw Winifred's death certificate and fax it to the ship? I'll text you the number shortly."

"Let me guess, you need this right now?"

"Sorry, it can't be helped. It should be in the office safe. If you can't find it there, call my lawyer Felicity. She'll get it sorted."

"Yes, no problem. I wish I could be there. Will you be coming back here afterwards? Or St. John? I can set up a small party for your return."

"Oh, Jackson, that would be wonderful. I don't know our schedule yet. After the cruise, we'll likely go to Gertie's to pack her things before heading home. We'll have to play it by ear."

"All right. Congratulations. Send my love to Gertie."

Cudlow walked over to Gertie and whispered, "Jackson sends his love."

She said, "Yes, same to him."

Cudlow relayed the message and they wrapped up the call. He put away the phone and looked at the marriage application. "It looks like you filled out your part. Here, sign the bottom. I'm sure you want to get your hair done." He looked at Margery behind the desk. "Could you set up some pampering time in the salon for my beautiful bride?"

"Yes, of course. Ms. Brown? Come, follow me."

Gertie smiled and kissed Cudlow on the cheek before she departed. "See you later."

Cudlow rubbed his palms together. Everything was falling into place. He and Freddy would be together for the rest of their lives. And he couldn't wait to get started.

* * *

After Gertie's hair appointment, they met up outside the small jewelry shop on the ship to look for wedding bands.

Cudlow greeted her with a kiss on the cheek.

Her hair was wrapped under a silk scarf, with some curls tucked away with bobby pins. She looked at her watch. "I tried to call Johnnie. No answer."

"He'll find out soon enough. I spoke with Jackson again. He wanted me to 'live-stream' it, but I don't know how."

Gertie smiled. "This is our day. Let's keep it simple."

"Yes, of course."

"I only have twelve minutes until my makeup appointment."

"Shall we?"

They walked in and examined the cases. The selection was small.

Gertie held up her hand with the sapphire engagement ring. "Cudlow, this ring is stunning, but I can't imagine wearing it every day. Especially gardening. Maybe only for special occasions. Would it bother you?"

He kissed her hand. "Of course not. Yes, I can see how it isn't the most practical option."

"Thanks for understanding." Gertie peered at the tray of wedding bands the salesperson brought up to the counter. "What kind of ring do you want?"

Seeing the assortment of men's bands, he recalled how his old wedding band became too loose to wear after he lost weight living on the beach. For a time, he kept it around his neck on a cord. But a year later, it went missing after the cord frayed and broke. He never found it despite his searches.

He choked back his past sorrow and put on a brave face, reminding himself of the future, which he hoped meant great joy. "Why don't you pick one first, and I'll find one to match?"

Gertie's attention went to a ring inside the lower case. She pointed. "Can I see this one?"

The salesperson confirmed which one and placed it on the black velvet pad. It was a thin ring with a gold flower on top and a tiny blue stone at the center.

Gertie fitted it on her ring finger and it was loose. "What do you think?"

He smiled. "It suits you."

"I love it."

"Good." Cudlow picked up a thin gold ring to match. "I'll take this one."

Gertie asked, "Do we have time to have this re-sized?"

The salesperson said, "We could do it tomorrow."

Cudlow nodded, "Yes, fine. In the meantime, we'll make these work."

Gertie kissed him on the cheek. "I should get going. See you later?"

He chuckled, "I certainly hope so!"

She laughed. "I love you."

A warm sensation flooded his face as he watched her walk away. Only two more hours and his life could begin again.

He paid for the rings and headed back to his cabin. A hot shower, a clean shave and perhaps a brandy to calm his nerves.

Cudlow drew in a long breath as he opened the cabin door. The next time he entered, he'd be married to an angel.

Please be happy for me, Freddy.

I need your forgiveness now more than ever.

* * *

At seven-forty-five, Cudlow and Gertie arrived, arms linked, at the Darwin reception center. He wore a tuxedo he had packed for formal nights and she, her hair in loose waves, wore the gorgeous one-shoulder white gown from Paris. A small crowd had arrived for the usual nightly reception but a few people seemed dressed more formally, making it seem like a typical wedding.

Cudlow placed his hand in his pocket, feeling for the wedding bands to ensure they were still there.

The ship's photographer introduced himself. While they waited for the captain, they took several pictures. One in front of the three-foot-tall ice sculpture of a sea turtle. A few posed sipping Champagne or kissing.

As more reception guests arrived through the outer doors, a powerful gust of wind slammed the door shut behind them; paper napkins from the dessert table took flight through the air and across the floor.

Gertie's hands flew to her hair. "Oh no. Does it look alright?"

Cudlow reached behind her head and smoothed her locks. "Never prettier."

She smiled. "You cut a fine figure in that tuxedo."

"Don't get used to this. These shoes are cutting off the circulation in my toes. After tonight, it's shorts and flip-flops for me."

She pecked his cheek. "I love you no matter what you wear."

"Are you sure? I still have those brown shorts..." He recalled how his butler Hugh offered to set them on fire in the yard after he returned to the Bahamas.

Gertie huffed, "Please...for the love of God, no!"

Cud shook his head. "I'm just teasing."

Captain Ramos strode into the room, creating a hush among the crowd. Margery, the woman who helped them with the paperwork, directed the Captain towards them.

"Mr. Loughton, Ms. Brown, I'm sorry to be on such a tight schedule. Did you prepare your own vows? Or should I go with the standard routine?"

Gertie looked at Cud and giggled. "Prepared? I didn't even have time to shave my legs!"

Cudlow laughed and said to the Captain. "I think we'll use the standard vows."

Ramos asked, "Do you have witnesses?"

A short brown woman raced up to them, waving her hand in the air. "I'll be a witness."

Cudlow turned to Gertie, who was laughing.

Gertie said, "Cudlow, meet Lisa."

"How do you know…"

Lisa said, "Gertie and I had a wild night. I'm so happy for you two. See Gertie, I knew you loved him."

Cudlow chuckled. "That's what I told her, too!"

Ramos said, "We need a second."

Gertie said, "I'll be right back." She walked across the room and began talking with a woman with a large nose and muscular arms.

She returned with the tall woman. "This is Charlotte."

Cudlow squinted at Gertie, "How do you know everyone?"

She laughed. "I get around."

Ramos cleared his throat. "Let's take our places." He guided them to the windowed wall looking over the ocean.

Cudlow and Gertie held hands and took deep breaths as Ramos began. "Ladies and gentlemen, we are gathered here today to witness and share in the joy of this special occasion. With solemn commitment, Cudlow and Gertrude have come before us today to proclaim their love and enter into the lasting bonds of matrimony. If anyone has cause to object to this union, speak now or forever hold your peace."

Gertie looked uneasily around the room.

Cud rubbed the top of her hand with his thumb. Maybe Gertie was having some jitters. He glanced around. Only smiling faces.

The captain looked at Gertie and continued, "Repeat after me. I, Gertrude, take Cudlow to be my lawfully wedded husband."

She repeated the vow, "I, Gertrude, take Cudlow to be my lawfully wedded husband."

Ramos said, "Promising to love and cherish him through good times and bad, sickness and in health, for richer or for poorer…"

She repeated the words, focusing her eyes on Cudlow.

Ramos said, "Forsaking all others, for as long as we both shall live."

Gertie completed her vow, "… shall live." She let out a long breath and squeezed Cud's hand.

Ramos turned to Cudlow, asking him to repeat his vow.

With his heart beating fast, he couldn't get the words out quickly enough. "I, Cudlow, take Freddy to be my lawfully wedded wife, promising to love and cherish her…"

An odd hush came over the room. Gasps were audible.

Gertie pulled her hand away, her eyes wide. "What? NO! I can't believe…"

Why was she upset? What had he done?

She pulled the blue engagement ring off her finger and placed it in Cud's palm. Without another word, she ran toward the door. After a few steps, her shoe caught on the front of her dress and she fell forward, landing on her chin. She screamed. As she pushed her face and torso off the floor, gobs of blood flowed bright red from her jaw onto the front of her dress. Her mascara ran down her cheeks and she sobbed as she muttered, "Damn" and "Ow, ow, ow." Lisa ran up and grabbed her arm to help her up.

Cudlow strode over. "Oh, God. Gertie, my love, are you alright?"

Gertie held her chin to catch the blood and eased up to stand. With her face turned away, her sobs stopped and she growled. "You…you stay away from me." She grabbed the fabric on her skirt and jogged out of the room.

Lisa turned to face him. "Mister, you really fucked that up."

The air left his lungs. He gasped, "I don't understand."

Lisa waved her hands at his head like she might strike him. "You called her Freddy."

He took a step back. "I did?"

Lisa shook her head and frowned, then jogged after Gertie, calling towards her. "Wait! Let me help you."

Captain Ramos grimaced. "I'm sorry, Mr. Loughton. I should get back to the bridge."

Cud nodded in a daze. *Did he really get her name wrong again? What did it mean?*

He dug a finger under the band of his bow tie, loosened it and threw it on the floor. "Bollocks!"

Charlotte came up to him and put her hand on his shoulder. "Don't worry. She loves you. Men screw up all the time. Believe me. She'll forgive you."

Cud exhaled and closed his eyes. The blue diamond ring was still in his palm. "No. She's right." Without waiting for a reply, he headed out a side door to the outdoor deck. The cool air and strong wind hit his hot cheeks. He kept walking. At the front of the ship, he stared at the ocean and distant lights of the coast.

What the hell was wrong with him?

He looked up at the brightest star and asked, "Freddy, why can't I let you go? Please let me go."

Cudlow walked over to a chaise lounge and curled up in a ball. The hard white plastic reminded him of his nest back on St. John.

He hit his temple with his fist. Over and over. And began to weep.

Chapter 35

n the last night of the cruise, Cudlow packed his suitcase and affixed the green sticker to the handle. He eased his door open, mindful to not make any loud noises, and placed it outside in the hall.

Gertie's door opened. Before he could duck inside, she said, "Wait."

Without making eye contact, he said, "Hello."

She placed her suitcase in a similar position in the hall, then turned to him, propping open her door with one foot. "Hello."

He noticed the bandage under her bottom lip. "How is your chin?"

"I didn't need stitches. But I chipped a tooth slightly. How are you?"

He wrung his hands. "Gertie, I'm so sorry."

"I know. I'm fine. But what about you?"

He had ruined their future together with a stupid slip of the tongue. He wanted to crawl under a rock and stay there. But even a rock would be too good. Maybe he could throw himself into a lake of fire. Cudlow couldn't hold his breath any longer. "Are we telling the truth?"

"If you want to."

"I'm knackered and miserable. And you?"

"I've been better."

She wasn't wearing any makeup and dressed in shorts and a thin long-sleeved sweater. Her hair was tucked under a print scarf. Even with her damaged chin, she was still dazzling. He wanted to caress her cheek and hold her close. *Make amends.* But it was too late for that.

He left his door. "Gertie, I've been doing some soul searching."

"Do you want to take a walk?"

"Around the top deck, perhaps?"

"Let me put on long pants." She popped back into her room, shutting the door.

He wondered if she would reappear, or if she would leave him waiting forever. He leaned against the wall, wondering if he could say what he must. A minute later, although it seemed ten times that, she opened the door. "Ready."

They walked in silence to the elevator and rode it to the top level for the walking track. The wind was strong, likely due to the speed at which the ship was traveling to make their morning dock schedule. Teams of workers power-washed the chaises and ship walls. Cudlow and Gertie gingerly stepped over the water hoses. The stars above were in full display. In the glow of the moonlight, Cudlow glanced at Gertie, appreciating how radiant she looked, even with her bruised face. When they arrived at the bow of the ship, they stood, shoulder to shoulder holding the wooden hand rail, gazing into the dark sea.

Gertie said, "I'm sorry. Maybe I overreacted."

Cudlow said, "No. It's not your fault. I've spent the last twenty-four hours thinking."

"And?"

"I think I'm a sentimental old fool."

She darted her eyes and nodded. "Hmm. Not gonna disagree."

"I wanted to say thank you."

She shook her head and stared at him, one eyebrow raised. "For what?"

"For being the voice of reason. And I'd like..." He took her hand. "I'd like us to remain good friends."

"Friends..."

"Yes. I wasn't prepared for this. Too many years alone. I let my heart run amok. Letting myself think I was in love. Which clearly makes no sense."

"Wait...what?"

"I mean, look at you! You're absolutely brilliant. And I suppose I was overwhelmed." He walked behind her and hugged her around her shoulders. "I want to say I'm sorry. Can you forgive me?"

"I..."

He released her. "Can you?"

"Yes?"

"Wonderful. I'm so glad." He let out a long steady breath. "Whew. Thank you. That is such a relief. Now, friend, do you want to walk a bit more?" He gestured to the track. "I'm thinking of going a few laps." He looked above. "The stars tonight are spectacular, don't you think?"

She squinted at him. "Um, okay?"

He held out his arm and she linked hers. They walked in silence for the next full lap, although Gertie seemed to stare at the ground instead of the beautiful night sky. Cudlow pointed above at the constellations, "Do you see Cassiopeia?"

Gertie stopped. "Don't I get to say anything?"

"Oh. Sorry. Yes, what is it?"

She crossed her arms. "When you say friends, what do you mean?"

He was afraid of this. Because she was right, perhaps 'friend' wasn't the correct word. He'd done enough damage and needed to let her move on. "You know, like neighbors. Not that we'll see each other much, living on different ends of the island."

"Not *close* friends."

"I was thinking maybe I'd start attending your church on Sundays. I'm sure we'll see each other there."

"So, you're not going back to the Bahamas?"

"No. I rather like St. John. I miss my nest. And nightly swims."

"Hold on. You're going to live on the beach?"

"I was happy there."

Gertie clasped her hand to her mouth. "No. You can't put that on me."

"What are you talking about?"

"I leave you at the altar and you decide to remain homeless? That's not fair."

"No, no, no!" He took her hands in his. "Oh, my, your hands are ice cold." He rubbed her hands in his. "We should go inside."

She pulled her hands away. "Cudlow! Don't change the subject."

He drew in a breath. "Right." He walked to the railing and gazed at the sea. "It has nothing to do with you."

"The hell it doesn't."

"I've told you. I've been soul searching. It's the only way to get my feet back under me. I was happy there. I don't resent what happened."

"You don't?"

"No. And I wouldn't go back in time and change anything. Would you?"

Gertie came up to the railing next to him and sighed. "No, I wouldn't either."

Feeling forgiven, he sighed with relief. "Good."

They watched another cruise ship sail parallel to theirs off in the distance.

Gertie said, "Do you want to get a night cap?"

He couldn't keep up his brave face much longer. "We have a big day tomorrow. I'm going to get some rest. Are you coming?"

Gertie stared at the ocean. "I think I'll stay up a little longer."

"See you tomorrow." He ducked into the nearest door to the inside and walked towards the elevator bank. Through the window, he looked back at Gertie. It was a convincing performance, he hoped. Inside, his heart felt torn to shreds. But it didn't help to think about what could have been.

Cud made a bee line back to his room and turned out the lights.

Moonlight through his balcony door bounced across his darkened room. Tucked into bed, he whispered, "I'll always love you, Gertie."

* * *

Dave Jones arrived on the ferry at Cruz Bay at nine o'clock at night. The darkness of the evening was excellent cover, in addition to his new face and name. In the morning, he would pick up the handgun Ren mailed to the St. John P.O. box. Walking among the other passengers down the dock, he still stuck out in his all-black attire. Maybe he needed to dress more festively if he were to fit in. Again, another task for tomorrow. At the street, a man standing beside a black Jeep Cherokee held a sign with the word, "Jones".

He walked up to the man. "I'm Jones."

They did some paperwork and he signed his most recent name at the bottom of the clipboard.

The rental agent asked, "Where are you staying?"

"With a friend."

Soon he was on his way. He couldn't stay at the big resort like last time. Instead, he chose the remote eco-lodge to the southeast, close to his prey, but obscenely inconvenient to stores and the post office. But he wouldn't be staying long.

On the ride to the eastern end of the island, he stopped into Calabash Market for some nourishment. Conveniently, there were no other cars in the parking lot. He picked out a few items, like some razors, instant coffee, yogurt, a plain blue t-shirt, and packets of protein powder.

He paid with cash.

The man at the register asked, "Are you visiting?"

"Yeah."

The man bagged his items. "This is the loveliest time of year, if you ask me."

"No one asked you."

The older man in the apron appeared confused. "I'm sorry. Is everything alright?"

Jones shook his head and grabbed the bag out of the man's hands. "Goodnight."

He noticed the security camera above the door as he exited. *Damn.*

Still, no one was looking for him and his face was different. He was probably fine.

Yes, everything was fine.

As he pulled out of the parking space, he saw the cashier through the plate-glass window talking on a cellphone.

A wave of disgust gripped him. *Was the check-out dude calling the police? No. Impossible.*

He continued on, pulling onto the road, now heading due south. Winding his way along the narrow road in the dark, the turn for the eco-lodge came into view. The steep rocky terrain made him thankful for the all-wheel drive of the SUV.

As he rounded a corner, a donkey stepped out in front of him. He slammed on the brakes but the car slid on the loose rock, sending the car sideways. He turned the wheel frantically, but hit the donkey. The animal crashed through the front window; broken glass sprayed across his face and neck. The vehicle continued to slide and careened on two wheels before it rolled onto its right side and came to a stop.

Jones passed out. Upon awakening, he found himself dangling in his seat, held in by the belt. He opened his eyes to see a dead donkey face, inches from his, enmeshed in the deflated airbag. The smell was horrific. Donkey blood and saliva oozed through the animal's open mouth onto his bare arm. He didn't know how much time had passed since the collision. His face had a sticky substance, probably dried blood, with pebble-sized shards of glass penetrating his nose and forehead. All of Ren's intricate plastic surgery was likely ruined.

Vehicle lights sent shadows across the vertical dashboard. In the rearview mirror, a white pickup truck rolled up behind.

A short slender, dark-skinned woman with high cheekbones and a yellow dress exited her truck and approached. She pressed her hands on the Jeep door to boost herself to peer into his driver's side window. "Are you all right?"

It hurt his face to talk. "No. Fuck."

"Don't worry. Dottie's here. Don't move."

"I'm fine. Help me open the door."

"Sorry, Thomas. I can't do that."

His mind raced. *How did she know…?* "Who the fuck are you?"

She grinned. "I'm the bitch who's taking you down."

How was this possible?

He was out of options. Trapped and hurt without an exit plan.

And no gun to end his own misery.

* * *

Dottie considered her options. She could call the police and an ambulance. Or let Smith bleed out like a damned dog. It was only fitting for a murderer and kidnapper. She'd been so focused on the chase, it never occurred to her what she would do if she caught him.

This might explain how Smith ended up on LeDuck Island. Maybe someone, like Johnnie, also captured Smith but didn't know what to do with him either.

Smith groaned. "Lady, if you are going to call the police, do it already. Someone better get this fucking donkey out of my face!"

"Shhh. Shut up." She had to think. And she didn't have any waffles to help clear her head. Dottie leaned against Smith's vehicle, arms crossed, looking up at the stars.

"Lady, I can give you a million dollars if you help me."

"Ha! Like I'd believe you."

"I still have the bitcoin."

Dottie didn't care about money. Only justice. But she couldn't leave him here in case another car came by.

She peered over the side of the hill. The slope was steep and there was little vegetation in the way. With a little momentum…

God could decide.

She got back in her white pickup truck and started the engine. With light pressure on the gas pedal, she inched past the black SUV on the right side, heading up the road which continued to climb in elevation. About a hundred feet beyond, she checked her rear-view mirror, carefully aligning her vehicle in a straight line with Smith's vehicle.

Crossing herself, she whispered, "Jesus, take the wheel."

Dot put her truck in reverse and gunned the engine. Accelerating down the hill, four seconds later, her rear tail gate slammed into the SUV; as she neared the edge of the hillside, she stomped on the brake with her entire weight, nearly standing on the pedal.

Smith's SUV continued its descent down the hill, toppling over, the metal crunching against rocks all the way down the ravine. Despite the dark of evening, she saw a large furry mass fly off; likely the headless donkey.

Leaving a spectacular swath of broken vegetation, with dust spewing, Smith's vehicle came to a halt sixty feet down.

It was unlikely the assassin survived.

Not that she cared to find out.

She did a cautious K-turn and headed back north, toward Calabash Boom, and ultimately, toward Cruz Bay. But all this excitement made her hungry.

Dot stopped into the Calabash Market.

"Good evening, Mario," she said as the door chimed above her.

He waved. "Good evening, Dottie. Did you locate the man I told you about?"

"Yes, but it wasn't him. Maybe next time."

"Well, I'll keep my eyes out."

"Thanks, Mario. I'm starving. I know it's late, but do you have any rotisserie chickens left?"

"Sorry, we sold out."

"That's okay." She went to the baked goods aisle and picked up a package of chocolate chip cookies. At the small fridge by the checkout counter, she got a small bottle of milk.

As she placed her items on the counter, she said, "You know? The more I think about it, Smith returning to St. John doesn't seem likely. I mean, he has all that money. What would you do if you got away with thirty million dollars? Hypothetically?"

Mario bagged her items and took her cash. "If I were so rich, I'd travel the world."

She nodded. "Yes. I would too. I guess I love a mystery."

He laughed. "But tell me if you locate Elvis. I still have my old vinyl records."

Dottie smiled. "Will do. You have a blessed evening now."

She walked out and the door chimed.

Part of her wanted to swing by Gertie's place, aching to tell her the good news. But for once, she could keep a secret to herself.

Chapter 36

ohnnie finished his errands, trying to put his life back in order: laundry, food shopping, and picking out the rotten vegetables in Gertie's garden. For good measure, he re-hung her house's shutters like she had asked two months ago. Tomorrow he was due back at work. There was one more task on his to-do list: visit Greta.

He parked outside her apartment. It was now or never.

Taking the stone steps in twos, he was breathing hard when he reached her doorbell.

She answered the door. "Johnnie!" In gray knit shorts and a black tank top, she stood there in white ankle socks.

"Hi. Did I come at a bad time?"

She leaned her back against the doorframe and twirled a lock of hair. "No, I was just thinking about you."

"I can come back another time…"

"Silly, come in." Her eyes twinkled.

He stepped inside. Her apartment was small. A cottage tinier than his own place. With a murphy bed in the living room, tucked against the wall to the right. A small couch opposite a television. A kitchen with smaller appliances than his. But the walls were bright white, with macrame wall hangings. A pink fluffy rug anchored the room. A series of floor-to-ceiling white laminate shelves held hundreds of books, mostly paperbacks.

Part of him wanted to inspect the books. But they needed to talk. "Nice place."

Greta looked like she might hug him, but said, "Sit." She gestured to the loveseat.

He wasn't sure. *Would they be sitting too close?* "I…I'll take the chair." A wooden kitchen chair next to the television was an uncomfortable distance from the sofa, but it was better than the first option.

She sat on the sofa and twirled her hair. "Tell me everything."

"Hey, first, I heard you had coffee with my sister, Robin?"

"Yes, we were so worried. Your sister is amazing. You should have heard her on the phone with the Coast Guard. She doesn't take no for an answer."

"What did she tell you? About me?"

"She said you have memory problems and headaches after your accident. How far you've come. How you saved your convoy by charging a Taliban vehicle. She said you're the bravest person she's ever known."

"Robin said that?"

"Yes. She also mentioned you struggle with depression."

He bit his lip. "I was going to tell you…"

"No, it's okay. I have a sister with anxiety. It's not something to be embarrassed by."

"It's just I feel broken most of the time. Like a mutant. An idiot mutant."

"Come here." She got up and took his hand, guiding him to the sofa.

He sat, but kept the maximum distance from her, staring straight ahead.

"I can't imagine what you've been through. But I think you're pretty special."

"Greta, I like you. Really like you." The pit in his stomach ached. He had to tell her before he lost the nerve. "But I'm too damaged to be your boyfriend."

She crossed her arms. "Kiss me."

Not the reaction he expected. "Are you sure?"

Instead of a reply, she pulled his shoulders towards hers and kissed him on the mouth. Her cherry lip balm threw his senses into a frenzy. The kiss intensified. His hands reached around her waist. He felt movement and pulled away, gasping for air.

"Was that so bad?" she asked.

"Greta, I need to tell you something." *Maybe this would change her mind…*

Her wide eyes met his. "Yes?"

"I usually can't."

"Can't what?" She stroked his neck.

Should he tell her? Everything felt so right…

He blurted, "I haven't been with a woman in years."

She leaned away. "Oh."

"My mood stabilizers, they dull everything."

"*Everything?*"

"Well, not right now, I've been off my meds." He gestured with a tilt of his head toward the bulge in his shorts. *No! Wrong thing to say…*

With wide eyes and mouth agape, she said, "I see. It's been a couple years for me also. Do you want to?"

This wasn't his intention. He wanted to tell her the truth, not jump her bones. *But only a fool would say no…* "I can't promise anything. It's up to you." Instantly, he knew he should leave. *Only a creep would…*

"Yes."

She said this like a business transaction. His lungs stopped working. This was no way to start a relationship. *Where was the romance? Seduction?* "Yes? Like, *now?*"

Greta bounced up from the loveseat. "I've been having this hot pirate fantasy." She went to her walk-in closet and pulled out a couple hangers. "I'm going to change. I'll be right back. Don't move." She turned on the overhead light in the closet and shut the door.

He had no idea what to do. How was he supposed to role-play when he wasn't sure if this would work at all? And did his confession turn this into a pity fuck? His erection subsided as the terror in his mind grew.

This was all too strange. And too sudden.

From the closet, he heard the screech of hangers dragged aside, grunts, and the rustle of fabric. Greta reemerged a couple minutes later, wearing a low-cut, navy blue midi dress, with a wide black leather belt, still in her white socks and a pink satin scarf on her head. Her right earlobe held the companion gold hoop earring to the one he'd lost in the shipwreck. She was an adorable pirate lass.

"Avast ye! Care to help me rig my dungbie?" She posed with a sly grin, hand on one hip, the other lifting her skirt suggestively. She turned and flashed a lacy thong.

His throat felt tight. He didn't know exactly what a dungbie was, but if context clues were correct, hers looked amazing. "Greta, I love your outfit. But…" The voices in his head screamed at him to run. Fast. But no, she would take running away as a rejection.

"It's the socks, right? Yeah, I know they're not sexy. See, I have this mild hammertoe…"

He had to be honest. The truth was, he was terrified. But he couldn't tell her that. "I think we should wait. Get to know each other better."

The blood drained from her face and she whipped off her headscarf. "Oh, gosh. I'm sorry. I'm too weird. Yes, I didn't mean to come on so strong. Stupid Greta!" She smacked her forehead.

Greta slunk down onto the sofa beside him. "How about this? Tell me a bedtime story. I'll close my eyes and you can tell me all about your shipwreck?" She grabbed a throw pillow and placed it on Johnnie's lap. Greta took off the belt and earring. She curled up on the sofa with her head on the pillow, like a bug in a rug, and closed her eyes.

Yes, he could manage a story. He gazed down at her serene flushed face with long lashes. *God, she was pretty.* "Where should I start?"

"Anywhere you want. I'll just listen." She intertwined her hand with his and rested it on her waist. Her fingers were warm.

He began his story at the point he found Mo on the back deck.

She asked a few questions here and there, like a sleepy child.

With his free hand, he stroked her hair.

Greta sighed contentedly. "That feels nice."

When he got to the part about the pirates chasing them into the storm, Greta opened her eyes.

"How did you survive?"

He smiled. "I had a promise to keep."

"Really, what's that?" Greta propped herself up to face him.

"I wanted to tell you a great pirate story."

She smiled. "Johnnie, you can tell me a story any time you'd like."

He couldn't resist any longer and kissed her. A long kiss that started softly but escalated to the point where his mind violently fought his primitive urges to press further.

She whispered, "Aren't you going to tell me the rest?"

"Maybe later." He kissed the base of her neck. His fingers left hers and wandered across her dress towards the crease of her rear end. Half of his brain shouted, "No! Too soon." The other half said, "Shut the fuck up!"

"Captain Johnnie," she whispered, "I'm having…a shiver in me timbers." She unzipped the back of her blousy dress and wiggled the puffed sleeves off her shoulders, revealing a lacy white bra. Night was falling and the room was dark now. But her porcelain skin glowed.

Her silky red hair fell across her cleavage. In a breathy tone, she said,

"We can just mess around…if you want." Greta traced the scar above his ear and kissed it. So close, her rose-scented perfume made his mind blank. She whispered. "We don't have to go further than second base."

He nodded. "Yes, that seems safe."

They kissed and fondled each other over their clothes.

A few minutes later, Greta whispered, "Maybe third. We're grown adults. Third isn't *so* bad, right?" She grabbed the bottom of his T-shirt and pulled.

"Yes, third," he whispered. His thoughts became gummy. With a chuckle, he asked, "Um, what's third again?"

She let go of his shirt. Her eyes widened and she stared at the ceiling. "You know what? I don't remember!"

Johnnie laughed, his shoulders collapsing, his eyes tearing.

Greta belly laughed. "Gosh, we are *terrible* at this." She got off his lap, hitched her top back onto her shoulders, walked over to the table by the front door and grabbed her phone. "I'm a frickin' librarian. I'll look it up." She seemed to be typing; the screen light cast her shadow on the wall.

Johnnie exhaled to control his laughter. He wiped his eyes with his palms. "You know what, I think if we keep our clothes on…"

Greta bounced back over to the sofa. "So now what?"

"We could watch television."

She chuckled and ran her fingers along his stomach to tickle him. In a silly gruff voice, she ordered, "Just talk pirate to me and kiss me ye landlubber!"

Orders were orders. They messed around some more. Now, he realized, all the pressure was off. Being with Greta was fun in a way he hadn't thought possible. There were smiles and giggles among delicate kisses—interspersed with corny pirate jokes about 'walking his plank' and 'plundering her booty'—making him feel at ease.

It was all coming back to him. Like a memory he didn't have to work to remember.

Although something Mo said came flooding back. *It was all about being truthful.*

And he could find no better truth than the desire and acceptance he found in Greta's eyes.

Chapter 37

The next morning, Johnnie woke well before sunrise. He kissed the still asleep Greta on the forehead and headed to his apartment to change into this park uniform. The sun hadn't risen yet but there was sunshine in his heart as he rode the Pig along the winding roads.

A light was on in Gertie's house, meaning she was home. He quickly showered and changed, and packed his lunch: a sandwich, a couple apples, some cheese puffs, and two granola bars. Back on the Pig, he turned the ignition key.

Gertie's front door opened. She waved.

He turned off the engine. "Hey, when did you get back?"

She walked out in her slippers and bathrobe. "Last night. What have you been up to?"

"I was at Greta's." He noticed a bruised lump on Gertie's chin but otherwise she seemed okay. *Best not to ask...*

"Overnight?"

Johnnie grinned.

"Good for you! Did you, you know?" She raised an eyebrow.

"We did a few things. Watched television, had dinner..."

She crossed her arms and laughed. "You know that's not what I'm asking."

Johnnie shook his head, "We didn't *exactly* have sex. I mean..." He recalled a certain point where they came very close... He smiled. "It's complicated."

She placed her hand on his shoulder. "Well, I'm still proud of you."

"Jesus, you sound like Robin."

"I have your mail. There's a letter from the Bahamas. Someone named George?"

"Yeah?"

"Hold on." Gertie stepped back inside her house for a moment and emerged with a stack of mail. "It's on top. Who's George?"

"A friend. Thanks." He took the stack, with mostly bills and advertising circulars. The letter seemed to be in Mo's handwriting. "Hey, what happened with you and Cud?"

Gertie shook her head and hid her hands in her robe pockets. "We broke up."

"Aw. Sorry." Alarms went off in his head. "He didn't do that to your face, right?"

"No. I fell on the ship."

"Oh. Good. I mean, not good. Um. I was hoping you two would work it out."

Gertie sighed. "Part of me did too."

"Where is he?"

"Not sure. We took different flights. He said he was moving back to the beach."

"Really?"

She shoved her hands into the front pockets of her house coat. "Could you look in on him? Let me know if he's okay?"

"Yeah. No problem. Hey, I need to get going. Don't want to be late on my first day back."

"Take care. Do you want to come for dinner tonight? I feel like cooking a feast. I can make mashed potatoes."

"Sorry. Maybe another time? I'm going to Greta's tonight."

"Oh." Gertie sighed. "Well, have fun."

Johnnie waved goodbye, sifted through his mail and put all but one item in the seat compartment of his scooter. He was already running late, but he set aside the letter from Mo and opened it.

It read:

> John, thank you for everything. I know it isn't much, but I wrote some new lines for your pirate song. I hope Greta likes it.

He grinned. The song lyrics were classic Mo and still sounded like the Macarena. Greta would truly adore it. He locked his apartment, got on his scooter and drove to Hawksnest Beach.

The beach looked the same. As if he'd never left. The sun was coming up behind him. As he walked to the toolshed, he saw a man's silhouette sitting on the sand, near the water's edge. *Not bulky enough to be Smith.*

Johnnie crossed the beach towards the figure.

Cudlow, sitting cross-legged, turned. "Hey, good morning, Johnnie!"

"Hey." He took a seat on the sand next to Cud. He noticed Stumpy resting his head on Cud's bare foot.

The trio looked out across the water. The sky brightened to the east.

In a soft voice, Johnnie said, "Cud, I'm sorry it didn't work out with Gertie."

"Who?"

Alarm coursed through Johnnie's brain. "Gertie. She told me you broke up."

In a nonchalant voice, Cud said, "Well, I can't say we were ever *truly* together."

Johnnie faced him. "What? Are you feeling okay?"

"Fine as rain." Cud began humming. "Stumpy said women are trouble."

"Cud, you're scaring me."

Cud gestured with both arms gracefully toward the bay. In a lyrical tone, he said, "Life is wonderful." He continued staring straight ahead like a zombie. Or a lobotomy patient. He had stopped petting Stumpy and instead he twiddled delicate gold flower ring, focusing on it. "So pretty."

"Wait. I don't get it. You love Gertie."

"Ha! What is love? Stumpy says love is an artificial construct that deludes the mind." Cud rose, stretched his back, and rolled his neck. "Do you want my help this morning? Stumpy and I can rake the seaweed or sweep the changing room."

There was a glossiness in Cud's eyes that made the hairs on his neck stand on end. Johnnie backed away from the pair. His friend was not right in the head. "Cud, I think you should talk to someone."

"Why? I want to be useful." Cudlow turned to Stumpy. "Right, Stumps? We can be useful." Cud danced like a hula girl in the sand, waving his arms and singing, "We are useful. We are useful. La, la, la, la, la." He twirled in place.

Cud had always been odd, but a fun and *with-it* kind of odd. Not completely off his rocker as he appeared now. In the VA hospital, he'd seen vets with the same far off looks and bizarre manic speech. Perhaps he himself had been that way at times…

Johnnie's phone chirped. Another text message from Kemper with a long list of chores he needed to accomplish today. It was clear many of the small repairs piled up during his absence. "Cud, I'll catch you later. I have stuff to do."

Cudlow waved, "Bye, Johnnie. See you tomorrow." His friend walked toward the mangroves and disappeared.

Johnnie headed toward the tool shed, trying to decide what chore to tackle first. But as he opened the lock on the plywood door, he stopped cold. A dark thought nagged at him. *Was his best friend really off the deep end?*

Still, Cud seemed cheerful. Certainly not a danger to himself. *He hoped.*

Maybe all Cud needed was time.

Time fixed many things. Or at least made them better.

Because he was living proof.

Epilogue

~Mo's Letter~

John,

Thank you for everything. I know it isn't much, but I wrote down some new lines for your pirate song. I hope Greta likes it.

John and Greta live on the sea-ah
Battle dragons and try not to flee-ah
Rubies spell trouble so give them to me-ah
HEY, Captain Johnnie

Yo-Ho-Ho, he gives to the poor-a
Treasure map means they'll all go explore-a
Mo's got moves but loud when he snore-a
HEY, Captain Johnnie

Stumpy's bad, he's a gnarly iguana
Parrots are lame so he sits on John's shoulder
Won't poop in his box, but you know that he's gonna
HEY, Captain Johnnie!

Drug lords are fierce and act real orn-ry
The ocean's rough and turns crazy stormy
Johnnie's brave and wins all the glory
HEY, Captain Johnnie

Cannons are hot and balls are so heavy
Grog tastes bad, not good for your belly
Dance every day with friends and get sweaty
HEY, Captain Johnnie

Don't be a stranger and see you on the flip side,
Your friend, Mo.

ABOUT THE AUTHOR

DS Whitaker is a Virginia author who loves quirky, contemporary stories with oddball twists. Johnnie the Pirate King, is the second book of the Johnnie Series.

The first Johnnie book, Johnnie Finds a Dead Body, was a 2021 National Indie Excellence Award finalist for comedy. Her debut novel, Antigenesis, was a finalist in the 2020 National Indie Excellence Awards.

Follow her on Twitter at @ds_whitaker. To get updates about the next books in the Johnnie series, subscribe to her mailing list at www.dswhitaker.com.

Other works by DS Whitaker:

> Antigenesis
> Planet of the Creeps
> Shower of Lies
> Johnnie Finds a Dead Body (Book 1)
> Johnnie the Pirate King (Book 2)
> Johnnie in Miami (Book 3)
> Johnnie & the Tempest (Book 4)

Dear Reader!

While I have your attention,
please consider leaving a book
review on Amazon or Goodreads!

Thank You!

www.ingramcontent.com/pod-product-compliance
Lightning Source LLC
Chambersburg PA
CBHW051432170626
46809CB00006B/2433